COPYRIGHT

Copyright 2022 author Delaney Foster

No part of this book may be reproduced or stored in a retrieval system or transmitted in any form or by any means, electronic, mechanical, photocopying, recording or otherwise without express written permission from the author. This book is licensed for the purchaser's enjoyment only and may not be re-sold.

The story in this book and all the characters are the intellectual property of the author. No one, except the owner of said property may reproduce, copy or publish, in any medium, any individual part of this story or its characters without express written permission from the author of this work.

Translation: It is ILLEGAL to distribute this book or its contents or resale this copy in ANY form. Stealing books is not cool. Plagiarism is not cool. All pirates will be hunted down and burned at the figurative stake.

Cover design: Dez Purington with Pretty in Ink

Edits: Nicole McCurdy with Emerald Edits, Dawn Alexander with Evident Ink, Elizabeth Gardner

Proofreading: Lunar Rose Editing

DEDICATION

To all the belles who fell for the prince when he was a beast.
This one's for you.

CONTENT
WARNING

The Obsidian Brotherhood series is a darker romance series dealing with the inner workings of a fictional secret society. The world I've created within this series is dark, ominous, and oftentimes not pretty. There will be topics, such as drug use, dub-c0n, intimate interactions with a minor, hunting for sport, etc. that some readers may find offensive or uncomfortable.

I trust you to know your limits and turn the page at your own discretion.

I personally love a good morally gray main character and a storyline with no boundaries.

Now that you've been warned, will you keep going?

WAIT! One more thing!

Before you begin, if you'd like to find a reading buddy or simply join a group of readers who have decided to go down the same path where morals don't exist and sanity is questionable, I'd like to invite you into The Chamber Facebook group. Just remember, what happens in The Chamber, stays in The Chamber. ;) I hope you enjoy the ride.

Somewhere in the darkness of the forest the enemy waits. He's patient. He's silent. He is the predator and she is his prey. The brittle tree branches crack and sway in the bitter night wind. The moon hides behind the clouds, too afraid to watch. Tonight, it ends—generations of hate, a centuries-old feud. Tonight, the forbidden becomes the desired. There is no escaping a fate that was sealed in blood, etched in scars. She stands alone under the midnight sky, waiting, anticipating. The chill of the wind prickles her skin and whispers softly in her ear.

"Run."

ONE

Tatum

age nine

I was six years old when I first met Caspian Donahue.

I was playing dress up at a wedding, and he was being... *him.*

You shouldn't do that, Tatum.

Come here, Tatum.

Stay with me, Tatum.

Just because he was four years older than me didn't make him the boss. So what if he was friends with my older brother? So what if his family had more money than God? So what if all the other girls thought he was cute? None of that made him special. He was just another boy.

Even though he wasn't.

Caspian was different from the rest, and everyone knew it. All because of his last name.

And since that day at the wedding, it seemed like he was everywhere, all the time, following me around and telling me what to do. Like now, when he'd pulled me out of bed, dragged me to his cabin, then disappeared.

He'd told me to stay put, and I'd rolled my eyes at him. I didn't want to sleep in Caspian's bed. I wanted to go back to my own.

To most people, Crestview Lake was the perfect place for a weekend getaway. The still water and tall trees were a peaceful change from where we lived in New York City. But there were things out there, things in the woods beyond the row of cabins, things that might hurt me. At least that's what my dad always said. I was supposed to stay away from the woods.

Once a year, we all got together for the Crestview Regatta. Twelve families. Twenty-four cabins all lined up around a massive lake. The grown-ups had their side, and the kids had ours.

Caspian's cabin was just like mine. It had a full-sized bed with a plaid comforter, a fireplace, leather chair, and a dresser with a TV on top. He'd left the lamp on for me, but I didn't want to be here. I didn't want to be at Crestview Lake at all. I wanted to go home.

I waited.

He never came back.

I waited longer.

Finally, I decided I wasn't waiting anymore. Whatever Caspian wanted could be taken care of tomorrow after the regatta. I was going back to my bed.

It was quiet when I stepped outside into the darkness. Not the peaceful quiet I usually liked but the kind of quiet that made me think something bad was going to happen—the kind of quiet we had after my pet hamster died and no one knew how to tell me.

It was late, after midnight if I had to guess. The sky was dark, darker than usual because the stars were hidden behind the clouds. Like even they knew better than to be out right now. Everything was still, including the branches on the tall trees behind me. Nothing moved. Nothing made a sound. Nothing was there to warn me if trouble wanted to chase me into the forest. I knew I shouldn't be outside alone. This wasn't our home, where I was always safe.

I should've just waited for Caspian to come back.

The grass was wet against my bare feet, making me wish I had grabbed my slippers in case I needed to run. It was cold, too cold for June. My favorite Hannah Montana nightgown suddenly felt too thin, too small. I wanted a blanket to wrap around my body, to protect me from the chill in the air. Mostly, I just wanted to go back to bed. I wanted to climb under the covers and pretend like it didn't feel as if someone was watching me. I hugged my arms around myself while the wind started to whisper, like it was trying to tell me its secrets.

The flickering of flames down by the water caught my eye. *Why was there a fire in the middle of the night?* Everyone should be asleep.

I took a step closer, hoping to feel some of its warmth from here. My eyes narrowed, focusing on the fire, trying to see if that was where Caspian had gone. I took another step, creeping closer and closer.

But there was nothing.

No one.

The fire was just… there, and I had no idea why, or who started it. My heart thumped faster and faster as I watched the flames dance against the night sky. With every breath, it seemed like they grew bigger and bigger.

A gust of wind blew my long, dark hair across my face and sent a shiver all the way to my bones. I tucked the strands behind my ears and stared past the fire onto the glass surface of the lake. There were boats on the water, three of them total, all in a line. Each boat had one person standing tall in the middle. Their faces were hidden in the shadow of a dark hoodie, but I saw their figures in the moonlight. All three of them were boys, and all three about my brother's size. *What are they doing?* It looked like they were about to jump into the water. I wanted to scream at them, to tell them not to jump, but the sound got stuck in my throat.

One of the figures turned his head. *Is that Lincoln?* Why was my brother on the lake?

We were here for the regatta. And my brother was on one of the rowing crews. But they didn't race at night. *Did they?*

No. It was too dark. And nobody raced standing up. Something was definitely wrong.

I squinted again, but they were too far away and the shadows kept them hidden. Maybe that's where Caspian went. Maybe he was in one of those boats. It still didn't explain why he'd dragged me to his cabin.

A strong hand gripped my arm, and the scream that was lodged in my throat sliced through the darkness.

"Sssh, Tatum. It's just me."

I looked up. "Daddy? What are you doing out here?" He wasn't in his pajamas. *Shouldn't he be in his pajamas?* I pointed out to the water. "Is that Lincoln? Why is he in the boat?"

Just as I pointed, the person in the boat turned his head and looked right at me. The moonlight pushed away the shadows, revealing Lincoln's face. I held my breath as he slowly brought a single finger to his lips. *Sshhh.* I could almost hear the sound from here. For some reason it sent an even colder chill up my spine.

Dad scooped me up into his arms and brought me back to my cabin, then tucked me into bed where it was nice and warm. "Go back to sleep, sweetheart." He kissed my forehead. "When you wake up in the morning this will all be just a dream."

Right. Just a dream.

The funny thing about dreams was that sometimes they haunted you long after you woke up.

One year later…

It was our annual weekend at the lake again, and everyone else was up on the bank at the party celebrating the regatta. Well, everyone except me. I came down here to be closer to the lake. The water was calm and peaceful, but I had this strange feeling there were things under the surface that people couldn't see, secrets that belonged to the lake.

Every time I tried to ask about the fire, about why Lincoln was in that boat in the middle of the night, Dad gave me this reassuring smile then changed the subject. I wasn't crazy. I didn't dream it. But no one seemed to want to talk about it, so I let it go.

Even though it gave me chills, it was quieter by the lake after the race, and I liked the quiet. I liked watching the sun behind the trees and the way it bounced off the water.

Part of me expected Caspian to follow me down here and tell me to come back to the party. He didn't. Not yet, anyway. But I knew he would.

I never asked him why he dragged me to his cabin that night or where he went afterwards, and he never said. Part of me was glad about that because something told me I probably didn't really want to know.

Being around him made my heart feel weird—the way it did when I was learning a new dance routine or like riding a bike with no hands. Scary, but exciting.

I stopped thinking about Caspian and listened to the sound of birds chirping in the distance, competing with the music floating from the tent. Sometimes I wondered what it would be like to be a bird, to be surrounded by beautiful songs all day and go wherever I wanted to go instead of only where my parents told me. To be free.

A long walkway that looked like wood but felt like plastic stretched from the embankment all the way over the water until it joined with the boat launch—a big square platform where all the rowing boats were lined up.

A voice came out of nowhere, making me jump. "Hey. What's your name?"

I spun around to see a girl about my age walking down the boat launch with a bright green shaved ice in her hand. Her blonde hair was pulled up into a high ponytail. She was wearing denim shorts and a light pink T-shirt with sparkly sequins on the sleeves.

"Sour apple." She got to the end of the long walkway and held the styrofoam cup toward me before I had time to answer her first question. "Want some?"

I blew out a breath and twirled the hem of my baby blue sundress. "I'm good. Thanks."

"Lyric," she said, pointing a finger at her chest. "Like the words of a song."

Lyric. She wasn't shy, that was for sure. And she wasn't like the other girls that came for the regatta.

I smiled. "I'm Tatum."

"Whatcha doin' out here, Tatum?" She looked out across Crestview Lake.

From the other side of a nearby tree line, you could hear laughter, conversations, and music. My parents were there, hanging out with the other families under big white tents filled with linen-covered tables and fancy foods.

I shrugged a shoulder. "Just looking for someplace quiet. You?"

My family knew everyone on every crew. My brother had been rowing with the same group of guys all his life. We didn't let outsiders into our world. I wondered who this girl was and what she was doing here—and where in the world she got that snowball.

She scooped a bite of colored ice into her mouth then squinted like she'd gotten a brain freeze. "My dad's doing a concert for some rich kid's birthday, and my mom flaked, so I had to come."

She pointed at the racing shells lined up on the launch. "What's that?"

"Those are racing boats."

"Boat racing? Like, with oars?" She scrunched up her nose. "That doesn't sound like fun."

It wasn't. Not for me, anyway. But my dad was in politics, and according to him, *family is important in politics*. I'd heard him say that at least a hundred times.

"My brother rows." I paused a beat then smiled. "And it's his birthday, so I had to come."

She stopped just before the white plastic spoon disappeared inside her mouth again. Her lips and tongue were stained green, contrasting her pale skin. "Oh, God. Your brother's the rich kid, isn't he? I'm sorry. I didn't mean—"

I laughed and waved my hand. "Don't worry about it. He's been called worse."

"My dad says rich people don't have morals." She took another bite of her shaved ice. "You're cool, though. You're not like the rest of them."

I wondered what else her dad had to say about rich people.

She pulled a cell phone from her back pocket then snapped a picture of me.

"What are you doing?"

"Taking a picture of my new best friend."

I smiled because I liked her. She didn't ask where I bought my outfit or where we were going on vacation this year. She didn't care about money, and she didn't drool over Lincoln the way most other girls did. I'd never been anybody's best friend, but I wanted to be hers.

She walked over to one of the shells and hopped inside. The boats were all secured between two metal rails on the edge of the launch, but it still rocked when she jumped in. "Come on. Come sit with me." When I stood there pursing my lips, she sighed.

"It's not like you have anything better to do." She jumped up and down. "And see? We won't go anywhere."

"Don't even think about it," a male voice said from behind me.

I looked over my shoulder and watched as Caspian stalked down the walkway of the launch. He walked with his shoulders squared and his back perfectly straight. My ballet teacher would love his posture, but I thought it made him look more like a grown-up than a fourteen-year-old boy. He had his usual serious, *I'm-the-boss-of-everything* look on his face.

Well, he wasn't the boss of me, even though he liked to act like he was.

I stuck my tongue out at him, then moved closer to the boat.

"I mean it, Tatum. Your parents are either going to kick your ass or you're going to fall in and drown."

He said ass.

Fourteen-year-old boys had no business saying ass.

A few loose strands of hair fell out of my ponytail as I ran to the end of the launch, where Lyric was watching us with wide eyes from inside the boat while she finished eating her snowball.

Caspian let out a loud groan that sounded more like a growl.

I'll show him who's boss.

I hurried to hop into the boat, but my foot got caught on the rigger. I reached out for support, but there was nothing to grab onto. The sound of Lyric's voice yelling my name was followed by the stomping of footsteps on the launch. The hull of the boat scraped my leg as my whole body fell forward into the lake. All the air was squeezed from my lungs the second I hit the cold water. It felt like knives were stabbing my skin. I tried not to panic as I pushed my way to the surface. I knew how to swim. I was just surprised by the chill, then I thought about the secrets, all the secrets that might be under here. I pushed my legs harder.

Out of nowhere, a strong arm wrapped around my body, pulling me close. My heart beat faster as I squeezed my eyes shut, praying the secrets hadn't gotten hold of me. *Please don't take me down to the bottom.* They didn't. They pulled me up and up until we broke through the top of the water. I sucked in a deep breath, then opened my eyes to find Caspian staring at me. The water made his dark hair stick to his forehead, and tiny droplets trickled down his face. We stayed there like that, treading water with his arm around me.

I finally shoved at his chest, but he only held me tighter. "Let me go."

"One day you're going to listen to me." He heaved a breath. "Even if it kills us both."

TWO

CASPIAN

age sixteen

The only time my father ever smiled at me was when my crew crossed the finish line first at Crestview Lake, and that was only because that meant we'd beat Lincoln's crew. Like we just did for the third year in a row, but who was counting.

"Heads up, Donahue," Lincoln said as he eased his shell up to the launch.

I smirked. "Try not to trip over my dick when you get out."

He flipped me off, then spit into the water. One of his friends, Ethan Williams, clapped him on the shoulder and said something I couldn't hear.

Fucking pricks, both of them.

Our fathers hated each other, and somehow that feud had trickled down to us. We still all hung out together because it was easier to watch your enemies if you kept them within eyesight. Our dads acted like they were tighter than brothers while wishing each other dead behind their backs. Lincoln and I didn't give two shits about appearances. We wore our contempt on our sleeves.

There was only one good thing about the Huntington family. And she was sitting at the edge of the boat launch, like she always did after the race. Her hair was pulled back in a braid.

She cheered for her brother during the regatta, but I always caught her watching me. I knew this because I watched her too.

Tatum Huntington always managed to find trouble—or maybe it found her. Either way, she was always right in the fucking middle of it.

The first time I ever saw her was when I was ten and she was six. We were at a wedding, some big event for a high-profile celebrity couple. Come to think of it, the only reason kids were allowed to attend was because the couple was famous for adopting a shit ton of them. Any other time, we'd have both been stuck at home with a nanny. I was looking for a place to piss, and Tatum was in the bridal suite doing what I supposed all little girls did—spinning around in front of the mirror with the bride's veil over her head—probably imagining herself as the bride. Where the actual bride—or any other adult—was, I had no idea. I didn't care. All I knew was that there was a little girl cloaked in white, dripping in innocence as she smiled and twirled, and I had the overwhelming urge to make sure she stayed that way. I yanked the veil off her head before she did something stupid like step on it and rip it, or worse, got caught by someone other than me. She rubbed her hands through her long brown hair then poked her lip out in a pout. "You're mean," she'd said. I wasn't, though. Not then. Not yet. I grabbed her wrist and dragged her back to the main area where all the other guests were. She'd called me names the whole time, but I didn't care. From the moment I laid eyes on that girl, I had this all-consuming need to protect her, this underlying current sweeping me toward her. Even when she was yelling things like *stupidhead* at my back while I dragged her down the hall.

Two years ago, I'd caught some asshole watching her from the woods here at the lake. I had the urge to protect her then, too. And I did. Even though she would never know it. She wouldn't be able to look at me with those same innocent eyes if she knew what kind of person I truly was.

It was always there, this basic, primal need to keep her safe.

Even at a young age, I recognized that she wasn't like the rest. She didn't belong in this world. People like me—like my father—would devour Tatum Huntington.

I quickly learned the only way to protect her from the monsters was to become one of them.

She looked so innocent right now, staring out onto the water. The sun hadn't set over the lake yet, and the adults were already up on the embankment with their alcohol and live music under the tent.

I walked over to her, pulling my shoes and socks off as I went. "You shouldn't be out here by yourself." *You're vulnerable when you're alone.* I sat down, letting my legs dangle off the launch.

She gripped my knee. "Don't." Her eyes were wide with panic.

I was wearing khaki shorts with a blue polo. Her fingers dug into my bare skin. *The fuck is that about?*

"You don't know what's down there." She glanced at the lake, then slowly pulled her hand away.

I knew exactly what was down there, and it was nothing we needed to worry about.

I played her game, though, and crisscrossed my legs the same way she had. "Okay."

We sat there, quiet, for the longest time. Music floated down from on top of the hill. The surface of the lake rippled in the breeze.

"Lyric's mom left," she said, breaking the silence.

That didn't have shit to do with me, but something told me Tatum just needed to say it, to talk to someone.

"That's why she's not here." She kept staring forward, not looking me in the eye. "She doesn't want to be around anyone. Her mom wasn't great, but..." her breath hitched, "...now Lyric is alone."

I didn't say anything. This conversation wasn't for me. It was for her, another way for me to watch over her.

She swallowed. "I mean, she has her dad, but..." Her words trailed off. "I have both of my parents, and I still feel alone. If it wasn't for Lyric—" She cut herself off. "What if she stays sad? What if she never wants to come back?"

"You will *never* be alone." I didn't know why I promised her that. I just knew the words were out before I could stop them. And that I hated her family even more now after hearing how they made her feel. She was a twelve-year-old girl. She should have felt loved, happy, safe—never *alone*.

Her gaze shot to mine. Her eyes welled with tears. "Would you just sit here with me for a minute?"

This was a rare moment, one of those that you tucked away in the back of your mind for later. Tatum was always fighting me, always defying me. Right now, she was letting me in, and it damn near fucking broke me. If I thought I needed to protect her before, that was nothing compared to what I felt now.

"Yeah, Little Troublemaker. I'll do whatever you need."

THREE

CASPIAN

> **This chapter contains graphic scenes of hunting for sport. It may be skipped over as its contents are implied in other chapters.**
> age eighteen

Throughout the world certain people practiced their religions in chapels, synagogues, and cathedrals. In my world, power was the religion, and there were five gods—my father, Kipton Donahue, along with Malcolm Huntington, Pierce Carmichael, Winston Radcliffe, and Grey Van Doren. Each of them was a key player in the Obsidian Brotherhood. These five families were bound to the Brotherhood by blood. They all worshiped on the altar of the almighty dollar, and instead of saving their souls, the power swallowed them whole.

The entire Brotherhood consisted of one-hundred men from around the globe—all bankers, tech engineers, real estate moguls, diplomats, and politicians. There was enough collective money and power in this one organization to run the world. The only way in was by formal invitation from a current member, followed by an initiation sealed in blood—either yours or someone else's. Preferably someone else's. The only way out was death. And no one within the Brotherhood talked about the Brotherhood.

To these men, authority was a privilege, not a right. Hundreds of years ago, the founding fathers—my great-grandfather included—established a secret society devoted to keeping power where power belonged. There was an order to things, a balance between dominance and subservience, and it was their job to maintain that balance, by any means necessary. These men didn't dance with the devil. They bent over, dropped their pants, and let him defile them.

Everything, *everything*, was the result of a meticulously constructed plan set in motion long before our time. From secret meetings in hidden rooms to controlling the media, all the way down to a fucked-up ritualistic ceremony they liked to call Judgment Day in which the single men in the organization chose their wives—there was a doctrine that these men were willing to die for, to *kill* for.

Since I was old enough to walk, I'd witnessed it all from a distance—the rise and fall of empires, of fame, of governments. I'd watched my father, the puppet master, pull strings in countries around the world, in languages I didn't understand yet, all from the sleek black, Italian leather chair behind his Dalbergia wood desk. I memorized every facial expression, soaked in every word—not just his but those of everyone around me. The world was my classroom and experience my favorite teacher.

By the time I was eleven, I could smell a lie from a mile away and manipulate a conversation with a con man three times my age. At thirteen, I saw the world for what it was. By sixteen, I could charm the panties off a nun.

Today was my eighteenth birthday, a rite of passage, the threshold into manhood. All my friends got parties at The Boulevard, the most exclusive club in New York City's posh neighborhood of Chelsea. Not me. I was the only son of the almighty Kipton Donahue. We didn't do parties.

Everything my father did was an exertion of power, including birthday celebrations. You didn't prove you were a man by lining up shots and doing keg stands. *Manhood* was a label that had to be earned. I'd already earned mine years ago, but out of tradition, here we were, thousands of miles from home, in the middle of the African savanna with two of Dad's business associates hiding behind brush and studying our prey. Deer and rabbit were for amateurs. You weren't shit 'til you'd taken down an elephant or a wildebeest. Hunting the Big Five. This was what my father called *sport*. Fine with me. I'd rather be here than at a party anyway.

It was mid-August, so most of the leaves had begun to fall, making the animals we hunted easier to spot from two-hundred-fifty feet away. The ground was dry and dingy brown, nothing but a dusty path beneath our feet. The grass was tall but dull and yellowed. The branches were brittle, leaving very little green to be seen on the treetops.

"Everyone wants to eat, but no one has the balls to hunt."

I'd heard those words countless times when Dad would slam down the receiver after an intense business call or slip his tie from beneath his collar and toss it onto the kitchen counter after a long day at the office.

It meant everyone wanted something, but no one was willing to work for it. People wanted wealth, fame, and happiness but weren't willing to make the sacrifices that came with it—sacrifices I knew all too well. Sacrifices I'd spent most of my life watching him make.

"The world is a jungle, Son. You're either the lion or the antelope. You either run or you take."

I was a taker, and today I was going to prove it. After all, that was why he brought me here—to hunt—to prove I'd earned my seat at the fucking table. I wasn't just another pretty-faced fuckboy who needed to be spoon-fed from a silver platter. I was the one here to kill the beast and serve it for dinner.

We all watched quietly as a Cape buffalo chomped leaves from a bush less than fifty yards away. Dad's friend, Pierce Carmichael, was the first to raise his rifle while grinning ear-to-ear. Dad pointed and whispered something as Pierce slowly aimed his gun. The beast must have heard us because it turned its head and stared right into Carmichael's eyes. Jet black orbs that matched the animal's skin narrowed in on us, daring any one of us to make a move. It all happened in slow motion. The buffalo shook its head as if in warning, its solid black horns moving from side to side as a puff of dusty air flared from its wide nostrils.

Tick.

Tick.

Tick.

It was like watching glass shatter just before red wine spilled all over the floor.

The buffalo charged. Its massive frame headed straight for us, but not one of us moved. No one took as much as a single step backward. Then a shot cracked through the air, quickly followed by another. Birds scattered from the tree branches. Dust filled the air.

And my father clapped Pierce Carmichael on the back and grinned at him as if he'd just secured the deal of a lifetime.

He'd never looked at me that way. Not once.

I clapped Carmichael's other shoulder. "Five more seconds, and we'd be pulling your spleen up out of the dirt." I winked. "Good thing you have steady hands."

Dad shot me a glare, and I flashed him a smile. *Fuck you, old man.* He wanted to know if I had the balls to hunt? I was ready to whip my dick out and put them all to shame.

The professional hunter tagging along with us pulled his camera out of his backpack and took some obligatory shots of Pierce squatting next to his two-shot kill. Dad jumped in the pic for good measure.

Fuckers. Both of them.

I stopped giving a shit about Pierce Carmichael the day I walked in on one of their brotherhood meetings and heard him talking about putting price tags on women.

Now, we were walking down another dirt path to a less dense part of the savanna. A Bushpig grunted somewhere off to our left, and Dad nudged me with his elbow. Like he paid seventeen-thousand dollars and brought me all the way to South Africa to kill a fucking Bushpig. I'd have laughed in his face if his suggestion wasn't such an insult.

One of the other men, Malcolm Huntington, started rambling on about taxes and chemical warfare. He was a senator on his way to the White House. I couldn't care less about his political agenda, but the second he said *her* name, the hairs on the back of my neck stood on end.

I whipped my head around and pinned him with a stare. "What did you just say?"

"I was just telling your father how I think it would help my campaign if Tatum married someone like Khalid Falih."

Tatum. *My* Tatum. The girl I vowed to protect from the time she was six years old.

I belted a laugh. "Khalid Falih? The oil guy." *From Saudi Arabia*, I wanted to add but didn't because it was redundant. We all knew who he was and why that marriage would be beneficial for Huntington—and a nightmare for us. We also knew how men like him treated women.

He nodded, swallowing hard because he knew too. He knew what that meant for his daughter. He just didn't care.

We all stopped walking now. My father was shooting daggers at my back. I could feel it. Didn't stop me, though. Dad hated Huntington as much as I did. They'd been frenemies since the day Huntington got into politics, a mutual dislike as thick as it got. But they needed each other like matches and gasoline. Alone, they were dangerous, but together they were lethal. When your families had spent generations fighting for the same cause, you put on your mask and played the fucking game.

Now this dude was standing here talking about pawning his youngest daughter off to some asshole like she was a piece of property to be traded. An asshole ten years older than her, might I add. I was five seconds away from shoving the barrel of my rifle up Malcolm's ass.

"Married?" I raked my fingers through my hair and tipped my head back, looking up at the clear blue sky. If there was a God, I wished He'd send a mountain lion to rip this man's throat out right fucking now. "She's fourteen fucking years old. Has she even hit puberty yet? For fuck's sake." I dropped my head and narrowed my eyes at him.

He palmed the back of his neck. His dark brown eyes closed for a brief second, and I caught the clench in his squared jaw. "I didn't mean right now, Caspian." His eyes opened. "Jacobs just got elected, and I'm sure he'll win re-election another term. It will be at least eight years before I can add my name to that ballot." He sighed as though I exhausted him. "I was making plans. Thinking out loud."

Yeah, well, think that shit quietly from now on.

I nodded once but kept my eyes locked on his for a moment longer before I started walking again.

"I think an alliance with the Middle East is precisely what we need," Carmichael said, more to me than to Huntington.

Of course, he would think that. Women were a commodity. Feelings were liabilities, and marriage was just another business transaction. I didn't disagree with him completely, except when it came to this, to *her*.

A movement caught my attention from the corner of my eye. Well, fuck me. There were no mountains here, but there was definitely a fucking lion. I chuckled to myself and tightened my grip on my rifle. Without motioning for anyone else in our group to stop, I stood still and watched the majestic creature one hundred yards away. He was lying under a tree, licking his paws as if he'd just finished a good meal. His golden mane blended in with the long, wispy blades of grass and moved with the breeze.

The smart thing to do would have been to keep moving. The lion wasn't concerned with us. But thanks to Huntington here, my blood was rushing through my veins, and thanks to Pierce, I had a point to make to my father. I practically heard his words in my head. *Lion or antelope?*

I wasn't fucking running. That lion didn't stand a chance.

The group stopped walking once they saw what had my attention.

Dad leaned in close to my ear. "I know you're eager, but this is your first time. If you miss—"

"I won't." I wouldn't.

He heaved a breath then stepped away without another word.

I lifted my rifle. The world closed in around my scope. It was just that lion and me. I held my breath as my heart raced. The cool metal of the trigger was like a delicate pulse against my finger, a lifeline under my control. The butt of the gun rested against my shoulder. I lived for this feeling, the power high, and this was the ultimate. I closed one eye, zeroing in on the five-hundred-pound natural-born killer through the scope. Dad was right. One wrong move and that animal wouldn't hesitate to rip our flesh from our bones.

I had no way to know exactly, but I was pretty sure no one else was breathing at this moment either, not even Wexley, the guide we'd hired to accompany us on the hunt. The world was still, quiet, captivated with the anticipation of who would end up at the top of the food chain.

Three.

Two.

One.

I took aim and squeezed the trigger.

The lion bolted up the second the bullet hit him. His thunderous roar echoed across the open land as he spun around in circles then roared again.

"Fuck," Pierce yelled. "You missed."

Only, I didn't. I hit him exactly where I'd meant to—his front leg. I always made it a point to learn from other people's mistakes. I knew there was no such thing as a one-shot kill, not out here, not for a beginner like me. And I wasn't about to let that lion charge at us the way the buffalo did. It would only take a beast like that four seconds to cover the one-hundred-yard distance between us.

I ignored the curses behind me and brought my finger to the trigger again.

The lion stopped spinning and finally spotted us. His mouth opened wide with another roar, exposing razor-sharp teeth and making the air around us vibrate.

I looked back at him and smiled.

Then I took my place at the top of the food chain.

FOUR

Tatum

Two years later…
age sixteen

There was something to be said about the ocean. On the surface she was calm and captivating. Her waves beckoned to us, calling us like a siren's song to come closer, *closer*. We were lured by her beauty and the serenity she offered. But in her depths, in the places dark and deep that we couldn't see, she held the power to drag us into the darkness and never let us go. She was a soft embrace and a dangerous predator. She was majestic and terrifying.

I'd always been fascinated by the ocean.

I leaned against the rail, staring out at the vast, blue water. The lights from my father's yacht lit up the surface. Behind me, below me, and all around me, people were celebrating my birthday. They drank, laughed and danced in honor of the day I was born. I wanted a weekend trip to the house in the Hamptons. Dad insisted on throwing me the biggest and best Sweet Sixteen New York had ever seen. Unless I was onstage in my pointe shoes and leotard, performing the perfect variation in front of a nameless crowd, I hated being the center of attention.

Unfortunately, when your father was a major player in the game of politics, *attention* was a way of life.

Right now, he was in one of the interior cabins that he'd turned into a poker room, waging bets and rubbing elbows with some of the nation's most powerful men. Mom was on the lower deck, drinking champagne and comparing lifestyles of the rich and famous—with the rich and famous. Here, on the upper deck, a DJ worked his way through a playlist of my favorite songs while people I'd known my whole life but never really *knew* paraded around in bikinis and swim trunks, hopping in and out of the pool in between sipping drinks and making out. Some of them used the thirty-foot slide on the side deck to plunge into the ocean. I loved the water, but not after dark. Never after dark.

"Sweet sixteen." A familiar voice came from behind me, wrapping around me like an unwelcome stench.

I turned and smiled. "Senator Polluck. I know my father is glad you came." *Be polite but say nothing to lead him on.* The senator was older than me by at least twenty years. He was attractive by normal standards with his perfect white smile and country club style. According to high school cafeteria whispers, he'd gone through more young, female housekeepers than was appropriate, and his beautiful wife was probably downstairs swapping interior designer info with my mom and the other wives. Someone was always adding on, redecorating, or remodeling. It was their idea of *staying busy.*

He inched closer. "My daughter will be sixteen next year." My skin crawled when he ran a finger along the column of my throat. "Any idea what a sixteen-year-old girl might want for her birthday?" His hand slid down my back, his fingers stopping to fumble with the strings of my bikini top before resting right above my ass. "Is there anything special *you* might want for your birthday?"

Bile burned my throat as I shifted my weight to the other foot, easing away from his touch. Cool air caressed my skin when his hand slipped off my back.

"My parents got me a car." A Mercedes Benz E450 Coupe with a shiny black finish and all-leather interior. I would have been fine with a Jeep, but the car was still gorgeous.

"Ahh, the Benz. We named her Katniss because she's a bad bitch." Lyric popped up beside me with a red plastic cup in her hand.

My best friend.

My little firecracker.

The Kimmy Gibbler to my DJ Tanner.

And right now, my favorite person in the entire world.

A deep frown etched his picture-perfect face. "You certainly have quite the mouth." His voice was like acid as he switched his attention to Lyric.

She shrugged one shoulder then brought the cup to her lips. "People say I take after my dad."

Her father was a world-famous rapper known for his take-no-prisoners, give-no-fucks attitude, bleached-blond hair, and widely renowned diss tracks—most of them aimed at his ex-wife and fucked-up childhood. And just like him, Lyric was an outcast in our world because she had no filter. The ties of etiquette and well-bred genetics didn't bind her.

"Yes, I suppose you do." A slow smile crept over his lips as he grabbed my hand and let his gaze settle back on me. "Any plans after graduation?"

A high-pitched shriek followed by a loud splash resounded from the side deck, stealing our attention for a moment. Lyric's eyes narrowed when she spotted my brother, Lincoln, laughing after he'd obviously pushed a girl down the slide.

My brother was kind of a dick, so none of that surprised me. Truth be told, the girl probably liked it. They flocked to him like moths to a flame.

I turned back to the senator. "Juilliard." I faked a shiver in order to pull my hand back to rub my arms. "Then the New York

Ballet."

Another splash followed the first, then deep, male laughter.

Lyric slid in and draped her arm over my shoulder, dragging me against her side. "After a wild week in Belize with fruity drinks and cabana boys." She waggled her eyebrows then took another drink.

The senator lifted his chin and shifted his eyes to something over my shoulder.

Fervent energy threaded around me, a salacious cord pulling, tugging, and twisting until the air felt tight until *everything* tightened. My heart beat faster. It was *him*. I felt it. I was inherently aware of his presence before he ever spoke a word.

I angled my body to see him.

Caspian Donahue.

Sin personified.

Caspian was a dangerous kind of beautiful, like a garden full of wolfsbane or oleander. His dark brown hair was always styled to perfection and his chiseled jaw was smoothly shaven. He had full, kissable lips and golden-brown eyes. His faded jeans and casual white button-up shirt did nothing to hide the fact that there was an impeccably toned body underneath. Everything about him screamed polished, but beneath the silky surface lurked something ominous, something dark. Confidence seeped from every pore. When he was near, the air even had a pulse, and it quickened at the sight of him.

"Senator Polluck." Caspian handed him a clear glass full of amber liquid. "You look a little thirsty."

Lyric choked on a laugh at the veiled insult.

"Caspian, I'm surprised to see you hanging around at a teenage party," the senator said with brazen arrogance.

Why would he be surprised?

Caspian may have been four years older than me, but so were at least a dozen other people hanging out on this deck. Age wasn't a requirement for an invitation. Status was. And Caspian's family was about as high on the totem pole as it got.

"Likewise. I figured you'd be on the lower deck playing high-stakes poker with all the other dads." Caspian boomeranged the insult to his age.

Lyric cleared her throat as she fought another laugh.

Senator Polluck's eyes crinkled with his tight smile. "Right. Well, I suppose I should be going." He placed a hand on my shoulder. "Happy birthday, Tatum. I hope you'll get back to me about that gift."

Tension rolled over me as I watched the senator walk away then shot my gaze to Caspian. "I had it handled." I hoped my glare burned right through him.

His eyes flashed dark as he tightened his jaw. "Yeah. I saw."

"What she means to say," Lyric broke in, giving me the same look my mom gave on the rare occasion I'd forgotten my manners, "is *thank you*."

Caspian never moved his eyes from mine. There was electricity in his gaze, a steady force that demanded attention. His tongue ran easily over his bottom lip. "Nah. I know her better than that."

He didn't know shit.

Or maybe he did.

As far back as I could remember, Caspian had always been there. He was *everywhere*. Always. Fundraisers. Galas. The annual regatta. There was nothing in our world that he wasn't involved in, no place I could go where he wouldn't also be. He watched me as if watching me was the very essence of life. He watched me as though I were his to watch. Over time, the watching had become a familiarity. I'd almost begun to rely on it. Sometimes I was even disappointed if I looked around a crowded room and he wasn't there.

Sometimes I watched him too.

FIVE

Tatum

Malum Noctis, otherwise known as Mischief Night, was the one night when rules were irrelevant and consequences didn't exist.

Every year on the eve of June 20th, the sons and daughters of the nation's elite gathered underground in a place called The Chamber, concealed inside a mausoleum at New York's Green-Wood Cemetery. The other three-hundred-sixty-four days, it was nothing more than a memorial. But today it was a catacomb of sin.

Green-Wood was a four-hundred-acre tribute to the dead with its elaborate memorials, rolling hills, groves of trees, and four lakes. During the day, families came to walk its trails and revel in its medieval beauty. But the night air carried an ominous whisper in its breeze. Tonight, I knew my life would change. I just didn't know how yet.

Lyric held my hand as we waited beneath a pavilion near one of the lakes. Our only source of light was the moon streaming through the trees and illuminating the water. *No cell phones, no exceptions*, the invitation had said.

The cemetery was alive tonight—if that could be said about cemeteries. There was a heartbeat here. I felt it, magical and mysterious. Among the gothic memorials and tall, looming trees, there was something more... something powerful beneath the surface. I was just about to take Lyric and walk back to my car when a man in a blood-red, hooded robe grabbed my arm.

"What the fuck, dude?" Lyric said, and he slowly turned his head in her direction.

His identity was hidden beneath a white *Phantom of the Opera*-style mask that covered only his forehead, one eye, and one side of his face. I had this feeling I'd seen him before, like I should know him.

His mouth curled into a wicked grin when he looked from her to me. "We've been waiting for you..." He let go of my arm and licked his lips. "Tatum."

I glanced at the invitation in my hand, black cardstock with a serpent shaped to form the letter "O" engraved in red ink. I'd seen the same emblem before on my dad's desk but had no idea what it meant. The back of the card had only my name, Tatum Huntington, and the rule regarding the phones printed on it.

"This way," he said, then guided us down a paved pathway to a monument that resembled a white stone chapel. The appearance didn't fool me. Nothing holy ever happened here.

We followed our guide inside the monument and down a stone staircase lit only by flaming torches fastened to the wall.

I fought the urge to turn around and run. I didn't belong here. My last name got me an invitation to the elusive gathering, but I wasn't one of "them." I'd never been one of them—no matter how much my parents had tried to groom me for their lifestyle. I didn't want to live my entire life by some ridiculous playbook that was established generations ago. I didn't want to force a smile that never reached my eyes. I didn't want a fabricated life. I wanted *real*. Yet, here I was, driven to the heart of it by either madness or curiosity... or both.

The closer we got to the bottom of the stairs, the more my body vibrated with anticipation. A nervous tightness gripped my chest. *What waited for me on the other side of that door?* The walls hummed with a formidable energy. Apprehension and excitement were two forces pulling on the same thread. My nerves were so alive with energy that it felt as though I might snap. I'd even started counting my breaths to keep my mind from wandering. Music echoed from down below, an evocative mix of Gregorian chants blended with the steady beat of low bass and electronic violins.

We stopped at a heavy, wooden door covered in intricate carvings, all gothic and celestial. Another guy in a similar hooded robe and mask pointed to a large steel bowl filled with red glass and fire. The flames licked the glass, bouncing reflections onto the ceiling and the walls around us. It reminded me of the firepit my mother had installed by our pool last year. The thought should have been comforting.

It wasn't.

I tossed my invitation into the bowl and watched it disintegrate to soot and ash, dispelling any evidence it ever existed.

The second guy opened the door but held up a hand, halting Lyric from going inside. "She doesn't have an invitation."

I reached for her hand. "She's with me."

Lyric stepped forward until she was toe-to-toe with the door guy. "Do you know who the fuck I am?"

Of course he did. Everyone knew who she was. She was the rebellious "hot daughter" of a rap god. Her last name made her infamous. Her provocative Instagram stories kept her that way.

"No one gets in without an invitation." His voice was firm. No inflection. No emotion. No concession.

"Okay." I grabbed Lyric's hand. "We'll go."

The door guy grabbed my arm, his fingertips digging into my flesh all the way through my jacket. "You stay." He nodded in Lyric's direction. "She goes."

I yanked my arm away, ignoring the throbbing ache where his fingers were, and narrowed my eyes at him. "She goes, I go."

He shared a look with the guide who led us here, and an unspoken conversation flashed between them. Finally, guy number two let out an exhale and brought his hand to my face, catching my chin between two fingers.

He forced me to look at him. "I know you're new to all this, so I'll give you a pass." He let go of my chin. "One pass, Huntington. That's all you get."

No one under the age of sixteen was ever invited to Mischief Night. I had no idea *why* they weren't, just that they weren't. I'd celebrated my sixteenth birthday two months ago. As far back as I could remember, this party was the topic of bathroom whispers and forbidden fantasies—the holy grail. Everyone knew *about* Mischief Night, even though no one knew *what* it really was. Each guest was hand selected by someone who had attended the year before. I was euphoric when I'd first gotten the invitation. Now I wished I had burned it long before I ever tossed it into that bowl.

We walked through the door and entered The Chamber. This place was an enigma. Until now, it was only as fantastic as my imagination would allow. My imagination had nothing on the real thing.

A throng of people—some of them fully clothed and some not—swarmed around each of the four corner bars. A pungent-scented smoke fogged the air. Black iron lanterns lit up gray cobblestone walls with an amber glow. Large stone arches separated the main area from the darker, more obscure places, hidden in the shadows. The dark corners of my mind itched to know what kinds of things needed to be hidden in a place where sins were allowed to roam free. A massive pool filled with sapphire blue water was in the center of it all. The blue of the water reflected off the walls and ceiling, making the entire place feel like an underwater cave or a hidden grotto. I half expected to look up and see Hades himself seated on a throne with a wide smile on his face.

From a platform suspended in mid-air, a DJ continued mixing his club beat with ancient Latin chants.

Da pacerne domine...

Thump thumpthump

In diebus nostris...

Thump thumpthump

It was there again, the heartbeat. It was in the music, in the mysterious humming vibrating off the walls of this crypt, in the sheer power that filled this room. That heartbeat intermingled with mine and made me feel more alive than ever. A shiver ran down my spine, even though it was the middle of June.

My attention narrowed on a blonde girl sat spread-eagle on top of a large boulder while a guy with jet-black hair buried his face between her thighs. Another girl, a brunette, drew a hit off a joint then leaned over and pressed her mouth to the blonde's. The blonde's cheeks hollowed as she inhaled, then the brunette grabbed her by the nape and pulled her into a kiss. Those same girls probably made millions influencing pre-teens with their work on the Disney channel.

So, this was why no one talked about it.

For some reason the scene enticed me. It lured the deeper parts of me, the parts that had hibernated in the darkness but now stirred to life. No one cared about the confines of etiquette. There were no boundaries to cross because boundaries were nonexistent.

Maybe I did belong here.

I glanced over at Lyric right as she pulled a cell phone from inside her black leather leggings and snapped a picture. The pants were so tight, I didn't even want to think about where she was hiding that thing.

"Are you kidding me right now?" My gaze narrowed in on her. "These people aren't your dad. You don't have to intentionally piss them off."

She rolled her eyes and shoved the phone back inside the waistband of her pants, then down another inch. *Ew.* "Chill out, T. It was one selfie." She threw her long blonde hair over one shoulder. "I'm not going to share it."

I held my pinky up in the air. Lyric was forever taking pictures of things and places she had no business taking pictures of. She said blackmail is a powerful weapon. I said she wouldn't need a weapon if she never picked a fight.

She heaved a sigh when I widened my eyes and shoved my pinky in her face. Reluctantly, after whipping her hair over her shoulder like the sassy bitch she was, she wrapped her pinky around mine, making me grin.

Then she yanked my hand and dragged me through the crowd. "We need drinks."

Yes. Drinks. Plural.

I'd never been drunk before, but I completely agreed. It was Mischief Night, after all.

Someone grabbed a handful of my hair from behind, jolting me to a stop. "Oh my God, it's so soft," her voice cooed in my ear.

I spun around to find a girl I'd never seen before rubbing my hair across her face. Her features were illuminated by the colorful glowstick necklace she wore.

Lyric pulled on my hand, yanking me—and my hair—away from my new admirer in a painful tug.

"She likes my hair," I shouted at her as I rubbed my scalp.

She glanced over her shoulder. "She's rolling. She likes everything."

Rolling. The love drug. I'd heard Lincoln talk about what that felt like. No wonder the girl was getting off on my hair.

Lyric shoved and pushed, clearing a path across the concrete floor to the other side of the room.

Was it a room? I'd heard stories about the guy who was buried here. The legend said he threw some of the most elaborate—and raunchy—parties New York had ever seen. The guest list was exclusive to the elite and kept top secret. In a time when *raunchy* was the equivalent of *sinful*, attending these parties was quite the scandal. Before the tomb was fully constructed, when it was nothing more than a concrete slab on a dirt clearing, he'd brought those same parties here as a celebration of life before death. Somewhere along the way, someone decided to embrace his legacy and keep the party going.

I swerved to the side to keep from bumping into a tall guy with blond hair who was hunched down over a girl's chest. "Wait, was that—"

Lyric looked over her shoulder at me. "Jake Ryan whiffing snow off Geneva's tits? Yes."

So that's how he manages those all-night gaming sessions. Jake had a record-breaking YouTube following thanks to his online video streams.

The more I saw, the more I envied their freedom. My world always felt bound by obligation, but now I was curious, so fucking curious. Now, I wanted to *feel*.

I was so preoccupied with the scene behind me that I didn't notice Lyric had stopped walking and let go of my hand.

"Easy, Helen Keller. Watch where you're going," she said when I ran into her. "You almost made me spill our drinks." She handed me a clear plastic cup filled with bright blue… *something*.

The bar in front of her was lined full of cups just like this one, no limit, free for the taking. The guy behind the bar was filling cups as quickly as they disappeared.

I took the drink but kept my eyes focused on my chest. My boobs spilled over the black, sleeveless corset I wore underneath my favorite leather jacket of the same color. I had cleavage, sure. I wasn't an A-cup, but I wasn't blessed by any means, not like Geneva. My tits would never be deemed snow-worthy. I would also never win a Grammy thanks to golden vocal cords like she did, but I was more upset about my boobs.

I cupped my free hand over one of my breasts and sighed.

Lyric placed one hand over mine and gave my boob a squeeze. "You're perfect. Your tits are perfect. You don't need some dude with a bad habit and greedy nostrils to tell you that."

That was why she was my best friend. She knew what I was thinking without me ever having to say a word.

Two seconds later, she was grabbing a lemon slice from a bowl on the bar and shoving it in my cleavage. Before I could stop her, she leaned down and placed it in her mouth, taking a moment to suck some of the sour juice.

Kyle Blankenship walked up as Lyric pulled the lemon from my cleavage. He was minus the robe and mask, but my mind immediately made the connection. Kyle was the hooded guy who led us from the pavilion to The Chamber's entrance. His eyes gave him away.

"Holy shit. That was hot as fuck. Damn, Tatum. I didn't know you were into chicks," he said.

"I'm not."

His eyes bounced to Lyric, who had her full lips wrapped around the lemon and a rebellious gleam in her eyes. "So, Lyric's into chicks?"

"Lyric is into Lyric." She wasn't homosexual. She wasn't heterosexual or bisexual either. She was just... sexual.

His lips quirked up into a grin. "What about Tatum? What is Tatum into?"

Kyle was hot. He'd been a model since he was in diapers. Everything about him was flawless, from his dirty blond hair and emerald green eyes to his washboard abs and perfect ass. He was older than me by a few years, but everyone knew who he was. Any girl in her right mind would've answered with an immediate, *"You. I'm into you."*

Not me. I brought the cup to my lips, stopping long enough to answer before I took a drink. "Why do people have to be put into boxes? Why can't we just be into what we're into?" Bold statement coming from a virgin who'd never even been kissed. But Kyle didn't need to know that.

He ran his thumb across his bottom lip, and I wondered if tonight would be the night that all that changed.

The music shifted. The beat dropped low, followed by a faster background of violins and electronic sounds.

Lyric downed her drink in one long pull, then tossed her empty cup into a round plastic barrel. "I'm going to dance." She threw a wink over her shoulder as she moved into the crowd. "You kids behave."

Kyle started to say something, but I overestimated my tolerance for the taste of alcohol and started coughing.

I brought a hand to my chest and swallowed hard, then cleared my throat. Good God, what did they put in this stuff? It tasted the way gasoline smelled.

Kyle chuckled and took a sip of his own drink. "You don't do this often, do you?"

"Is it that obvious?"

He smiled. "Nah. I just don't see you out much."

I lifted a brow. "So, you've been looking for me?" I took another drink. This one went down a little easier.

"You're kinda hard to miss."

I might not have gone out much, but I knew what flirting was, and he was definitely flirting.

"Is that why you sent me the invitation?" It was a hunch. The invitation had been placed under my windshield wiper a couple of weeks ago while I was at ballet. Until now, I'd had no idea who put it there.

"How'd you know that was me?"

I smiled. "You just told me."

He leaned in close to my ear. "Is it wrong to want to drag the princess out of her tower?"

I laughed him off. "There's no tower. I'm just busy." I searched the room for Lyric, finally spotting her sandwiched between two guys I vaguely recognized from Instagram. One of them eased his hand up the front of her shirt while the other ran his tongue along the side of her neck. I shook my head and took another drink.

"Too busy to have a life?" Kyle asked.

"I guess that depends on your definition of a *life*."

He looked up at me, his bright emerald gaze now dark, as he brought his hand to my collarbone, then traced a fingertip across my chest. "Doing things that make you feel alive."

That made me feel something. I just wasn't sure if it was excitement or unease. I wanted it to be excitement. I wanted some of what Lyric had—of what the blonde on the rock had. I wanted a raw, uninhibited passion for life, even if it was just one night a year.

"Dancing makes me feel alive. I love dancing." I started taking ballet classes the minute I could put on a pair of pointe shoes. Nothing made me feel more alive than when it was just me and the music.

"Yeah? Show me."

"Right now?"

"Right now."

I finished the last of my drink then handed him my empty cup. Game on. The alcohol was already messing with my head, making me fearless. I slipped my jacket off my shoulders and tossed it to him. He caught it with a grin then threw it over his shoulder. I walked backward, careful not to bump into anyone behind me, until I was far enough away from him to give him a good show but close enough to watch his reaction.

My hips rocked from side to side with the rhythm of the chants. My gaze was focused on Kyle, but my body was hyperaware of a *different* set of eyes on me. His heated gaze penetrated me from across the room, like a touch blazing across my skin. The familiar pulse I'd always felt when he was near began thrumming through my veins. A low, steady hum as powerful and deep as the bass vibrating in these walls.

I knew who it was before I ever looked in his direction. I felt him, the same way I always felt him whenever he was near. The energy was different when he was close. The air was charged. Electric.

Something dark and sinister swirled in my belly knowing *he* was watching me here in this place that manifested sex and sin, in this place where morals didn't exist. My heartbeat thrummed against my ribcage, and my hips began to dip and roll on pure instinct. Every single one of my senses peaked, magnifying *everything*. The corset hugging my body, the way it tightly cupped my breasts, the friction of black denim rubbing between my thighs, the cool air caressing my hot skin—all of it magnificently intense, all of it intimate. My hands roamed my curves, gliding from my stomach to my breasts, up my neck, and into my hair as though they had a mind of their own, as if my body knew what it wanted and was willing me to take it. I closed my eyes and tilted my head back, letting myself get lost in the rhythm, in my own touch, in the way the bass vibrated from the floor all the way through me.

When I brought my head back down and opened my eyes, my gaze landed directly on Caspian Donahue.

My lips parted in a gasp. A bead of sweat trickled down my back, evidence of the heat radiating through the room.

Beside him, a girl was pinned against the wall, her legs hooked around a guy's waist while his thighs and ass tightened and flexed as he pounded into her. The girl gripped Caspian's shoulder, fisting his shirt in her hand as if she needed something, anything, to hold onto to keep her from going over the edge, as if with this one carnal gesture, she was inviting him to join their pleasure.

He never gave them as much as a glance. His gaze never broke from mine. His mouth didn't move. His hands remained tucked into the front pockets of his jeans as he casually leaned against the stone wall.

I tore my eyes from him and walked back to Kyle.

He handed me a fresh cup of blue alcohol poisoning, and I drank it like my throat was on fire.

"I could watch you all night," he said.

I opened my mouth to respond, only to let out a yelp when my body was lifted up and hoisted over a broad shoulder. The cup fell from my hand, coating the concrete floor in bright blue liquid. Strong arms held a tight grip across the backs of my thighs and hard muscle dug into my stomach with every step he took. I reached down to grab hold of the back of his shirt. All I saw was the curve of a firm, round ass as I was carried through a crowd of people and back out the wooden door.

SIX

CASPIAN

The end of this chapter contains a graphic description of a sexual situation with a minor. (She is sixteen. He is twenty.) It may be skipped over as its contents are implied in other chapters.

The last time I saw Tatum was at her Sweet Sixteen when her dad threw a big party on his Lurssen yacht. I knew Tatum. I'd been watching her for years. I knew her mannerisms, her facial expressions, and her quirks. She hated that party. But she loved the boat. She loved the water—with the exception of Crestview Lake, for obvious reasons—and she loved her parents, so she flashed her perfect, red-lipped smile, and she made the world believe it didn't get any better than it was at that moment.

In life, I gave zero fucks.

Tatum gave too many.

At that party, one of Tatum's father's pervy friends kept pawing at her and making awkward conversation. Touching her all over the fucking place—her arms, her back, her face, tucking her hair behind her ear. Sick fucker. She was sixteen. He was at least thirty-five. She would smile and entertain him, but her body language told me all I needed to know. So, I slipped him some

Ambien—not giving a single fuck about mixing it with alcohol—and watched his perverted ass pass out.

It wasn't that I was some cockblocking douchebag who kept Tatum from dating. That wasn't what this was about. It was about not letting predators, like him or that dickhead Kyle, take advantage of her. She already had enough shit to deal with from her own father trying to marry her off to boost his career. If a nice guy with a solid GPA and maybe an investment portfolio wanted to ram his dick down her throat, who was I to stop him? Fuckboys and perverts were off limits, though.

Which was why I had her hiked over my shoulder, carrying her through the cemetery to my car right now.

Fuckboys.

I was ninety percent sure Kyle dropped a Molly in her drink right before she downed half of it in one gulp. How she acted within the next thirty minutes or so would tell me if I was right.

"Caspian?" She said my name like she wasn't sure who had scooped her ass up.

I didn't answer her. Who else would it be?

Her fists beat on my back. Fucking cute as shit.

"Let me down."

I kept walking. *Not a chance.*

"I mean it. I need to throw up."

Nice try. "Then throw up."

She growled. It was like a miniature Yorkie standing toe-to-toe with a Rottweiler. Her hands pounded my back again. Then as if she'd given up and sagged forward, there was a subtle slap on my ass. Then a gasp.

"Oh God. That was your butt."

Yes, it was.

"I touched your butt."

Yes, you did.

I followed the path past the second lake and the creepy-as-fuck church. We passed an all-white pavilion with a dome top and round concrete columns, then walked through the gothic, arched gates and to my car.

Chandler Carmichael was leaning his ass on my hood with his long legs stretched out in front of him. Chandler was my closest friend and the only person in this world I truly trusted without hesitation. His father was a world-class prick, and I couldn't even tell you how many times his mom had tried to ride my dick. But Chandler was nothing like the rest of his family, thank God.

I slid Tatum down the front of my body and set her on her feet.

She wobbled a little, then brought her fingers to her temples like she was trying to regain focus after being upside down so long.

I slipped my hand in the front pocket of the tight-ass black jeans she was wearing.

Her eyes popped open wide. "What the hell are you doing?"

I grabbed her key fob and tossed it at Chandler's chest. He caught it with ease. "You didn't actually think I'd let you drive, did you?"

Her mouth fell open. "What about Lyric? She can drive. I'm not letting him..." she jammed a finger in Chandler's direction. "...drive my car."

I opened the passenger door of my Audi R8. "You don't have a choice." I nodded toward the car. "Get in."

Her big doe eyes locked on mine. "I can't leave Lyric."

"Lyric is fine. Everyone in The Chamber knows you left with me, and Chandler will come back to take her home."

She stood there staring at me for what felt like an eternity. I saw Chandler push off my hood and walk behind us.

"Later, bro," he said as he passed. "Good luck with that one."

I didn't need luck. I needed her to fucking listen.

"Thanks, man," I said back without moving my gaze from the girl in front of me. My jaw tightened, and my hand clenched the door frame. I inhaled a breath through my nose and waited. Thank fuck I was a patient man.

Tatum finally heaved a sigh then plopped down in the passenger seat.

I ducked into the passenger side, reaching over her body to buckle her in.

She threw her head back against the headrest and groaned. "I'm not a child."

I angled my head toward her as the seat belt clicked. She lowered her head, bringing our faces centimeters apart. Her chest heaved with every breath she took, but her eyes never moved from mine.

"No. You're not." *Not with tits like that.* I ducked back out of the car, closed the door, and walked around to the driver's side.

This was going to be a long fucking drive.

"You aren't taking me home?" Tatum asked as she watched me drive through the heavy iron gates then up the driveway.

"No." I cut the engine. "You're wasted, and your dad would shit." *Or ship you off to Saudi Arabia and let some rich prick sober you up.*

I led her through the foyer and living room, then up the curved staircase and to my bedroom. The walls in our home were an ivory color and the floors a light swirled marble. Even with high ceilings and soft uplighting, at night, it still felt ominous. Maybe it was the silence. It was always so quiet here.

I'd never "hung out" with Tatum, never held more than a five-minute conversation with her at a time, never tried to be her *friend*. Since I was ten years old, I'd watched her from a distance—mostly—spoke when I needed to and made sure she stayed out of the kind of trouble that often seemed to find people in our world. Now, here she was, standing in my room in the middle of the night wearing tight black pants and a silk corset that cut off just above her belly button and pushed her tits up. Her dark brown hair was draped over her shoulders in long waves. Red lipstick was painted over a perfect pair of pouty lips, and thick dark lashes framed brown doe-like eyes.

Fuck.

Everything I did for Tatum was always instinctual, never sexual. Not that I had never thought about what her tight little cunt would feel like. I just knew I'd never act on it. Even if our families didn't quietly hate each other, she was four years younger than me. I was twenty. She was sixteen. But right now, my cock twitched, growing harder by the second, and I was having a really hard time giving a damn about any of that.

I reached in my dresser drawer and pulled out a T-shirt then tossed it her way. "Put that on and get in bed."

She caught it with one hand. Maybe she wasn't as fucked up as I thought. With one shoulder leaning against my dresser, I watched her walk over to the bed. She dropped the T-shirt on top of the plush blue comforter, then reached down to unfasten her heels and slide them off her feet. My blood rushed through my veins with a fierceness I hadn't known since the day I looked a lion in the eye. Tatum met my stare, then brought her hands to the top of her jeans and unbuttoned the top button. My eyes cut to the other side of the room. I gave a slight nod to where an open door led to my private bathroom. She followed my line of sight, then looked back at me, shaking her head.

Tsk. Tsk. What are you up to, Little Troublemaker?

I pulled my bottom lip between my teeth at the sound of metal against metal when she pulled down her zipper. She shimmied out of her pants then kicked them off to the side with her foot while I stood here motionless. Her bright red panties were a stark contrast to her creamy white skin. She moved her hair off her shoulder then reached around to her back.

That should have been the first red flag, but apparently, I was fucking colorblind.

I lived in a world where power reigned supreme, and my father wore the crown. There were libraries in universities across the globe with our family name on them. I was a firstborn male, fourth-generation Donahue, which meant one day, the legacy would be mine. I was twenty years old with the power of the world at my fingertips, and still, I was powerless to stop myself from standing here watching Tatum Huntington undress.

In one fluid motion she unzipped the corset and tossed it onto the floor next to her pants and shoes. I was breathless, fucking speechless, at the rapid rise and fall of her chest, at the perfect swell of her breast and her bare stomach. My hands itched to roam all over that delicate curve from her hips to her waist and up to her tits. Pale pink nipples begged to be pulled between my teeth.

God.

Damn.

My dick grew hard and heavy, pressing against the confines of my boxer briefs. This was wrong. I didn't bring her here for this. I was supposed to protect her, not burn with the need to devour her. Apparently, my dick couldn't give two shits about ethics.

She grabbed the T-shirt and slipped it over her head, then sauntered over to me, sexy as fuck. An instant, violent twinge of possessiveness gripped my chest. Fuck what I said about the guy with the perfect GPA. I wanted to know how many times she had done this. How many other guys had seen her this way? The urge to completely ruin her, to erase every other touch from her memory, pulsed through me at a blinding force.

"Are you always this ready to fuck, or should we blame it on the alcohol?" I asked when she stopped inches in front of me. *"Or the drugs,"* I should have said but didn't because I saw no reason to freak her out.

She propped one hand on her hip and glared up at me. "Are you always this big of a dick, or should we blame it on the stick up your ass?"

I gripped her chin between my fingers. "Keep fucking with me and I'll show you the dick you seem to be so curious about."

"Fuck. You."

Her words challenged my demons. She'd always been defiant, but this was the first time she'd done it while standing in front of me half-naked.

I let go of her chin and trailed my fingertip along her jaw, then down the column of her throat, gently, tentatively, a contradiction to the harsh way I gripped her a second before. Her pulse thrummed under the pad of my finger, so delicate, so fragile. "Careful. You're inching dangerously close to the fire."

She bit her lower lip and brought her hand to my shirt, unbuttoning the first button. "Maybe I'm tired of standing alone in the cold."

She was fucking provoking me. She had no idea who she was dealing with. I wasn't a normal man with normal needs. When you lived your life with your every desire at your beck and call, the only thrill came from chasing things that didn't want to be caught, taking what didn't want to be had. I craved the unattainable. I was addicted to the forbidden, to the push and pull. My last name was enough foreplay for most women. In my world, a good fuck was always just a smile and a nod away. That wasn't my thing. Easy access was for the weak. Give me a challenge, and my dick got hard.

I swallowed a groan. "You're sixteen fucking years old. You don't know what you want."

"I know I want to feel what it's like." She continued unbuttoning buttons, and I didn't stop her. "To be kissed." Another button. "To be wanted." Another button. She pulled my shirt open, then her hand traveled over my bare chest, letting her fingertips trace the tattoo that spread from my pec to my shoulder. "To be touched..." A pause. "*That* way."

Hold up. What the fuck did she just say?

I circled my fingers around her tiny wrist, halting her movements, and looked down at her. "You've never been fucked?"

She was definitely high. Virgins didn't act like this. Virgins who had never been kissed damn sure didn't. Fucking Kyle just bought himself an ass whipping.

She shook her head.

"Never been touched?"

She shook her head again.

"Never been kissed?"

Another shake of the head.

The possessive jealousy from before unraveled then wrapped back around me as something else, something more primitive, like a clingy vine morphing into barbed wire. It dug at me until I almost couldn't breathe.

She was untouched, unkissed, innocent. Part of me envied that. Most of me wanted to take her innocence and devour it. But I also wanted to protect it, to protect her from men like me, men who would destroy her. It was all one big mind fuck that was making it difficult to think straight.

I clenched my teeth. "You should get some sleep."

"If you won't show me, then will you at least tell me what it's like? So I don't look like a fool when it finally happens."

When it finally happens. Just like that, she was the six-year-old girl in the wedding veil again, dreaming about her wedding day. There was a vulnerable girl underneath the smart-mouthed exterior. Except now, instead of dreaming about her wedding, she was fantasizing about being touched... kissed... fucked. She was both hellfire and holy water, and that made her dangerous.

"You want me to tell you what it's like to be kissed?"

"Please."

I was rock fucking hard with my demons practically clawing out of my skin, ready to be unleashed, and she wanted me to *tell* her what it was like to be kissed. She might as well have asked me to strike a match and set myself on fire. The fucked-up thing was that I would, because if she thought *she* was ready to burn, I was already engulfed in flames.

"Okay," I agreed.

"Okay?"

"Yeah. I'll tell you what it's like." *Even if it kills us both.* I held her stare. "One minute, everything will be normal. Nothing in the universe will seem out of place. You'll be watching TV or sitting across from each other having dinner or… standing in the middle of his bedroom."

She swallowed hard at my last remark.

"Then, all of a sudden, the air will shift. It will feel charged, and that charge will swirl around your body like a tornado. Your heart will beat faster. Your breath will come harder. And there will be a moment, right before it happens, right when the air shifts, that you'll feel it here…" I reached between our bodies and cupped her pussy. She sucked in a breath. My long middle finger sank into the thin fabric of her panties, teetering on the edge of dipping into her tight little hole even through the lace. Her tiny hand fisted my shirt. Fuck, she was wet already. I pulled my hand away and brought it to her lips. "…before you ever feel it here." She inhaled her own scent. Christ, this was going to be harder than I thought. "He'll look at you. He'll look at you and know."

"Know what?" Her voice was a breathy whisper.

"That you want him."

She let out a long exhale, then licked her lips.

"He'll touch you, probably like this." I brought my hand to the side of her face and continued. She leaned into my touch. "His gaze will fall from your eyes to your mouth. He'll sweep his thumb over your cheekbone, then over your lips." I followed my words with a demonstration. Her skin was so fucking soft. Her lips were so fucking full. It took everything in me not to rub harder and smear her red lipstick across her pretty face. "Your lips will part." Her lips parted. "He'll lean in and touch the tip of his nose against the tip of yours." I leaned in and brushed my nose along hers. She closed her eyes and breathed in. "Then across your cheek, letting his breath whisper over your skin." *Just like this.* "Finally, he'll bring his mouth to yours." I moved my lips above hers. "And stop."

Her eyes popped open, and I grinned.

I wet my lips. "He's waiting for permission."

"Oh," she breathed.

"He might bring his tongue to the seam of your lips and steal a taste." I traced my tongue over her bottom lip. "And as soon as your lips part to invite him inside, he'll know you're his."

She parted her lips. The demons inside me demanded to be freed. My dick was painfully hard, and the control I'd so artfully mastered began to slip from my grasp. I had to remind myself that this was just a demonstration. If it were real, I'd have had one hand wrapped around her throat and the other fisted in her hair.

"You'll open that pretty little mouth and let him suck the soul right from your body and into his own," I said against her lips. Then I lifted my head and stepped away.

Tatum fisted my shirt tighter and pulled me back. Her gentle hands moved to cup my face as she looked up at me with those fucking eyes. "I want it to be you." She leaned up on her tiptoes and brought her mouth to mine. "I want you to be the one to take my soul."

I lost the battle between dick and mind. Every ounce of self-control evaporated into thin air. She offered me her soul, and I wanted to take it. It wasn't enough to simply protect her anymore. I wanted to have her, own her, claim every part of her from the inside out as mine.

"I will destroy you."

A challenge glinted in her eyes. "I dare you to try."

A good man wouldn't steal her innocence.

A good man wouldn't take advantage of a wasted girl.

A good man would have sent her to bed then jacked off in the shower instead of lifting her up and wrapping her legs around his waist.

I lowered my mouth to hers and did exactly as she asked. I kissed her until she came undone, until she was grinding her sweet pussy against me and moaning in my mouth, begging me to fuck her. I kissed her until our souls were one. Then I walked her over and tossed her down on my bed.

She yanked the shirt over her head while I pulled the panties over her hips. Her sweet little cunt glistened for me as I unbuttoned my pants and freed my cock.

"Is this what you wanted?" I leaned down and swept the head along her seam, rubbing up and down with the tip. Christ she was so fucking wet.

She swallowed hard then bit her lip.

I should've held back. I should've eased from between her legs and rolled over instead of pushing my pants the rest of the way off and waiting at her entrance.

My thumb swept over her cheek, making her breath hitch. That right there, that innocent little gesture made my balls draw up so tight they ached. She caught her bottom lip between her teeth and all I could think about was covering that mouth with my cum then watching her lick it off.

I moved my hand to her hair, tightening a handful in my fist and forcing her head to tilt back. "This is the one and only time I'll ask, so I suggest you answer me." With my other hand, I reached between our bodies and coated the pad of my thumb in my pre-cum and her slickness. And then I smeared it across that fucking lip she loved to chew on. "Is this what you wanted?" My words were precise, deliberate, and very, very clear.

She let out a breath, ragged and slow.

And then she licked that goddamn lip and smiled.

Fuck.

Me.

I braced myself with my hands on the bed. "Time's up, Little Troublemaker. You're mine now." She looked so vulnerable when I pushed into her, burying my dick all the way to the root.

She pressed her hands against my shoulders but never pushed me away. "Oh, God."

Not quite. But she did feel like fucking heaven.

I gave her a second to adjust because I might have been an asshole, but I wasn't a sadist. And then I gave her what we both needed, what no one else would ever be able to give her again. I drilled into her like the animal I was, like the motherfucking king of the jungle. Her perfect round ass would probably leave an imprint in my mattress. We easily fell into a rhythm, like her body was made for fucking, like it was made to be fucked by me. Her hips lifted to chase me. Her legs hooked around mine, pushing me harder, deeper. Beads of sweat trickled down my back and pleasure burned in my veins. Her pussy clamped around me, and she looked up at me with tears spilling from her eyes as the last shred of innocence tore from her sweet little body with the sound of my name.

It turned out I was not a good man after all.

SEVEN

Tatum

Thick, inky blackness. My mind was a voided slate with random splashes of colorful memories. My eyelids were heavy, and it felt as though I'd been sleeping for days. I was in a bed, but not my own. Tiny threads of sunlight crept through the cracks in the curtains. The sheets felt cool against my skin, and my head settled into the plush pillow. I clutched the comforter in my fist and brought it close to my body, clinging to it like a security blanket. I blinked away the heaviness until everything began to come softly into focus.

White.

The comforter was white.

I could've sworn it was blue last night. And the walls were a different color. They were a darker shade of gray than the one I was staring at now.

It all looked so different. It all *felt* so different.

Because it was.

This wasn't the same room I fell asleep in. At least I remembered that.

This room had white and taupe *everything*. Soft brown curtains made of heavy velvet kept most of the sunlight from coming in. There was an oversized chair and ottoman in one corner by the bed and a tall, three-door armoire painted ivory but trimmed in gold. A solid crystal chandelier hung over the bed. The other room felt dark and cryptic, at least from what I remembered. This room felt elegant and formal, noble even, like a princess should be sleeping here instead of me. I looked all around, then toward the door, trying to remember how I got here. Nothing. Just patches. I had all these separate pieces with no knowledge of the puzzle.

Images of Caspian flashed in my mind in one of the more vibrant memories. I remembered the way he took me—if you could call it *taking*. I offered myself to him. I knew that. All he did was accept. That part came back to me clear as day.

He wasn't gentle. There was no coddling, coaxing or asking if I was okay. He fucked me, savage and fierce, like he was determined to make his mark on my soul. Then again, I didn't expect anything less from him. Caspian had always felt distant and dangerous, but he also felt safe. I knew with him I was protected—from everything but him. He didn't make me feel delicate or fragile. He made me feel powerful and cherished all at once. My body sang for him. I was already addicted to the way it felt.

My virginity wasn't ever something I dwelled on, not like most girls I knew. Lyric lost hers a few months ago, and I lived vicariously through her. I never felt the urge to rush into the kind of unrelenting need for release that she always talked about. I never wanted to crave anything the way she craved sex. In my eyes, it was a handicap. Dancing was my passion. It was my future. I didn't want anything to get in the way of that. But last night, being in The Chamber, stepping outside of my comfort zone and into a world that didn't revolve around structure and etiquette, stirred something inside of me. It awakened a part of me I didn't even know was sleeping. There was an intoxicating thrill in walking on the edge of forbidden.

That's what Caspian was.

He was forbidden.

My father hated his family. My brother hated him.

Maybe that's why I wanted him. My whole life, I'd been groomed to like the respectable things, speak the proper words, follow the appropriate path, be the perfect angel. Sometimes the halo got heavy. Sometimes I just wanted to take it off and hand myself over to the darkness. I wished I could say it was the alcohol, but that would be a lie. There had always been a current flowing between Caspian and me. I just never knew what it meant until last night.

I rolled over, not believing I'd actually find him sleeping beside me but still feeling the need to check. The bed was empty. There was only me. Something about that made my heart feel heavy. Was it twisted to wonder if he stood at the edge of the bed last night and watched me sleep? Was it even more twisted to wish he had?

I pulled the comforter back and climbed out of bed. Oh my God. My whole body hurt. My muscles ached the way they did after I'd spent hours trying to execute the perfect pirouette. And my lady bits… God. I reached my hand down and cupped my hand over my pussy, seeking some sort of relief from the throbbing soreness. How in the world was I going to pee without wanting to cry?

How in the world was I even supposed to walk?

Where in the world were my panties?

My head throbbed and my legs struggled to hold up my weight as I circled the bed to find the bathroom. I ran my hand along the wall until I found a light switch. My aching muscles almost cried out in relief when I spotted a deep garden tub in the middle of the room. A gold chandelier with crystal teardrops dangling from each arm hung from the ceiling over the tub. A hot bath. God, I wanted a hot bath.

I stood in front of the vanity mirror and took in my appearance. Other than the fact that my hair was a mess and I was wearing nothing but a black vintage Rolling Stones T-shirt, I didn't look any different than I did last night, but I felt like I'd been transformed. I combed my fingers through my long brown hair, remembering the way Caspian's fingers were wrapped in it, the way he tugged and pulled while he stretched and filled me until tears rolled down my cheeks. There had to have been something seriously wrong with me for wanting him the way I did, but I couldn't make myself *not* want him, *not* wish he would walk through that door right now and rip me open again.

The air shifted, and for a moment I thought he might actually do just that, but when I walked back into the room there was no one there, nothing but a white serving tray on the bed.

My clothes were folded neatly on the oversized chair. Splashes of bright color spread across the white bed tray—a bowl of fresh fruit, a cup of coffee, a glass of orange juice, two tiny, clear plastic cups—one with two pills inside that I immediately recognized as Advil and the other with just one pill I had never seen before but assumed was for the soreness between my legs. Next to the fruit there was an unopened toothbrush and a note written in crisp, precise handwriting.

Take the pills. All three of them.

Then, down at the bottom, *Remember, Little Troublemaker, your soul is mine to ruin now.*

He left the tray.

Why?

Why would Caspian take the time to do all that with the tray and the note, even sending me a toothbrush, if he was just going to ignore me?

I swallowed the pills down with some orange juice but left the fruit and coffee alone. Then I took the toothbrush and my clothes —except for the corset because I was keeping this T-shirt—to the bathroom and contemplated soaking in that tub.

Okay, maybe not. That would be weird, right?

Definitely weird.

I mentally scratched *soaking in the tub of the man who took your virginity* off my to-do list.

My muscles groaned in protest, which reminded me I definitely needed to cancel my ballet lesson for today.

After brushing my teeth, I walked back into the bedroom then pulled on my jeans, minus panties because those were missing. I was so engrossed in my thoughts that I almost didn't hear a knock on the door.

The door opened slowly, and a man peeked his head inside the room, startling me. "Miss?"

I hurried to fasten the button on my pants. "Yes?"

He pushed the door open the rest of the way. His dark hair was styled to one side and there wasn't a speck of lint on his tailored black suit. "Your car is ready."

His words sent my pulse skyrocketing. *Caspian was telling me to leave, and he didn't even have the balls to say goodbye.* I narrowed my eyes and rushed past Suit Guy then out the door, only to end up on the mezzanine overlooking the massive foyer. There were at least twenty other doors out here, and I had no idea which one was Caspian's room. For all I knew, it wasn't even on this floor. It wasn't like I remembered walking upstairs last night. Bracing my hands on the polished wood railing, I stared down at the swirled, black "D" design etched into the center of the white marble floor below. Everyone knew the Donahues. Their money was as old as money itself. My family was old money, too, but not like this. Our home was nice. Theirs was a museum for interior design.

Was I pathetic enough to search every room until I found him just because he bruised my pride? Then what? I beg him to let me stay? My father had always said that begging was beneath me.

My father.

Panic filled my chest. My family could never know about this. It would destroy everything.

I didn't let my thoughts linger on that for long. Instead, I did the smart thing and went back into the guest room, grabbed my heels and corset off the chair and pulled the jacket over my shoulders.

"My car is here?" Not a driver hired to bring me home. *My* car.

The man in the suit pulled his lips into a thin line and nodded once. "Yes, Miss." Suit Guy was obviously not here to make friends. Or maybe he grew tired of escorting Caspian's conquests out the front door when he was finished with them.

Was I a conquest? Did Caspian have conquests? I tried to remember any rumors I'd heard about his sex life but the guy was a mystery with secrets as dark as the bottom of Crestview Lake.

"All right then." I inhaled a breath then tossed my heels onto the bed. He might have been able to send me off without as much as a goodbye, but I wasn't leaving without giving him something to make sure he didn't forget last night. I looked back at Suit Guy. "Lead the way."

The large iron gates at the end of the driveway eased open as I approached.

"Call Lyric," I told my Bluetooth as I pulled out and headed toward West Street.

No answer.

"Text Lyric."

A male voice with an Australian accent—which was so much better than the factory-set robotic female—answered back. "What do you want to say?"

"Answer your phone, hooker. You're never going to believe what I did."

She was going to die once she found out. She'd been teasing me about Caspian since the first day I met her, the day he pulled me out of the lake.

I touched the Spotify icon on my display screen and turned up the volume to my *Got me in my feelings* playlist the rest of the way home.

The minute I walked in the door I was suffocated by a thick sense of dread. My chest tightened, making it hard to breathe, though I wasn't sure why. Perhaps this was what guilt felt like. Until now, I'd never done anything to feel guilty about.

My mother was sitting on the sofa with her back straight and one leg crossed over the other. She looked as though she were ready to drag out a cigarette and start smoking again any second now. My father was pacing back and forth, running a hand through his hair. There were two policemen standing behind the sofa with notepads in their hands.

All this because I stayed out all night without texting them first.

Dad rushed across the room and grabbed me by the shoulders, studying my face and staring into my eyes. "Tatum. Thank God." He pulled me into a hug, apparently satisfied with my appearance.

I gave him a brief hug then backed away from him because I was almost certain I still smelled like sex, but he kept his hands cradling my face.

"I'm fine, Dad. We got in late, so I spent the night with Lyric." *Lie.* But there was no way I was telling him a truth that would start a war.

The muscles in his jaw ticked as he dropped his hands and took a step back. His gaze burned through me like fire, searing me all the way to my bones. He never looked at me like that, like he was furious and heartbroken at the same time.

He knew.
But how?

No one talked about what happened at The Chamber, so no one would have told him I left with Caspian. I'd left my phone in my car, so the Life360 app didn't give me away.

Life360.

Shit.

My phone was in my car, and my car was at Caspian's, even though I would've sworn I didn't drive it there. One click, and my dad would've known exactly where I was.

This was it. I was caught. That was why the police were here. He was going to press charges—sex with a minor. Every heated discussion I'd ever heard my father have, every promise I'd ever heard him make, years of resentment and animosity—it all boiled down to this moment. I would be the weapon to make our empire fall. All because I gave myself to the enemy.

It was too late. The lie was already out. There was no taking it back now.

My mother bolted up from the sofa and rushed over to where we stood. She pulled her soft yellow cardigan closed around her petite frame, wrapping her arms around herself. I saw then that she'd been crying. Her eyes were red and puffy, and she wasn't wearing makeup—a first for her.

One of the police officers made his way across the room, stopping a few feet from us. "You said you spent the night with Lyric?" His voice was level, but the look in his eye said he was holding something back.

I nodded. "Yes, sir. So, you can leave now. Close up your missing person's report. I've been found." I looked over at Mom, then smiled and attempted a joke, trying to lighten the tension in the room. "Tell me you at least used a good picture of me for the Amber alert." This was about as awkward as that time my dad sent me to school with a bodyguard because someone had just murdered one of his lobbyists.

Mom closed her eyes and inhaled a deep breath.

The cop cut his gaze from me to my dad. Dad blinked and nodded. Oh God. Here it came.

Dad stuffed his hands into his pockets and smirked. The worry was gone, replaced by an expression I'd never seen on his face before. It was almost as though he were challenging me. "You're going to have to try harder than that, sweetheart."

I looked around the room for my brother, Lincoln, but all I saw was the other cop saying something into the device clipped to his shoulder. Why was he talking so quietly? Adrenaline pumped through my veins, and my legs felt weak.

Determined to stay strong, I met my father's stare. "What are you talking about? I'm not trying anything."

I would make up an excuse about my phone later, say I left it at a party and Caspian picked it up. After all, the app tracked my phone. It didn't track *me*.

"Honey," my mom said as she wrapped her arms around me and nuzzled her face into my hair. Her voice was quiet when she spoke her next words. "Lyric is dead."

EIGHT

CASPIAN

Taking Tatum's virginity may not have been part of the plan, but that didn't mean I didn't enjoy every second of it. I tried to be tender and careful the way most guys would have been, but the instant I sank into her, that thin thread of humanity snapped and the monster broke loose. *Tender* wasn't in my nature. It hadn't been since the first time my father laid his hands on me.

I gave Tatum a glimpse of who I was, and she welcomed me with open arms. She never pushed me off. She never asked me to stop. She opened up for me and let me take her *my* way. The faces she made when she finally got used to me and let me push deep inside... God help me, those faces would make Aphrodite jealous. And when she cried... Fuck. When she cried, I damn near lost it. Then I saw my dick coated in blood—her blood—and I knew what sharks must feel like the moment they catch the scent of their prey. Instinct, animalistic and carnal, kicked in, and I had to stop myself from doing things to her that I would regret. It wasn't enough for me to take her virginity, to steal all her firsts. I wanted to corrupt her, to ruin her. I wanted to make it so she would never crave gentle and sweet, that she would only want the kind of depravity I could give. I needed it like a dying man needed air.

Which is why I hauled her ass to the guest room as soon as she went to sleep. It was the only way to keep her safe... from me. I'd already done enough damage. The evidence was all over my sheets, my dick, and smeared between her creamy white thighs—at least until I wiped her clean. I loved that shit, but she didn't need to wake up and see it.

Chandler was blowing up my phone before I was up long enough to take a piss this morning. He'd called to tell me Tatum's brother was on his way to my house.

And he was furious.

Fuck him.

I could handle him, but the last thing I needed was Lincoln Huntington showing up and finding his sister here. There was already enough beef between our families.

"One day, I'll have that motherfucker assassinated. Just wait," my father would sometimes say.

The crazy thing was, I believed him. Dad had no limits, no boundaries. He'd already taken care of two of Huntington's lobbyists because they were pushing bills that would affect our business. That thing most people had that separated right from wrong in their brains? It wasn't in our gene pool. Huntington wouldn't be the first politician to go down for pushing a Donahue too far and probably wouldn't be the last. He was just too stupid to realize it. Or too arrogant to care.

So, I slid on a pair of gray joggers and a pink tee—no underwear because I planned on making Lincoln suck my dick if he started any shit. Which was another reason it was time for Tatum to leave. She didn't need to witness what I'd do to her brother if he showed up here asking for a fight.

After I texted Chandler back, telling him to find out if Kyle had spiked Tatum's drink and to fuck him up if he had, I dropped off her breakfast tray—complete with two Advil, a morning after pill, and a little reminder of who she belonged to. She was standing in the bathroom in nothing but my favorite T-shirt. Her hair was a mess. Her skin was still flushed, and there were fresh purple fingerprints on her thighs where my hands had been. She didn't look afraid or regretful, the way I'd worried she would. She looked sated. She looked like a woman seeing herself for the first time. She looked fucking beautiful.

A weaker man would have walked into that bathroom and taken her again right then and there. I almost did. But I had to care more about protecting her from what was about to happen than satisfying my cravings, so I made myself walk out of that room then sent my dad's butler to get her the fuck out of here.

It was a good thing, too because she hadn't been gone ten minutes when Lincoln made one hell of an entrance. I was waiting at the door for him when he showed up, which gave me a front row seat to the shit show. He climbed out of his car, followed by one of his friends—a card-carrying member of the Beans-for-Balls Club.

Our front door was tucked away underneath a covered front porch with large, white stone columns. I leaned against the tall, wooden door with my hands in my pockets and legs crossed at the ankle. Lincoln's stare met mine as he twirled a baseball bat in his hand like a baton. That was when I realized Tatum looked a lot like her older brother. I supposed I'd always known that. I'd just never paid attention until now. They had the same eyes and dark hair.

He flipped the bat, then raised it high and brought it down on the windshield of my car. Once. Then twice. The sound of shattering glass tore through the air. A thousand tiny veins spread over the tempered glass, making my windshield look like broken ice.

My mistake. I shouldn't have left my car in the driveway when I got home last night.

I clenched my jaw and pushed off the door. Lincoln tossed the bat onto the concrete, then stood up tall and wiped the back of his hand over his forehead.

"Consider that your warning, Donahue. Stay the fuck away from Lyric."

Lyric? What the fuck? I figured he was here because some needle dick told him I carried Tatum out of The Chamber last night.

I walked down the front steps and across the driveway. "The fuck are you talking about? The drugs finally make you lose your shit?"

He nodded his head toward the black-haired dude to his right and let out a laugh. "Nice try. Ethan saw her car pull into your driveway yesterday, asswipe."

Why did he care what—or who—Lyric Matthews did?

I glanced at Ethan. "It sounds like Ethan needs to mind his fucking business." I smirked because, fuck him.

Lincoln bared his teeth. "And don't think I don't know about my sister, about your little performance last night at The Chamber." *And there it was.* He smirked. "One teenage girl wasn't enough for you? You had to make my sister your whore too?"

The fuck did he just call her?

"You have five seconds to get the fuck off my driveway and go apologize to your sister."

"Yeah? Or what?" He snarled and lunged at me.

Lincoln was a savage.

But I was a god.

I grabbed him by the throat and slammed his head down on the windshield he'd just smashed. It hit the shattered glass with a sickening crack. The remnants went flying inside my car, across my hood and onto the ground.

Lincoln's hand flew up to grab my arm, trying to loosen my grip, but it only made me squeeze tighter.

Ethan came at me from behind.

I peered over my shoulder at him, rage seething from every pore in my body. "Touch me, and you're next."

As he backed away and the other guy watched from a distance, I lifted Lincoln from the busted glass and slammed him down on my hood. His lips were turning blue while the color slowly drained from his face. Trails of snot ran from his nose over his mouth, and tears leaked from his eyes.

I leaned down, stopping inches from his face, loosening my grip enough for him to gasp for air. "If you ever come to *my* house again with this bullshit, I will end you. Understood?" I kept my tone calm, sounding nothing like the feral beast brewing inside me.

He clenched his teeth in defiance. I squeezed his throat in return. Finally, he nodded.

"Good." I grabbed a piece of the broken glass and brought the sharp edge to his face, against his cheekbone, just below his eye. "But just in case you forget…" Then I applied enough pressure for the edge of the glass to break his skin, and I carved a trail along the side of his face. Nothing a decent beard wouldn't conceal but enough to remind him who he was dealing with.

I let him go with a shove, making him stumble backward. Blood trickled down his face and dripped onto his baby blue T-shirt. He let it fall. He didn't even try to wipe it away. He grinned and wore that shit like a badge of honor. Maybe he was as sick as I was.

He jabbed a finger in my direction and shouted. "This is far from over."

I walked over and picked the bat up off the driveway, inspected it for a moment, then gave it a flip. I watched in silence as he climbed into his car and drove away because a wise man once said… absolutely nothing. He let the fools scream the loudest while revenge spoke for itself.

Then I went back inside and helped myself to the fruit Tatum left behind without giving her brother another thought.

At the end of the day, threats were just fantasies until someone decided to make them come true.

"Do you have any idea how royally you've fucked up?" My father was standing in his study with his hands in his pockets while he peered through a wall of windows overlooking Mom's flower garden.

I never meant to do permanent damage to Lincoln Huntington. All I wanted to do was warn him to mind his own business. But the minute her name left his lips, I lost it.

"He got what he deserved." I walked across the Persian rug, stopping in front of his desk. My fingertip traced the beveled edge of the dark wood. Not a speck of dust in sight.

"Maybe." He turned around and lifted his chin then smirked, as though he enjoyed looking down on me. "But the execution was brutal."

I stood up straight and looked him in the eye. "As opposed to tampering with his brakes and making it look like an accident when he smashed into a tree?" It was a low blow and I knew it.

Dad never got his hands dirty the way I just did, but he was nowhere near the saint he pretended to be.

His jaw tensed. *Hit a nerve, I see.* "He's not going to press charges."

I folded my arms across my chest. "Oh, should I send him a *thank you* card?"

He pulled his hands from his pockets as he walked over to the opposite side of his desk. I stared at the rows of bookshelves lining the wall behind him. There were mainly law books and autobiographies, but some were actual classic literature. I spent hours of my childhood in here reading while he conducted his business.

"Jesus, Caspian. This is serious." He pinched the bridge of his nose. "And to top it off, now you're fucking his sister."

My eyes snapped to his.

He grinned. "You think I didn't see her leave this morning? Come on, Caspian. You have to be more careful than that if you want to pull one past me."

I wasn't trying to *pull one past him*. Otherwise, I wouldn't have had *his* butler escort Tatum to her car, which was parked at the front fucking door. I was just aggravated that he chose this moment to bring it up.

Dad walked over to the bar cabinet and poured himself a half-full glass of scotch. "And since you made a show of bringing her home, her father knows it too."

Fuck.

Apparently, the saying "The Chamber keeps its secrets" only applied to sharing with people outside of our circle. Anyone inside the circle was fair game.

I turned and propped my ass against his desk. "I'll talk to him."

He took a drink. "Not a denial."

I swallowed and held his stare. Was he expecting me to lie?

He took another drink, draining the contents, then set the empty glass on the cabinet. "All right, then." He took in and let out a deep breath as he walked back over to where I stood. "You leave in the morning."

I stood up straight. "Wanna tell me where I'm going? Should I pack my swimming trunks?"

"Ayelswick."

I damn near choked on my saliva. "Europe? Because I fucked a girl and beat up her brother?"

He gritted his teeth, then grabbed me by the shirt and slammed me against the front of his desk. Papers scattered and pens rolled onto the floor. "Because you fucked the *wrong* girl then mutilated her brother."

The hatred between the Donahues and Huntingtons was as deeply rooted as the feud between the Hatfields and McCoys, the Montagues and Capulets, Road Runner and Wile E. Coyote. The

Huntingtons had always been in politics. It was their bread and butter as far back as anyone could remember. Until my great-grandfather decided being an oil tycoon and real estate mogul wasn't enough for him and ran for the New York Senate. He beat out old man Huntington and started a war. It was the first time in history a Huntington wasn't in office. Gramps eventually got bored and stepped down to let Huntington have his seat back at the political table, but not without bruising his ego in the process. Ever since then, it was their mission to make our family's life hell. Every time we turned around, Huntington was proposing some bill restricting fracking in the U.S, shutting down pipelines, or imposing ridiculous taxes on people like my dad. Every time, Dad wrote him a check to keep him in line, each with more zeros than the last.

And I just fucked his daughter.

Dad let go of my shirt and took a step back. "It'll be good for you. You'll go to college, learn the ins and outs of business and finance. It will be better for everyone in the end," he said, calm and collected, as if he hadn't just looked like a rabid dog two seconds ago.

I steadied my breath. "Europe? Columbia University wasn't good enough?"

He brushed his hands over the front of his tailored suit, hands that I swore then and there would never touch me again. "That was the deal. You get as far away from here as possible."

"You made a deal with Huntington?" I huffed a laugh. "Un-fucking-believable. And if I don't agree?"

"You'll agree."

"But if I don't?"

He walked back over to the windows. "There are two flights leaving in the morning. Either you'll be on one going to Europe or Tatum will be on the other going to Saudi Arabia."

Saudi Arabia. I should have known Malcolm Huntington cared more about his pride than his daughter. He was probably waiting for her to screw up, so he'd have an excuse to ship her off to the highest bidder. Right now, that bidder was Khalid.

I raked my fingers through my hair, massaging away an impending headache. "She's sixteen! What the fuck is wrong with you people?"

"Yes, and you're twenty. That's statutory rape, in case you were wondering. Throw in an assault charge, and your life is one big fucked-up mess." He looked over his shoulder at me, his eyes ablaze with fury. "I will not let you ruin decades of progress for some pussy, no matter how young and tight it is."

Anger boiled within me, feral and hot. I closed the space between us in a heartbeat. Then I grabbed my father by the lapels and shoved him against the closest bookcase.

I leaned in, stopping centimeters from his face. His eyes darkened with his own rage. It was time to show him what Hell looked like when it was disguised as a human. I'd had enough.

"I'll go to Europe. But if you ever talk about Tatum that way again, you'll be eating through a tube and shitting in a bag. What I did to Lincoln will look like child's play. Am I clear?"

He shoved me off and straightened his suit jacket. "You think you're the first person to ever threaten me?" He laughed. "You're lucky you're my son. Now, go pack your shit."

The only thing *lucky* about being his son was carrying the Donahue name. I walked to my room smiling to myself, knowing that this would all be over in less than five years. I just had to keep my mouth shut until then.

The only thing I knew about Ayelswick was that it was a ridiculously wealthy, medium-sized country somewhere around England, Ireland, and Scotland. It was also one of the few places in the world that still had a monarchy. When I unlocked my phone to check the weather there before I packed, the news app lit up my screen.

Top Stories

People

Lyric Matthews found dead in her New York apartment.

My heartbeat thrummed in my ears as Lincoln's words came back to me.

"Ethan saw her car pull into your driveway yesterday, asswipe."

Lyric was seen at my house, and now she was dead—overdosed, according to the article I clicked on. What if Ethan decided to tell other people what he saw? Not that he actually *saw* anything, but I still didn't want to think about the damage those rumors could do. My plate was piled full of shit already with Tatum and her brother.

Shit. *Tatum.* Lyric was her best friend. There was no way she hadn't heard about this.

I imagined her body shaking with sobs until the sound disappeared and there was nothing left but the pain. This was the one thing I couldn't protect her from, the one thing I couldn't prevent.

I tossed my phone onto the comforter, no longer caring about Europe's weather, and fell back onto my bed. She was alone, probably afraid, and I was leaving. How fucked up was that? I'd spent most of my life shielding her from the ugly. Well, death was about as ugly as it got, and there wasn't a damn thing I could do about it. This was Fate's twisted way of testing how far I would go to protect her. I had no doubt Malcolm meant what he said about sending her away, so I got up and pulled my suitcase out of my closet.

"Across an ocean," I said out loud, as if Fate were waiting for an answer to her challenge. *How far would you go to protect her?* "I'd cross the ocean to keep her safe."

Even if it meant hurting her in the process.

Tatum was strong. She would get through this.

She had to.

NINE

Tatum

Drug overdose. "A deadly cocktail," they called it.

They blamed it on the fact that her mom was an addict who died of a drug overdose, so Lyric was bound to do the same, right? They showed pictures from Instagram of her "wild" behavior and quoted her Twitter feed, all to justify their story. And no one questioned it because those who knew differently weren't talking, and those who were talking didn't know shit.

Such a tragedy.

She was so young.

She had such a bright future.

I hated the news.

Today was her memorial. I sat on the front pew next to her dad, holding his hand. Michael Matthews was a man who'd built a legacy with his words, but today he was speechless, silent. Every once in a while, he would squeeze my hand, and I knew a memory had just flashed through his mind. They'd been flashing through mine all week. We stared at the picture on top of the closed casket. It was one from Lyric's sixteenth birthday. She was holding her white puppy, Casper, and smiling like a kid at Christmas. She was wearing a bucket hat and a bright yellow top. It was my favorite picture. That was the Lyric I knew. That was the Lyric I loved.

I looked at her smile and was grateful Lyric's dad took the funeral director's suggestion. He'd said sometimes it was easier to close the casket and display a photo. Seeing her there, cold, stiff, and lifeless would have been too hard. Mr. Matthews agreed. This way, we could remember her the way we wanted. I wanted to remember that smile.

People filed into the private room inside the cathedral. Some of them I knew. Some of them I didn't. All of them handed out hugs and false condolences. False because no one *really* liked Lyric. She spoke her mind in an elite world where people were paid for their silence.

But she was my best friend.

Now she was gone.

Lyric didn't do drugs. She saw what they did to her mom and hated them. Anyone who spent five minutes with her knew that. She was outspoken and confident in her skin. She was sarcastic and loud. That didn't make her an addict. Something else happened to her, something that someone with more money than morals paid to have swept under the rug. Maybe someone got a little too kinky. Maybe they were a little too rough. I wasn't a prude. I knew things like that happened. We were surrounded by powerful people, and where there were powerful people, there were other powerful people covering up their secrets.

A still, small voice whispered in the back of my mind. *Or dumping them in the bottom of a lake.* I shuddered at a distant, cloudy memory I couldn't be sure was real.

The pastor walked up behind the podium to speak and time slowed. I wasn't ready to say goodbye. My stomach did that thing, the thing it always did when my body searched for Caspian. I missed the pull in the air when he was near. I missed the comfort I found in his stare. It had been days since I gave him the intimate parts of me that until now, I'd only kept to myself. By the end of the ceremony, my mind had finally reconciled with my heart that he wasn't going to show.

After the memorial, my parents had a fundraiser event to go to. I didn't feel like forcing smiles while hearing about "how lucky I was that I came from a good family," so I went home. My father hadn't spoken to me since the morning I got caught lying to him—and the police. I eventually ended up telling them I went to a party and had too much to drink and was too ashamed to tell them. I made up a story about Chandler Carmichael taking me to a friend's house just in case anyone saw him in my car that night. It took a few tears, which was easy considering I'd just found out my best friend died, but the cops were convinced I was telling the truth. My father also convinced them to sweep the whole underage drinking thing under the rug. On the outside, he looked like a concerned father. On the inside, I knew he was seething.

When I walked in the door, Lincoln was sitting on the sofa with one arm draped across the back and a near-empty bottle in his other hand. His feet were propped up on the glass coffee table, and his shirt was unbuttoned halfway with his tie hanging loose. He didn't even make it out of the living room and to the service, probably because he was still butthurt that he and Ethan got in a car accident and botched up his face. That was what he got for drag racing with his friends. Lincoln said Ethan's car was a mess. Someone said Caspian's car was worse. Why were those two even racing? As far as I knew, they didn't even hang out with the same crowd.

I hadn't seen or heard from Caspian since Mischief Night. At first, it stung. His rejection made my soul ache. But grief quickly took over and swallowed the rejection whole. It took what was left of my heart and tore it to shreds. It rearranged my world and suffocated me. It transported me from pain to anger. If I hadn't left with Caspian, I'd have been with Lyric. If I had been with Lyric, she wouldn't be dead.

Now I had no one. My own family rarely talked to me anymore. Dad would rather pretend he was on the phone than look me in the eye. Mom stayed gone all the time. I hadn't seen Lincoln sober since the day he got in a wreck—the day I found out about Lyric.

My best friend was gone, and Caspian left me to deal with it alone.

Thanks to the Universe's sick sense of humor, I got to mourn the loss of my innocence and my best friend all at the same time.

And I hated Caspian for it. I hated him for all of it.

Then, I wished he were here to make me feel safe the way he always had.

It was a vicious cycle that I prayed would end.

I walked across the hardwood floor, stopping in front of the leather sofa. "You didn't go to the memorial."

Lincoln lifted his gaze without raising his head. "I can remember Lyric just fine from right here."

"You okay? You've been weird." Weirder than usual. Lincoln was a loose cannon on any given day, but lately, he was falling deeper and deeper into the darkness. It would have broken my heart if my heart didn't already feel shattered.

"So, because I didn't go sit in a room full of people pretending to give a shit about a girl they didn't even know, I'm being weird?" He tipped back the bottle, taking a long pull.

"It's not about those people, Lincoln. The memorial was for Lyric."

He scoffed.

"Do you think you could at least pretend to care about someone other than yourself for a minute?"

He held the bottle out so that the black label faced me. "I care about Johnnie."

"My bad. I forgot you carry your heart in a bottle these days," I said as I turned and walked away.

"You don't know shit about my heart," he shouted after me.

Yeah, I know you don't have one.

Lincoln needed help, but I didn't have the energy to give it to him right now.

I opened the door to my room, and a lifetime of memories immediately assaulted me, like a swarm of bees stinging my heart. I saw Lyric and me sitting on the floor, leaning against my bed while we gave ourselves pedicures, using blow-out brushes as microphones while we sang Taylor Swift break-up songs at the top of our lungs, and lying on our stomachs on my bed, crying over Nicholas Sparks movies. She was here. She was everywhere.

No. She wasn't. She was in the cold, hard ground, and I would never see her again outside of these memories.

I squeezed my eyes shut as if that would somehow lock the visions inside. Maybe if I closed them tightly enough, my memories wouldn't seep out. I would never lose sight of her.

"I promise, I will never let them forget you," I said into the air. "I promise *I* will never forget you."

It was too much, too suffocating. I didn't want to be here.

After changing into one of Lyric's tank tops she'd left at my house and a pair of leggings, I went to the one place I knew I could be free.

The lights were off in the studio. I knew they would be. No one came here after hours except me, even though it was located in a corner building on a busy New York City street.

My parents leased this space for me to practice ballet with a private instructor, some world-famous dancer from Russia. I appreciated their effort, but it made me feel isolated and alone, so a few years ago, I asked them to bring in other instructors and open the studio to the public. They agreed, but only if I also agreed to start taking classes at SAB, The School of American Ballet. Dancing was my lifeline. I wanted it to be other people's lifeline too, so I said okay. I didn't use books or movies to escape the way most people did. I used music.

For a moment, I stood in the darkness and waited for my thoughts to quiet.

"I'm sorry I didn't save you." I finally said the words out loud that I'd been holding in my heart for days. "I wish I could take it back. I wish I could have you back."

I wish I'd never left with him. Even though leaving with him made me feel things I never knew I was capable of. Things like confidence, strength, and passion. Things I didn't know if I would ever feel again. But I wasn't selfish enough to mourn the loss of something so trivial when I was consumed with mourning the loss of something so much bigger.

Tears filled my eyes, but I blinked them away. I took a deep breath, then I flipped a switch and the place lit up. The large, open room was light and airy. The walls were off-white and the floors a soft gray. Heavy, blue velvet curtains covered floor-to-ceiling windows and separated the studio from the busy street on the other side. The darkness of the fabric matched my mood.

I pressed *Play* on the sound system remote, and the room was instantly filled with echoes of a sultry voice crooning over the sound of piano keys. I toed my tennis shoes off and pulled my hair up into a bun. I closed my eyes and saw Lyric's smile.

The music played.

The man kept singing his solemn tune.

I began to move.

I started off slow, letting the tension build, then release, in calculated, fluid movements. My arms gracefully tore through the air in perfect rhythm with my feet. My body moved across the floor—stretching, pulling, swaying with the music. Then I began to turn.

And turn.

My heart beat faster. All the weight of the last few days lifted from my shoulders with every move I made. The song built up to its crescendo. The music got louder.

I kept turning.

Faster.

More deliberate.

The blood rushed to my fingertips and toes, but I refused to stop. The music died down, and the dance became more about the breaths I was fighting to take than the way my body moved. I was exhausted, but I didn't stop until the very last note.

The song ended and I fell to my knees. Tears stung my eyes as I worked to steady my breathing. I glanced at the mirrored wall in front of me. My eyes were red. My face was splotchy. There were blisters on my feet, and I was gasping for air. But I felt free. For the first time in days, I looked in the mirror, and even though she might not have looked her best, I recognized the person staring back at me.

This was it. This was my therapy. All of my sadness, all of my anger, and all of my pain faded away the moment the music started. This was me.

My life had been shaken, rearranged, and flipped upside down all in a matter of days. But maybe that was the point. Maybe being turned inside out was the only way to see who we were always meant to be.

Looking in the mirror now, I saw who I was. I may be broken. I may be damaged, but I was strong.

TEN

Tatum

I had no idea what I was looking for when I went back to Green-Wood Cemetery. In the light of day, the statues looked more like broken angels than creatures lurking. Birds sang in the trees, and people walked the pathways around the lakes. The chapel, while still gothic, was less intimidating. As I walked up to the entrance of the tomb that led to The Chamber, two stone lions stared back at me. I wanted to ask them what all they'd seen, the secrets they kept. *Who did Lyric leave with that night?*

I didn't find any answers there, not that I expected to. Some part of me just wanted to breathe in the air of the last place I saw her alive, to see if I could still feel her here. As if somehow I would be miraculously blessed with a gift like those women who help cops solve murders by channeling dead people's emotions.

Ha.

If only.

Every time I asked Lincoln if he had heard anything about what really happened to Lyric, he got angry and told me I needed to let it go. People talked. There was no way he didn't know anything.

"Who did she leave with? Who gave her drugs? Was it Jake Ryan? Chandler Carmichael?"

"Leave it alone, Tatum. You're fucking with things you don't understand."

He was right.

I didn't understand it. Why else would I have asked?

Dad still wasn't speaking to me unless he had no choice, like at dinner or a social event. He never brought up my Life360 location that night, and I didn't either. Sometimes omission is the best part of a lie. If he suspected I was with Caspian, he never said anything.

Mom was Mom. She said all the things she'd been bred to say.

Be thankful for the memories you have, Dear.

One day it won't hurt so bad.

You're going to get through this.

Chin up. You're a Huntington, and Huntingtons don't give up.

She was right. I wasn't giving up. I needed to know what happened.

I went by Chandler Carmichael's house because I remembered Caspian telling him to take Lyric home. All I got was more vague answers.

Lyric made her own choices.

Stop looking for answers you'll never find.

Don't make her mistakes.

What did that even mean? What mistakes did she make? What choices?

I even bartered favors until someone finally gave me Kyle's number. The minute he heard it was me on the phone, he hung up.

Dick.

He wasn't so quick to dismiss me on Mischief Night. I'd heard someone jumped him outside of a club last week. At first, I felt bad for him. Now, not so much.

It seemed like the more I talked about Lyric, the less everyone else did. Within a week of her memorial, the media had moved on to the next piece of celebrity gossip.

I promised Lyric I wouldn't let them forget, and it seemed like that was the one thing they all wanted to do. She was my best friend. I knew everything about her.

Didn't I?

I went by her apartment one day after school. Her dad was there, standing in front of the floor-to-ceiling windows, staring out over the city. It was his penthouse, but Lyric might as well have lived alone. He was never home.

Now it was empty.

"Are you moving?" I asked when the elevator doors opened.

He spun around, seeming startled at my voice. "Yeah," he said simply. "I can't keep drowning in it, you know?" He meant the grief.

And yeah. I knew. Most days it felt like I was suffocating.

He'd dyed his blond hair dark brown and let his beard grow out to a rugged scruff. He looked like hell.

"Going to LA," he said, although I didn't ask.

My heart broke all over again.

I came here because I knew if anyone understood my pain, it would be him. Now he was leaving, and I had no one to share my grief with, no one who understood.

I was alone… again.

He walked across the room, his hands stuffed in the pockets of his charcoal gray sweatpants. "You were good for her." His blue eyes shined with unshed tears.

I swallowed the lump in my throat. "So were you."

He shook his head. "Maybe once. Not anymore." He blew out a small breath and smiled to himself. "I used to sing to her all the time when she was little. She fucking loved that shit." His smile grew. "We'd make up our own words depending on what we were doing. Stupid shit like, *the bubbles in my bath get big and bigger, big and bigger, big and bigger*—instead of *the wheels on the bus*. When she'd fall down and look up at me with these big, wide eyes, I'd just say *toughen up, soldier*, and she never cried." He pulled his hand from his pocket and raked it through his hair. "She never fucking cried."

I didn't bother with things like etiquette or all the things my parents drilled into my head over the years about appearances. This man was in pain. He was hurting more than I was.

I took a step forward and circled my arms around his waist, pulling him into a hug.

We stayed like that as the seconds ticked by in silence. We stood there as two people who shared the same broken heart. Until finally, I inhaled a deep breath and let him go.

"Take care of yourself, Tatum," he said as he stepped away from me. His blue eyes held mine. "And be careful."

I almost asked him what that was supposed to mean, but he turned his back and walked over to the window again.

And just like that, I said goodbye to the last bit of thread that held me to Lyric.

In a moment of weakness, I went by Caspian's house on my way home. I was hurt. I was angry. I needed someone to shoulder my pain, and the only logical person was him.

Right?

Wrong.

With grief, there was no logic.

He wasn't there, and the butler wouldn't answer my questions. Surprise.

Then a few days later during dinner, Lincoln let it slip that Caspian had gone to college in Ayelswick. *Europe.* It wasn't enough to ignore me. He had to put an ocean between us to make sure it stuck.

Stalking him was fruitless. His only social media was Instagram, and all he ever did was post inanimate objects with captions that quoted dead poets and philosophers. You would think giving someone your virginity was enough grounds for them to press the *follow back* button, but as usual, Caspian Donahue was the exception to the rule. Some girls might take his rejection and wallow in self-pity. I was fueled by determination. I refused to be the girl who was forgettable.

Huntingtons don't give up. If I had inherited any trait at all from my dad, it was his ruthless motivation to prove people wrong. I buried myself in school and dance, determined to be the smartest, the strongest, the best. I was invited to parties that I never went to. A few girls from school offered to hang out or go shopping. I always had a good excuse not to go. I wasn't interested in parties or friends. I had enough guilt looming over me like a cloud. I was here, and she wasn't. I would grow up, and she wouldn't. I couldn't add partying and finding a new bestie to the list of things that I could enjoy, but Lyric never would.

I landed a role as a soloist in *Sleeping Beauty* with SAB. Practices were brutal and free time was a delusion. One night after a particularly intense rehearsal, I found a small gold box wrapped in purple ribbon on the front seat of my car. Inside, there was a tube of Orajel with a note that simply read: *I heard this helps when you want to feel numb.*

I knew that handwriting. I'd seen it once before on a breakfast tray after the worst—and best—night of my life.

Why was Caspian leaving gifts in my car? Better yet, *how*? He was on another continent living his life while I merely existed.

On a whim, I slipped off my shoes and rubbed the ointment over and between my toes, surprised when it actually worked. The stinging pain from oncoming blisters disappeared. For the first time in months, I sat back, closed my eyes, and breathed. *How did he know I needed this?*

Because he always knew.

I still hated him, but I appreciated the gesture.

Too bad the Orajel didn't work the same way when I rubbed it over my heart.

ELEVEN

Tatum

Two years later…
age eighteen

Eventually, the minutes turned into days, the days into weeks, and the weeks into months. Before long, two years had come and gone since Lyric's death. I was almost finished with my senior year and about to graduate high school—without my best friend there to stand up and shout "Yasss, bitch" when I walked across the stage.

We were supposed to take our senior trip to Belize, where the legal drinking age was eighteen. Now, the scent of alcohol made me want to vomit. It brought back so many memories, so much heartache, so much regret. I would never drink again.

I grew tired. My mind, my body, my heart… all of it grew ineffably tired. Every day that passed was a day I was reminded I was building a life without my best friend in it. In some strange way, I supposed I believed that if I found out the truth about what happened to her, if I had someone, something, to blame, then I could stop blaming myself. I could move on. Mom told me if I kept going the way I was that I would eventually burn out. The ache in my soul told me she was probably right. I was searching for answers that just weren't there. Everyone had moved on with their lives. There was no blame to be found.

There was nothing left but my guilt, guilt I would live with the rest of my life, guilt that sometimes, when I woke up from a dream with tears streaming down my face, threatened to tear me apart. In my heart I knew there was no way a girl who hated drugs ended up letting them kill her. But if I ever hoped for any kind of *normal* in my life, I needed to give up trying to find out what happened. Instead, I made myself focus on the memories, on the good times. It was the only way I'd ever survive.

We didn't go to the same school, but Lyric was always at my house studying. Even though she was a year older than me, we were in the same grade. Her mom's death really hit her hard, and she ended up missing a lot of school and repeating that grade. She'd make fun of me and call me a sexy nerd, and I would watch her eat peanut M&Ms and drink Dr. Pepper instead of studying because she was the kind of smart that didn't need hours of recitation.

She was supposed to be my prom date.

I didn't even go.

She was going to Sarah Lawrence, and I was going to Juilliard.

I didn't even apply.

We had a plan.

Now all I had was old photos and text messages.

Today was graduation day. Excitement buzzed through the River Center as we all walked in a single file line to find our designated chairs on the main floor. Our friends and family sat in the stadium seats and watched on the jumbotrons hanging from the domed ceiling. We probably looked like ants from where they were—ants cloaked in royal blue robes and wearing square cardboard caps.

I sat between Dawn Holm and Jason Ingram while we waited for our names to be called. The Senior Choir sang the National Anthem. The people on stage, including my father who was there as guest speaker Senator Huntington rather than my dad, gave their speeches. I graduated in the top ten percent of my class and had a National Honor Society cord draped around my neck. For the first time in two years, my father looked proud when he saw me walk across the stage. When he stood up to give me a hug, I had to blink back tears. I blamed it on the fact that today was a major milestone and not that it was the first time in a long time that he'd welcomed me into his arms.

After the ceremony, we all drove out to the Hampton house where Mom had put together a massive graduation party—that I didn't ask for.

I loved it here more than anywhere else we ever went. It was only a two-hour drive from the city, but it felt a world away. Our house sat about three hundred feet off the Atlantic Ocean on six acres of perfectly manicured green grass. It was a two-story, gray shingle-style home with a white wraparound porch. A wall of neatly trimmed hedges separated the grassy yard from the white sand beach, but from the balcony off the upstairs master bedroom you could look out over the bright blue ocean. Tall, lush maple trees lined the edge of the property on both sides, making it feel secluded. This was my oasis. It had been since I was a little girl.

Dad even hired someone to build a cottage-style guest house with a small studio just so I would have a place to dance when we spent long summers here.

On the east lawn, by the tennis court, Mom had a large white tent set up. Under the tent, people gathered around tall tables and laughed and smiled while a band played modern songs with classical instruments. The salty scent of the ocean drifted around us with the breeze.

Lyric would have hated this.

I took my robe off before we made the drive here, so I fit right in with the rest of the guests in my slim-fitting blue dress and strand of heirloom pearls around my neck—and the delicate gold bracelet with a ballet slipper charm that I'd found wrapped and placed in my car on my seventeenth birthday. It had been the second gift Caspian sent, left in my car just like the first. I didn't even want to know how he'd gotten it in there. It had been a shit day, my first birthday without my best friend. My parents wanted to throw me a party, but all I could think of was my last party on the yacht and how Lyric went head-to-head with the perverted senator. Then I got this bracelet, along with a note: *Show them what you're made of.* He knew. Caspian knew exactly where I needed to go to find my strength, to find *me*. He always knew.

As I mindlessly rolled the ballet charm between my fingers, my mind flickered between relief and disappointment knowing he wouldn't be here. He wasn't *anywhere* anymore, not even on holidays. I stopped looking for him a long time ago, but my body still missed the warmth of his stare from across the room.

I let go of the charm and focused on the present. Caspian wasn't here. He wasn't coming. Judging by the guest list, my graduation party was more for my parents than it was for me, anyway. Out of the hundred or so people here, I could have counted the number of them that were my age on two hands.

Dad had just finished making a welcome speech when a gorgeous guy with sandy blond hair walked up to me with a drink in each hand. I recognized him as Brady Rogers, one of my brother's friends who got drafted into the NFL right out of high school.

He held one of the glasses in my direction. "They think they're doing us a favor by throwing these things, but they really have no idea every time we have to attend one, we die a little inside."

I accepted the drink with no intention of drinking it, and he smiled. It was one of those blinding, all-American boy-next-door smiles. "Pretty sure you've graduated from the whole parents-fawning-over-every-accomplishment stage in life."

He crinkled his nose. "Nah, they still fawn. My parties are just a little better now," he said with a wink.

"I'll have to take your word for it."

I sounded like a bitch.

I wasn't one. At least, I tried not to be.

There were just a lot of emotions wrapped up in this one day, and I was having trouble digesting them all.

A waiter walked by, so I set my still-full glass of orange juice and Prosecco on his tray.

Brady lifted a brow and watched me carefully. "Was it the orange juice? Or the Prosecco?" He swallowed. "Or the company?"

I forced a smile. "Not the company."

He smiled back.

This whole interaction should have flattered me to pieces, but it just felt misplaced. I didn't talk to guys, not like this. I wasn't opposed to dating. I'd even gone out with a few guys from my school. No one ever held my attention past dinner and a movie. Until today, I'd had a path to follow. I was focused on one thing only—getting *here*. Now that I was *here*, I had no idea what I wanted to do, where else I wanted to go. What was I supposed to focus on? Was this it? Was this my destination? Was I supposed to fall into the arms of a guy like Brady and become the trophy wife who cheered from the sidelines? Would I give up my dreams and become my mother? Did I even have a dream anymore?

Get a grip, Tatum. You're a mess. It's a conversation, not a marriage proposal.

I wondered if graduation day was like this for everyone. Did everyone feel as if they were standing on the edge of a cliff, staring out at the world with the world staring back, knowing that the second they took that next step they would either fall… or they would fly?

I wanted to fly.

I was terrified of the fall.

Brady waved at another waiter a few feet away. The young guy in the black tuxedo looked like he forgot how to walk but finally got his feet to work and made it over to us. I supposed Brady got that reaction a lot.

He set his champagne glass on the waiter's tray and flashed me a grin.

"You didn't have to do that," I said.

"I guess I didn't feel like being much of a drinker today either." His blue eyes grew darker.

A familiar heat crept up my neck and to my cheeks. Awkward or not, Brady wasn't the kind of guy my ovaries didn't notice, and the fact that he just did *that*... for *me*... raised the temperature about ninety degrees in my panties.

Maybe I needed to forget about falling or flying and let him hold me right here on the edge, at least for tonight.

Lincoln walked up and clapped a hand on Brady's shoulder before I had a chance to respond. "If you're hitting on my sister, you're wasting your time." His gaze moved to me, mischief twinkling in his eyes. "She's an ice queen."

I glared at my brother. "Not true. I happen to be very hot. You're just a dick, so I stay away from you."

Brady pursed his lips as if he were thinking. Then he smirked. "I'm going with your sister on this one."

On which part? That I was hot? Or that Lincoln was a dick?

Lincoln pointed between Brady and me. "You're both assholes." Then he nodded his head toward the band. "I hate to cockblock here, but my dad wanted to talk to you."

When Senator Huntington rang the bell, you went running, no matter who you were.

I was almost going to miss the quarterback's company, but it was nice to finally see Lincoln in a decent mood. He needed his friend more than I needed to get laid.

I hadn't been with anyone since Caspian, and something told me Brady—although sexy as sin—would never compare to my first. He was too nice, too thoughtful, too much of everything Caspian Donahue was not.

"I'll see you later?" Brady asked before he walked away, his deep voice interrupting my dark thoughts.

It was more of a question than a statement, so I gave him a smile and nodded. "Yeah. I'll see you later."

As always, Caspian had crept his way into my thoughts. I needed to get him out of my head, so I made my way around the space, flashing smiles and giving thanks to all the people my parents invited. I had no idea how my mother did this all the time. It was exhausting. Then again, I didn't know what was worse, forcing a smile or having to explain why you wore a frown.

The music faded as I walked to the edge of the property and looked over the hedges onto the ocean. Way off in the distance, the sky turned a pinkish-orange as the sun began to set. The deep blue waves crested then collapsed in a spray of white foam. The crashing of them against the sand made its own kind of symphony, almost as if the ocean itself were breathing. A flock of seagulls flew overhead then dipped down closer to the water, scouting for their next meal.

An immediate peace washed over me. I breathed it all in and tried to think about what would happen next. What step did I take? The only thing I was sure of was that I wanted to dance. I wanted to breathe. I was tired of suffocating from the inside of a box I didn't belong in.

"We haven't taken pictures yet, and you're going to smear your lipstick." My mother's voice scolded somewhere behind me.

I'd just taken a bite of the red wine arancini I stole from one of the waiter's trays and brought out here with me. I loved risotto. Cover it in breading and cook it in oil, and I was obsessed. What I didn't care about was my lipstick.

I finished chewing, then turned to face her. "Totally worth the mess." I held the other half of the arancini out. "Have you tried this?" I moaned. "It's amazing."

Her lips formed a thin line. "You have guests."

It was hard to tell if by *guests*, she meant actual guests or if she was referring to Brady. I'd caught her watching our conversation with a smile that mirrored the sun.

My mom had surrendered her dreams to my dad so that he could chase his. She was perfectly content being the trophy wife of a senator.

I was nothing like my mother.

I wanted more.

I finished the breaded ball. "I know. I'm sorry. I was just taking a minute to…" I shrugged. "…think."

She laid a hand on my shoulder. Mom was always touching my hand or hugging me. She always kissed me on the forehead before I left the house and ran her hand along my arm in that soothing way moms sometimes did. It was as if she had to become overly affectionate to make up for Dad's sudden lack of it.

"Anything you want to talk about?"

Actually, yes.

"I think I want to stay here." *Did I say that out loud?*

Her mouth spread into a small smile. "We are staying here. We aren't going back to the city until next week."

I did. I said it out loud.

"No. I mean, I want to *stay* here." I paused to gauge her expression. "After you go back."

"Tatum, you aren't serious. This is a vacation home. There's nothing for you here."

I pointed toward the cottage. "There's a studio for me to practice. I can take online classes during the week and go into the city and teach dance on the weekends. I feel at home here. I'd rather drink coffee on the balcony and watch the waves roll in than have brunch at Peacock Alley and spend the rest of the day buying shoes I'll never wear. I'll stay in the guest house if that's easier." I sighed. "I just want to stay." *My mind is quiet here.*

After a silence that felt like an eternity, she inhaled a deep breath. "Fine." She let out the breath. "I'll talk to your father."

I raised my eyebrows. "Really?"

"Yes. Really." Her expression was stern but amused.

My heart was ready to explode. I wrapped both arms around her and squeezed as tightly as I could. Then I kissed her on the cheek, hard and messy, leaving a bright red lipstick smear on her contoured cheekbone.

"Thank you. Mom. I swear you won't regret it."

"We haven't said *yes* yet."

No. But they would. They had to.

I didn't think I would survive the last two years. I was sure I wouldn't live through the pain of losing my best friend and the guilt of knowing I might have been able to save her. I thought I would let my anger consume me. But I didn't. I was here. I made it. And now I had a plan.

I was done surviving.

I was ready to start living again, ready to take that step.

I was ready to fly.

The future would take care of itself. Right now, I was enjoying the moment—starting with finishing the conversation Brady started before my brother interrupted.

I found him away from the crowd, staring out over the water and sipping on a bottle of Shiner Bock.

"I hope my dad wasn't too much of a ball buster," I said with a small smile.

He chuckled. "He just asked what a guy had to do to score tickets to the Superbowl."

"The Superbowl, huh? Sounds serious."

He took a sip of his beer. "I could stand here and bore you with football talk for the rest of the night, or you could just go ahead and agree to go to dinner with me."

I blew a long breath through pursed lips. "Man. That's a tough one." I fake-hesitated then smiled. "Dinner it is."

Yeah. I was definitely living in the moment.

One month later, I walked into my dance studio in the city and flipped on the lights. *My* dance studio. Man, that felt good.

I was dating a nice guy. My parents had let me move into the Hampton house. My father gave me this studio. And I hadn't woken up crying over Lyric in weeks. Life was good.

And then I saw it.

Sitting in the middle of the floor was a solid white rectangular box with a bright red ribbon tied around it.

My heartbeat faltered.

There was no way this was another one of Caspian's gifts. No one had access to this studio other than my parents and me. *Maybe it was from my parents.*

I tossed my keys onto the table by the door then walked over to grab the box. The ribbon slid off with ease as I pulled on it, then lifted the box top and removed a layer of white tissue paper.

Underneath the tissue was a thick, flesh-colored dildo inside a clear package labeled *Clone a Cock*.

This was clearly *not* from my parents.

Taped to the bottom of the dildo was a note—in the same pristine handwriting as the one I'd seen on a breakfast tray once upon a time.

Just a friendly reminder that the only dick that belongs inside you is mine. By the way, congratulations, Little Troublemaker. You made it.

My stomach dropped. A familiar heat began to simmer inside me as I looked down at the gift, at the intricate detail of it, the thickness and length, the full head and all the veins, then back at the label. *Clone a Cock.* Then back at the note. *The only dick that belongs inside you is mine.*

I should have known.

Until now, all his gifts had been thoughtful—well, as thoughtful as Caspian Donahue could be—nothing more than nice gestures reminding me he was still here, even though he wasn't. This was not a *gesture*. This was different. This was territorial. This was him pissing on his tree.

Why now? And why *this*, of all things?

Unless he knew about Brady.

Of course, he knew about Brady. Somehow Caspian knew everything. *Like the fact that I'd be at the studio this morning and how to get this box inside a locked door.*

So what? Who cared if he knew I had a date? Caspian had no power over me. I owed him nothing, and I was *not* a tree.

I brought the package to my desk and cut through the thick plastic with a pair of scissors. My fingers wrapped around the thickness as I pulled it from the package. Oh my God. It felt so smooth, so silky, so *real* in my hand. My lips parted as I wrapped my fingers around the dildo and imagined the body that went with it. I wondered what he looked like now, how he smelled, how he felt. I was too young and inexperienced to really soak in everything that happened the night I lost my virginity, but now… knowing what I knew now and seeing this, knowing that this was a reflection of *him*, as close to the real thing as it got… dear, sweet baby Jesus. My own fingers wouldn't be enough to satisfy me anymore.

I thought I was free of him. Now here I was, core throbbing, lips parted, breath erratic, and I knew I would never escape Caspian Donahue.

You didn't escape someone after you'd given them your soul.

TWELVE

CASPIAN

Two years later...
age twenty-four

Four years had come and gone, and I'd finally served my time. I paid my penance. I played the game. I kept my distance, just like I'd promised. *I kept her safe.*

Every Christmas and Thanksgiving, my parents flew to Ayelswick to celebrate the holiday, and we spent the summer breaks traveling the world. Dad popped in for visits while he was here for his annual Bindenberg meetings with the Obsidian Brotherhood.

When he wasn't here, he checked in every Sunday night for four years, just like a warden. Every Sunday night, I gave him the same report.

I'm staying out of trouble.
I'm going to all my classes.
I haven't talked to Tatum Huntington.

Sending her a mold of my dick wasn't technically *talking*. I made sure to send Chandler a sufficient thank you gift for making sure all my presents got delivered.

If she thought just because I was an ocean away that I wasn't keeping tabs on her, she was mistaken. I knew everything she did. I knew she moved to her parents' house in the Hamptons right after she graduated high school. I knew she skipped college and started teaching dance at the studio on the corner of Sixth and Twenty-third. I knew she stopped at a street vendor on cold mornings and ordered a hot chocolate with whipped cream and cinnamon. And I knew she'd been seen with Brady more times than I was comfortable with over the last couple of years. That shit would end the minute I stepped off the plane at JFK.

I took back all the things I'd ever told myself about being okay with her fucking another man as long as he wasn't a pervert. Brady Rogers was a good man. I still didn't want her anywhere near his cock. The dildo was a simple reminder that she was still mine, even though it might not seem like it right now. I thought about how many times she'd fucked herself with it. How her perfect pink pussy lips looked wrapped around it while it stretched her wide open. Did she fuck herself hard and fast or slow and easy? Did she close her eyes and moan my name? Did she bring it to her lips and suck her juices off when she finished?

Fuck. Just thinking about it had me reaching for my cock and pulling out the cunt tunnel. The blood rushed to my dick, making it throb with hot, urgent need while I pictured her pretty face like it was her I was about to fuck and not some overpriced rubber sleeve. I held the fake pussy on the bed with one hand the way I would hold the small of her back if she were here bent over in front of me. Would she lose her breath when I slid it in like this? Fuck, I hoped so. Would I hold back and go slow? Fuck no.

This was wrong. It should have been her that I was fucking. It should have been her tight little pussy wrapped around my dick. It should have been her feeling my swollen length stretching and pounding her until she cried.

I watched my thick, purple head thrust in and out of the toy's flesh-colored lips and thought about Tatum, about the way her tears trailed down her cheeks, about the way her breath hitched every time I knocked the bottom out, about that sexy fucking sound she made when she came. Fuck, I would give anything to hear that sound again, give anything to see her dripping wet with need.

Thrust.

This felt so fucking good, but I needed more. I tightened my grip and pounded harder. Faster.

Grunt.

I needed *her*, bent over and exposed with my fingers digging into her flesh until I left her marked with pretty purple bruises.

Thrust.

Fuck. I needed to come.

With one final grunt, I came all over the fucking bed the way I wanted to come all over her creamy skin—the way I *was going* to come all over her skin very soon.

During my time in Ayelswick, I'd eased my way from the outer rings of Prince Liam's inner circle all the way to the nucleus. I'd charmed diplomats and debutantes. And I did it all while maintaining academic excellence and soaking up everything there was to know about finance.

If my father thought I was a threat before, he had no idea the damage I could cause now. Wanna know what powerful people hid behind the masks they wore? Become friends with their children. Prince Liam had an easy demeanor, the way I would imagine a prince should. He had exquisite taste in women, which he sampled freely and often. People were drawn to him, as though they didn't have a choice. He was the epitome of charming—the polar opposite of me—but we clicked right off the bat.

I learned more about the king and queen in one drunken night on the quad than my father learned in years from his inside spies.

And now, thanks to my newly acquired college education, I knew exactly how to put that information to good use.

Fuck my father and Huntington with their threats. I wasn't the kid who bowed down to them anymore. I was the man who dared them to follow through.

The air back home felt different... in a good way. I'd missed this place. While Ayelswick was gothic towers made of stone with pointed steeples, walled gardens, and arched bridges, New York City was a concrete jungle with towers made of glass and steel, crowded sidewalks, and bright lights. Ayelswick kept her secrets behind wooden doors in stone towers. New York buried hers in elusive meetings and hefty bribes. Ayelswick had Summer's End. New York had Mischief Night. There they congregated in a grassy clearing with a massive bonfire, *Fight Club*- style competitions, and sex. Here we partied beneath a tomb with Celtic music, drugs and alcohol—and sex.

On the outside, it all looked different. From the inside, everything was the same.

"Just a quick stop on the way home," my father said as our driver pulled into the parking garage at 1 Donahue Plaza.

I continued looking out the window as the tall buildings disappeared and we became surrounded by concrete walls and fluorescent lights. "Of course."

Once we were in the parking garage elevator, Dad punched in the code that took us all the way to the thirty-sixth floor. Donahue Plaza consisted of three buildings our family owned in the heart of Manhattan, right off Fifth and Sixth Avenues. We rented out office spaces and entire floors to companies like NBC and *People* magazine. After all, it was easier to dictate what the press said about you when you sat them in your lap. The top three floors of 1 Donahue Plaza belonged solely to us, though.

This was where my father did business. This was where his heart beat the strongest.

The elevator opened up into the art deco style lobby. It was after four o'clock on a Saturday afternoon, so the offices were mostly empty. I followed Dad past the copper and silver sculpture of the Greek god, Apollo, trying not to smirk at the irony of the artwork as we made our way down the hall.

He stopped to open the door of an office directly across from his. "Welcome to your future."

He held the door as I walked past and into the space. I took one look, then glanced back over my shoulder at him, and he smiled.

What the fuck?

Since the day I turned thirteen years old, my father had always viewed me as competition. I physically felt the air shift the moment he'd transformed from loving father into bitter rival. I could have bet my life he'd never let me step foot in this building as an adult. Now he was giving me an office one month before my twenty-fifth birthday, the day all hell was destined to break loose. Something wasn't right.

It was open and airy with a row of floor-to-ceiling windows that looked out into Manhattan. The walls were painted a crisp white, and the floor was a sleek, charcoal gray marble tile. Black and white photographs of the city framed in bright red stood out against the white walls. The desk, a white geometric design made to look as if it were balanced on the tip of a triangle, sat in front of a solid black bookcase that covered almost the whole wall. There were two gray chairs in front of the desk and a matching sofa against one wall.

I might have thought this was a set-up, that he was baiting me, except there was one thing that caught my attention above every other detail in this office. On the ground in front of the sofa, there was a rug—made of lion skin. *My* lion.

Dad stepped into the office and clapped a hand on my shoulder. "You ready to eat?"

That depends, Dad. Are you ready to run?

I looked him in the eye. "I'm ready."

"Good. Your mother has this big *Welcome Home* dinner all set up over at the Skyline Room. She's been texting me for the past fifteen minutes."

Right. He meant *actual* food. I should have known Mom would make a production of my homecoming. She lived her life in camera flashes and wore confidence like diamonds. Attention was her Kryptonite, probably because my father never gave her any. But she had always been an amazing mother. She was loving and supportive. In the calmness of the night, when she'd taken off the mask she wore for the world, she'd sit at the foot of my bed and tell me stories about Greek mythology. It was her favorite. Over the years, it had become mine too.

She knew nothing of my father's secrets. She didn't resent me the way he did. I still felt his long-standing bitterness toward me. Even now, as we stood in the office he'd set up for me. Even after his smiles and promises of a better future, the sharp blade of betrayal was still there, poised at my back and ready to sink in. I saw it in the way his nostrils flared when he smiled.

I returned his charade with one of my own. "Thank God. I've been waiting four years for a decent burger."

The Skyline Room was on the top floor of the tallest building in Donahue Plaza. There were windows on all sides, looking out onto the Manhattan skyline—hence the name. It was a classic kind of modern with a large crystal chandelier in the center of the room and artfully designed floral arrangements on every white linen-covered table. A jazz band was set up where the grand piano normally was. Not exactly my idea of a good time, but it made Mom happy.

Most of the people were here for my mother, but a select few were actually here to see me. I walked in and immediately gave her a hug, making sure to say all the right things: how perfect everything was, how beautiful she looked, how grateful I was. Then I found Chandler Carmichael leaning against the bar, looking as *GQ* magazine cover model-worthy as ever. Chandler was always polished, always crisp, but I knew what he did in his spare time. I knew the places he'd been.

"The prodigal son returns," he said, his bright smile beaming as he held a bottle of Shiner Bock in the air as a salute.

I shook my head then waved for the bartender to grab me a beer too. "More like Apollo." Unlike the prodigal son, it wasn't my idea to leave.

Chandler scrunched his eyebrows together as he took a drink of his beer. The bartender handed me my bottle.

"The Greek god who was exiled from Olympus for pissing off his father," I explained, then took a drink. The ice-cold liquid was heaven.

His eyes widened as he caught my meaning. He pointed his bottle in my direction. "Or Romeo. They banished that bastard for fucking the wrong girl then killing her brother."

"Her cousin."

He stopped the bottle before it touched his lips. "Do what?"

"He killed her cousin." I took a drink. "But to be fair, the cousin killed his best friend, so an eye for an eye and all that literary bullshit."

"Speaking of best friends, I wanted to make sure you knew I did what you asked..." he looked over my shoulder, "...that night."

"I know you did."

We hadn't talked about what happened with Lyric after I'd asked him to bring her home. That wasn't something I wanted to do over the phone. In our circle, you had to be good at reading between the lines and hearing the words that were never actually spoken.

He looked back at me, his eyes dark and his tone deep and serious. "So, we're good?"

I met his stare. "We're good."

Chandler straightened back up and motioned for another beer. "But man, Lincoln Hunt—"

I pinned him with a glare. "Not here." I looked across the room and smiled at my father, who was watching our conversation with an intense expression on his face. I glanced back at Chandler. "Another time."

He grabbed his beer from the bartender. "Got it."

I finished my beer then set the bottle on the bar. The bartender was quick to pop the top and hand me another one.

Chandler leaned back and propped his elbows on the bar behind him as he scanned the room. "Have you talked to her? Tatum, I mean."

"Nah." *Not yet.* I pushed off the bar. "I'm going to make my rounds, then we're going to head out." I smiled at him. "And by *we*, I mean we're going our separate ways as soon as we're outside."

Chandler grinned back at me. "You got somewhere else to be?"

I took a long pull from the beer, finishing it off then placing the empty bottle on the bar. "As a matter of fact, I do."

THIRTEEN

Tatum

"First position, then plié." I stood with my feet turned out and bent my knees. "Hands in front, remember? Like you're holding a bouquet of flowers." I positioned my hands. "Now relevé."

Avery stumbled and huffed a breath, blowing a stray hair that had fallen from her bun. For months, I'd been working with her on her confidence. I even offered her private lessons. Avery was smaller than the other girls, so she tried harder to be perfect. I knew all too well what that was like—the need to be perfect.

I hated that she felt so out of place. Sometimes I wanted to lift her up, squeeze her in a hug, and tell her that size had nothing to do with talent. She could do this.

"It's okay, Avery. Look. Watch my form." I stood up with my back straight and tall. "See how my heels are planted on the floor?"

Avery nodded and the rest of the class watched in silence.

I slowly bent my knees until they were even with the tips of my toes, then I pushed myself gracefully back up. "Now, you try."

Avery took a deep breath and mimicked my movements.

"Awesome job. Now relevé." I lifted up on my toes.

The whole class clapped when she followed, then finished perfectly back in first position. Her smile lit up the room, even if she was missing one of her front teeth.

"Beautiful. Next, we'll try a bourrée turn. Relevé." I lifted onto my toes and arced my arms above my head. "Pull those tummies in nice and tight. If you can't balance with your arms up, you can just hold your waist." I demonstrated, then lifted my arms again. "Now, tiny little steps all around in a circle. Like you're tiptoeing on Christmas morning before everyone is awake." I stopped to watch ten little girls turn in a circle on their tiptoes and smiled.

And then I froze.

Someone was watching. I felt it in my veins.

I looked over the studio and out the windows. Sometimes I liked to leave the curtains open during class. People on the sidewalks would stop and watch with smiles on their faces. Some of them would even clap after a mini-performance.

This was not awareness caused by a crowd of spectators.

This was something else.

Caspian Donahue was close.

I knew it.

Anticipation and adrenaline sent goosebumps pebbling on my skin. Even though there was no one other than the usual sea of people streaming down the sidewalk, I knew it had to be him. No one else had ever made me feel this way. Four years and an ocean apart couldn't erase the power his presence had over me.

My whole life, I'd grown to crave the sensation of knowing he was near, ever since I was a six-year-old girl playing pretend at someone else's wedding. Somehow Caspian was always there, especially in the times when it felt like I needed him to be. Until he disappeared when it mattered most.

Over the last four years, I'd gotten good at not waiting for him to walk into a room or show up at an event. I'd trained myself not to hope for that feeling—*this* feeling. I'd convinced my mind it hated him, and aside from those moments when I was alone in my room with nothing but his custom-made cock and my memories of the way he'd fucked me, my body followed suit.

Until now.

I clapped my hands together then cleared my throat. "Okay, princesses, let's put it all together." I walked over to the window to pull the velvet curtains closed. But not before letting my gaze sweep the sidewalk one last time.

Just in case.

Nothing. Just a crowd of strangers and the unwelcomed sense of disappointment settling in the bottom of my stomach.

I straightened and focused back on my class. "From first position, we're going to do four tendus, two pliés, one relevé, and end with a spin." I demonstrated, and they followed. "Nice work, guys! Ready to put it to music?"

They all clapped their answer with a resounding "Yeahhhh."

This. These were the moments I lived for.

After three repetitions, I shut off the music and faced my girls. "Time for a cool down." I sat on the floor, pulling my legs into a butterfly position as I let out a breath. "Ready for some recovery stretches?"

Twenty minutes later, my studio was empty. My five o'clock class was my last class of the day. It was time to go home and disappear into a tub of bubbles.

After slipping out of my pointe shoes, I grabbed my cardigan off the back of my chair and slid it over my shoulders. I wore black leggings, a black camisole leotard, and a short ballet skirt. The cardigan helped me look presentable in case I had to stop anywhere on the way home, which I usually didn't.

My heart slammed in my chest as I slid my feet inside my sandals, taking one last look around the studio before I switched off the lights and stepped outside.

Breathe, Tatum. You're being ridiculous.

Right as I reached for the door handle to pull it closed, a strong arm wrapped around me from behind A hand covered my mouth, pulling me back into something solid—a body. Tall, hard, and unyielding. I was terrified beyond belief.

What if I was wrong? What if it wasn't him?

At the same time, anticipation flooded my veins.

What if I was right?

Why did that thought excite me? What the hell was wrong with me?

I was shoved back inside the studio, then the door slammed shut with a sturdy thud.

Oh God.

I instantly regretted closing the curtains. With the lights out, we were surrounded by complete darkness. I tried to scream, but my voice was weak, muffled by the force of the hand cupping my mouth. My arms flailed through the air, grabbing at the forearm that held me in place. An immediate hiss of breath ghosted my ear, letting me know I broke skin.

"Did you honestly think it would be that easy?" he asked, and my intuition was confirmed. "Did you think I'd just let you go?"

I knew that voice. I'd memorized it. It was Caspian. He was here.

I scratched at him again, this time reaching up and hoping to find his face. I missed. He growled against my ear, then grabbed my arm with his free hand and pinned it behind my back. A sharp pain tore through my shoulder at the force of it.

His voice rippled through the air again, sliding over my skin like silk. "Does he close his eyes when he fucks you? Whisper sweet things and ask if it hurts?"

Anger wrapped around me, clenching its fist around my heart.

He left.

He went four years without a word. Occasional presents with cryptic notes were his only means of communication. Now he had the balls to come in here and talk about things that were none of his business?

"See, that's the difference between him and me, Princess." His mouth moved, as though he were smiling against my throat. "I bet he calls you Princess, doesn't he?"

The sensation of his mouth against my neck sent a wave of searing heat straight to my core. This was wrong. I wasn't supposed to feel this way.

And no, Brady didn't call me Princess. He called me Babe. But Caspian was spot on with the other stuff. Brady didn't fuck. He made love. Which like I said, was none of Caspian's business.

I lifted my leg to try to stomp on his foot, but all I accomplished was making my sandal fly off and hit the floor with a slap.

He sighed. "I know you hate me, which is why I had to do it like this. I couldn't give you a choice to see me because I knew what you would choose."

He was right. I would have slammed the door in his probably still flawless face. I wished I could see him, know what he looked like now. Was his mouth still beautiful? Did his eyes still pierce through my soul?

But the wishing just made me angrier. I didn't *want* to want to see him.

Why couldn't he just stay away?

I was doing fine. I didn't need him here.

The sound of my labored breaths shuddered against the back of his hand. I tried to focus on breathing through my nose, but it was hard to concentrate on anything other than the pounding of my heart and my increasing lack of oxygen. Tears began to sting my eyes, but I blinked them back.

Caspian loosened his grip on my arm. Immediate relief washed over me as the blood began circulating again. "I needed to see you. I just wanted to talk," he said as if answering my unspoken question.

I closed my eyes and let out a calming breath. Maybe he was about to let me go.

He brought his hand to my hips, digging his fingers into the flesh there as he pulled my ass against him.

"But now you see my dilemma?" He pressed into me. The barrier of fabric between us didn't mask the thickness of his hard cock. "I like it when you fight me, Little Troublemaker."

A whimper escaped my lips, and I cursed the way my own body betrayed me.

"I think you like it too." His tone was laced in amusement.

I opened my mouth and bit down on the inside of his hand. Hard. The bitter taste of copper coated my lips and slipped onto my tongue. *Does that feel like I like it?*

Even though some part of me did. Deep in the pit of my soul, where I kept my secrets locked away, the idea of challenging him excited me. The idea of testing his limits made me feel powerful. The notion that the cords of control that bound him could snap… *for me*… was a rush like nothing I'd ever known.

Suddenly, the hand was gone.

I opened my mouth with a gasp, letting the air fill my lungs. The body behind me moved away, and I hated how lost I felt without him there. Until his large presence loomed in front of me, holding my hips as he backed me against the door. My head hit the wood with a thud, and his hand was right there, cradling it, lifting it back up. His fingers massaged my scalp, just the slightest hint of tenderness before he brought his mouth to mine.

My heart almost stopped beating when he paused. *Please. Don't stop.* His tongue traced the seam of my lips, and I wondered why he wasn't kissing me. Why the sudden shift in demeanor?

Then I remembered that night in his room—our first kiss—and his words.

He's waiting for permission.

I parted my lips. *Yes.* The moment I did, his hand fisted in my hair, pulling a handful from my bun and yanking my head back. He groaned low in his throat and pressed his mouth to mine. His kiss was rough and possessive. Scorching and all-consuming. The stroke of his tongue against mine was both a conviction and benediction. I moaned in his mouth as my body arched into him. *Stupid traitor.* His other hand held my face, smearing the slickness of what had to be his blood across my cheek. My hands slammed against his hard chest in an attempt to push him away, but I ended up clenching his shirt in my fists and pulling him closer instead. This was so much more than the kiss I remembered.

I was seconds away from melting into a puddle when he finally released me. His forehead rested against mine, and his harsh rush of breath ghosted my face. There was a faint trace of alcohol lingering on his breath and on his tongue, making me wonder where he'd been, who he was with. I didn't drink, but I wanted to taste it again. I wanted to get drunk on him.

There was the unmistakable sound of a hard swallow, then he reached over and fumbled on the wall beside us until the studio was flooded with light.

His dark eyes studied my face, dropped to my lips, then flickered down my body. He let go of my hair and trailed his fingers over my collarbone, then down to my breast, barely skimming my peaked nipple. This touch was delicate, concentrated, the antithesis of the way he was moments ago. With his other hand, his thumb swept across my cheekbone, smearing his blood deeper into my skin.

"See why I can't let you go? I need this." He licked his lips and looked back into my eyes. "We both do."

He was right. I hated it, but it was true.

It felt like I'd been holding my breath for the past four years, and now that he was here again, I could finally breathe.

That still didn't stop me from wanting answers. I needed to know why he left. I deserved that from him.

"You keep saying that, but you're forgetting one important piece of information."

"Yeah? What's that?" He brushed his bloody thumb across my bottom lip.

"You already let me go." I swallowed hard, challenging his steely glare. "You left me. Remember?"

His eyes narrowed and his jaw clenched. He dropped both hands to his side and took a few steps back but stayed silent.

My lungs felt tight as my heart pounded. "Can you at least tell me why?"

Did I really want to know?

"You know why." His voice was calm, the complete opposite of the storm brewing in his eyes.

"It's been a while. Refresh my memory."

"I went to college. It's what people do."

"And you didn't think to tell me you were leaving before I…" I closed my eyes and inhaled, then opened them again. "Before we—"

"Opened Pandora's box and unleashed a plague on both our houses," he finished with a smirk, then sighed and squared his shoulders. His expression hardened. "I didn't tell you because it didn't matter. It wouldn't have changed anything."

My blood boiled. I took a step forward until we were once again toe-to-toe. "It wouldn't have changed anything? My best friend died that night!" My whole body was shaking now. The adrenaline was still pumping through my veins from the kiss, and now this. All my emotion bubbled to the surface, and I was powerless to stop it. "I should've been with her, but where was I?" I shoved at his chest, but it was like trying to move a brick wall. "Where was I, Caspian? When Lyric took her last breath, where was I?"

His nostrils flared as he looked down at me, but he never made a move. He never said a word.

"I was with *you*." I spit the word as if it were laced in venom. "I left with you. I could have saved her. I left her there, and now she's gone." The first tear spilled over my cheek, followed by another, and another. "You couldn't just leave in peace, could you? You had to drag me out of that place like some kind of caveman. You had to ruin me before you left." All of the emotion, all of the rage, that I'd been holding in for four years was finally clawing its way out. I needed this *then*. That was why I'd gone to his house. I needed to set it all free.

But he was gone.

He ran.

He took the coward's way out.

But he was here now, and one kiss didn't wipe away years of questions.

We stared at each other for what felt like an eternity. Caspian towered over me. His presence was predatorial and intimidating, but I wasn't afraid. His features were still every bit as beautiful as they were when he was younger, just more defined now, more mature. My heartbeat calmed as I studied the sharp edges of his jawline, his full lips and fierce golden-brown eyes the color of whiskey. My heavy, rapid breaths slowed to steady and controlled. The tears began drying on my cheeks but I never moved to wipe them away.

"I deserve answers," I said, finally. My voice was softer and more composed now.

"You do." His voice was as smooth and silky as it has always been.

Finally. Progress.

He took a step forward, and his gaze darkened. He took another step, forcing me to move backward. Then another. Until my back was once again pressed against the door, and then

Caspian slowly slid his hands up my arms, stopping at my shoulders.

Every muscle in my body tensed, and my breath caught in my throat. I pressed my hands against his chest to stop him from leaning in any closer, but he ignored my protests.

His hand skated across my collarbone then wrapped around my throat.

I reached up and grabbed his wrist, and he squeezed, applying just enough pressure to send my heart rate spiking. My insides tingled as wetness pooled between my thighs. God, I was fucked up. Good girls weren't supposed to want bad things, and Caspian was very, very bad.

He leaned his head down, touching his cheek against mine. My breath stuttered. My anger was entirely dissipated and replaced with white-hot need.

His smooth voice was more of a growl, and his breath danced against my ear when he spoke. "You want answers? Fine. I'll give them to you. One: Lyric was going to die—whether it was that night or another one. Stop thinking you could have saved her. Her death was inevitable. Two: You're lucky it was me who dragged you out of that place and fucked you that night. Trust me, sweetheart. It could have been much, *much* worse. Three: We were going to happen. You have always been mine." He reached his other hand between my legs and cupped my pussy. "That was also inevitable. And four…" He tilted his head so that we were face-to-face. My body was humming, making it nearly impossible not to grind down against his hand. *More.* "You don't get to give your soul to the devil then ask for it back." He tightened his grip on my throat then opened his mouth and swiped his tongue across my lips.

I parted my mouth, asking for more, and a sinister grin spread across his face.

He let go of my throat then took a step back, dropping his hand from between my legs. "That's enough for today."

Enough? He gave me nothing. I knew no more now than I did before.

"You don't get to do that." I shook my head and pointed a finger at his chest. "You don't get to walk in here and uproot everything that I've planted, then leave me with half-assed answers and call it a day."

"You don't know what you're asking for, Tatum." He pinched the bridge of his nose. "I'm trying to protect you, for fuck's sake." There was an edge to his tone that would have sent a shiver of fear down anyone else's spine. Not mine. I wasn't afraid of him. Not really.

"I may not have figured out much else, but you know what I have learned in the past four years?"

He lowered his hand and raised a brow.

"I don't need you to *protect* me anymore." I straightened my shoulders, boldly meeting his stare. "I'm capable of protecting myself. Especially from guys like you."

He tilted his head, just a hint to one side, and his jaw twitched. "Tatum…"

The weight of his stare made my legs weak. I took a deep breath and swallowed back the sharp pang of hurt that wrapped around my heart. "Go." I pointed at the door as I stepped to the side.

He took a step toward me, sending a bundle of nerves jolting to life in the bottom of my stomach.

"Get. Out." My voice cracked.

His gaze lingered for a moment as though he were trying to see if I was bluffing.

For a split second, I thought he might touch me again, that he might decide to put me in my place.

He didn't.

If I was honest, I wasn't sure I wanted him to. I needed time away from him to process the fact that he was back and everything he'd just said. *Her death was inevitable.* I couldn't do that as long as my mind was clouded by lust—or whatever this was.

"You're wrong," he said as he walked past me and opened the door. "You'll always need me."

My heart fell to my stomach.

He stopped in the open doorway, standing with his back to me. "Just like I'll always need you."

My mind was screaming as I watched him walk away and disappear around the corner. Defeat settled over me as I closed the door to the studio then slid down the wood all the way to my butt. I wanted to see how far I could push him, and I ended up shoving him right out the door.

FOURTEEN

CASPIAN

Tatum thought she wanted answers. I knew firsthand what it felt like to know your father would throw you to the wolves in order to save his own ass. There was no way she could ever know the truth about why I left. It would crush her.

And those reasons didn't matter now, because I was back. She thought she didn't want to see me. She thought she wanted me gone. The damp spot between her thighs told me what she really needed was time to process the way I made her feel. Hell, I needed time to process how she made *me* feel. In all the years since I'd lost my virginity, I knew my… needs… weren't typical. I thrived on obtaining the unobtainable. It had been ingrained in my mind since I was a child. *Always the hunter, never the hunted.* Holding the world in the palm of your hand only made you crave the things that were just out of reach.

Until her, I'd always been able to control my urges.

Until her, I'd only tested my boundaries with a tightened grip around a delicate throat and a rough fuck against a brick wall in a dark alley.

Until her, no one ever put up a fight.

Christ, just thinking about it now had my dick hard. All I wanted to do was see her face, inhale her scent, and remind her the quarterback wasn't what she needed. But she awakened the beast.

I glanced down at the scratches on my forearm, then flipped my hand to inspect my palm. She broke the skin just below my thumb, enough to bleed but not enough to cause any real damage. The stinging sensation served as a reminder of her fire —a fire she kept hidden from the world and only showed me.

One month.

She had until my twenty-fifth birthday to sort her shit out, then I was coming after her with no holds barred. Which meant I had one month to come up with a solid plan because there was no way in hell my father, or hers, was going to let this happen. I had to be ready for them both.

She would have her peace—for thirty days.

I pulled my phone from the back pocket of my jeans and glanced at the screen.

Tick Tock, Little Troublemaker. I'm coming back for you soon.

I opened my contacts and scrolled down to Chandler's name.

"Damn, dude. After four years, I expected it to last longer than that," he said when he answered.

Fucker.

"What happened? She shoot you down for the quarterback?"

Now he was just asking for an ass whipping.

"Fuck off. She's not that stupid." *She knows I would deflate his balls.* "I'm two blocks from the office. Can you meet me? We need to talk." I had a plan.

Chandler's dad rubbed dicks with the elite, right along with my dad and Malcolm Huntington. They had their brotherhood. We had ours. While Pierce Carmichael was busy buying up property all over the country, Chandler ran the underbelly of NYC. If it was illegal, Chandler had his fingerprints on it. Not child prostitution or sick shit like that. He left that to the men our fathers associated with—men like Khalid. But guns, drugs, and gambling? That was Chandler's empire.

"Yeah," he said, "I'll be there in ten."

It took a week for Chandler and me to come up with a bulletproof plan and execute it without my father finding out. I spent the rest of the month sitting behind my desk in the office across from my dad's, crossing my t's and dotting my I's.

He currently had me working on something his brotherhood called the "weaponization of social media." Which was basically me creating an activist group on social media, establishing a cult following, then starting a bunch of shit to get the general population riled up. Then going back and doing the same thing, only this time creating an activist group with an entirely different viewpoint.

"Throw them a steak and let them fight over it," he said.

According to the Obsidian Brotherhood, people were expendable. There was an order, a food chain, so to speak, and we were at the top. Money talked the loudest, so everyone else just did as they were told. With elite members from around the globe, the Brotherhood was one of the most powerful forces in the world. Their influence extended from the media to the military all the way into the deep roots of the government. No one said shit, because no one knew shit, and those who did run their mouth never lived long enough to prove anything. Their fucked-up rituals and exclusive membership roster were shrouded in secrecy. It was a society strictly for men, and leadership roles were confined to the pure-blood descendants of the five main families.

I knew all about the Brotherhood because I'd been initiated into it at thirteen years old. I spent every minute hating the game my last name forced me to play.

But it was almost over. I was about to cash in my chips.

Today was my twenty-fifth birthday.

Normally, that wouldn't mean shit. Mom would order some elaborate cake from Ladurée, Dad would pick up the tab on a nice dinner, and we'd call it a day—except I was a first-born, fourth-generation, Donahue male.

To my father, to me, to the rest of the world that didn't mean shit. It was just a guaranteed seat at the head of the table. But on my thirteenth birthday, that all changed. I remembered that day like it was yesterday.

That day, I was sitting on the sofa in Dad's office, trying to solve a Rubik's cube while listening to him lecture someone about international trade tax, when his lawyer plopped a file on his desk. The moment Dad had seen what it read, I watched him transform. He'd looked over at me with the most intense hatred in his eyes. Then he stood up, walked across the room, grabbed me by the shirt and slammed me against the wall.

"I bust my ass. I sacrifice time with my family." He clenched my shirt tighter as he spit his words in my face. *"I sold my soul."* He lifted me up then slammed me again. This time my head hit the wall so hard, it cracked the sheetrock. *"And all you had to do was exist."* He let go of my shirt, sending me tumbling to the floor. *"I'll make sure you earn that money. You'll earn every single fucking penny."*

I had no idea what he was talking about, not yet anyway. Common sense told me Dad wasn't angry at *me*, but great-grandpa Donahue wasn't exactly around anymore for him to take it out on. And thirteen year olds didn't focus on common sense anyway. All I knew was that from that point on, my father was different. I became the son who was also an enemy. He treated me as though I'd stolen from him, so he stole from me. He stole the rest of my childhood by making me work with him instead of hanging out with my friends. He took my innocence by showing me the darkest depths of his world. And he robbed me of my dignity every time he laid his hands on me—until I was finally old enough to start fighting back.

He was right, though.

I'd earned every fucking penny.

It wasn't until years later, when I was eighteen years old, sitting in an attorney's office, where I'd been privately summoned—without my father's knowledge—that I knew exactly what that day had meant.

In 1911, my great-grandfather became this country's very first billionaire. Twenty years later, he set up a trust.

For me.

Of course, at that time, he had no idea of knowing *I* would be me. He'd simply set up a trust for the first-born, fourth-generation Donahue male. Every heir before me, including my father and grandfather, received stock in companies as their trust.

I got cash—*a lot* of cash.

John R. Donahue had set aside a hefty portion of his financial estate for this very day. While all the males before me had to strategize and manage their share of the Donahue family fortune in order to keep it alive, I just had to cash a check. The only stipulations were: I couldn't be in jail, I had to be mentally stable, and the trust didn't mature until my twenty-fifth birthday. My guess was he figured by then I'd either be smart enough to invest it back into the company or fed up enough to get the fuck out. That act alone gave me hope that at least my great gramps was a decent human. Money changed people. I'd seen firsthand how it turned men into monsters and women into whores.

I exited all my tabs and rolled my chair away from my desk. It was twenty minutes until one o'clock—fifty minutes until my meeting with family attorney. His office was on the seventeenth floor of the Roosevelt Tower, which was exactly eleven minutes from here. That gave me thirty-nine minutes to grab a sandwich from the deli downstairs.

"Caspian," Dad called from his office the minute I stepped into the hall.

I hid my frustration behind a smile as I walked over to his open doorway and leaned against the frame. "I was about to head out for lunch. We're up to fifteen thousand followers on IG."

There was no way I was telling him where I was going. I made sure no one would know about this meeting until it was over. No one, including my dad, knew I'd learned about the trust. Our attorney put his life on the line by even telling me it existed. Dad had spent every single day since he discovered the trust making sure I wouldn't find out what had pushed him over the edge. In his mind, if I didn't know about it, I wouldn't cash it in. If I didn't cash it in, and if for some reason I happened to die before my dad, the money went to him. All he had to do was make sure I checked off all the boxes in order for it to mature. That without a doubt explained why he was so eager to make a deal with Huntington to keep me out of jail. But now the boxes were all checked. I'd made it to twenty-five, and as far as my father was concerned, there was a three-billion-dollar price tag on every breath I took.

He smiled. "That's great. Come here." He nodded his head toward his desk. "I want to talk about your next project."

After today, there would be no more *projects*. In less than an hour, I was no longer a puppet. I would have enough money to cut my own chains and set myself free. The first order of business following that involved a dark-haired ballerina with a smart mouth.

"We'll have more time to go over it after lunch. I won't be long."

His eyes darkened and his smile tightened. "Come on, Son. This will only take a minute." He tapped the top of his desk.

I took in a deep breath and stepped inside.

His grin widened as he leaned back in his chair.

I ignored his request to sit, walking behind his desk instead. Whatever he needed to tell me, he could say to me while we both looked at his computer screen. I needed to be out of this building within the next fifteen minutes, which didn't leave time for secondhand explanations. He was already fucking up my chances of getting a sandwich.

He clicked around a few tabs then sat up straight. I followed his gaze as it flew to the television on the wall. Dad always had the news playing in the background, even though he'd already sifted through most of it before it ever hit the air. He grabbed the remote off his desk and turned up the volume. Something had caught his attention.

"Holy shit," he said as we both stared at the screen.

The blood in my veins heated as bile threatened its way up my throat. I had to clench my teeth to keep from showing any signs of a reaction.

"First responders are on the scene of what looks to be an explosion at the Roosevelt Tower. Officials are still searching for survivors. There is no word yet on what caused the explosion."

The news anchor's voice faded out with the ringing in my ears. Smoke and dust smothered the air in the background on the screen. Firefighters and police officers scrambled back and forth amongst the rubble.

Roosevelt Tower.

An explosion.

Well, fuck.

FIFTEEN

CASPIAN

At least nineteen innocent people died in that explosion, including Jonathon Bradshaw, the family attorney I was on my way to meet. The "cause" was still under investigation, but Dad and I both knew the truth.

Liabilities. That was what he would have called those people under any other circumstance, like getting rid of evidence in a criminal investigation. I'd seen enough *accidental* building fires and perfectly timed burglaries to know how it worked. This time he denied having anything to do with it. This time he had to lie to everyone, even me. This time it was personal.

"Damn," he'd said, shaking his head. "It will take months for them to sort through all that mess. I'm glad Jonathon didn't have anything important in those offices."

I wasn't sure if it was a veiled threat or if he was just being his usual unsympathetic self. People died. His attorney died. And he was worried about paperwork. If I'd had to guess, it was the former. He had no way of knowing I knew about the trust, but he had to have the last word just in case I did.

As usual, I showed no emotion. I'd trained myself well. I'd been wearing this mask for so long, I almost didn't recognize the man in the mirror when I took it off.

Knowing now that my strings were still tied, I went through the rest of the day with business as usual. I got my sandwich from the deli and spent the afternoon researching Dad's new project. As expected, Mom had a cake from Ladurée waiting for me when we got home. Dad offered to take us out to dinner, but I told my parents I already had plans with Chandler. Not a total lie.

I had plans.

And Chandler had helped me make them.

An hour and forty-five minutes later, I was pulling onto Seven Lakes Road in East Hampton. My name got me through the gate because our family had a house out here too. Ours was just located on Billionaire's Row.

One of Chandler's guys, a hacker who specialized in breaking into the Vegas point spreads system, was able to tap into the security cameras at Tatum's Hampton house and disable the feed. I still wore a black hoodie and parked down the road just in case.

In the darkness, landscape spotlights highlighted the colorful flower beds surrounding the front of the house, and wall sconces lit up the wraparound porch. There was a lifted Ford F-250 parked behind Tatum's Benz in the circular driveway.

Brady.

Had to be.

Was she fucking him right now? Was he touching her? Tasting her?

The demons inside me stirred to life, and the way I saw it I had three choices: I could climb into the backseat of his truck, wait for him to come out and fuck his pretty boy face up the minute he got on 27-E. I could walk through the front door and fuck him up, then jack off—because face it, the thought of fucking him up made my dick hard—and come all over his bloody face while Tatum watched. Or I could wait until he left, then go inside and remind her who she belonged to.

I wasn't trying to go to jail or make Tatum hate me any more than she thought she already did, so I walked around to the back of the house and waited. Thank God, I was a patient man because the minutes felt like hours.

The moonlight bounced off the ocean, and the crashing waves helped steady my raging heartbeat as I stared out over the hedges at the water. I took deep breaths and counted to myself.

Ten.

Nine.

Eight.

Seven.

"You should know that I have a gun."

I turned around at the sound of her sweet voice. She tried to sound intimidating, but it was actually cute as fuck. I couldn't imagine Tatum pulling a gun on anyone. She was too good for that. Unless it was a water gun. Then I imagined her with a water gun and me with mine. I'd soak her until her nipples poked through her clothes. Then I'd lick the water off every inch of her body.

A grin spread across my face as I looked up at her standing on the second-floor balcony. My face was shielded by my hood, but the way her mouth parted on a gasp when she saw me told me she knew exactly who I was. She stood there in a solid white, spaghetti-strapped dress that dipped in a low "V" between her breasts. Her hair was down, hanging over her shoulders. The soft amber glow formed a halo around her angelic body. If Shakespeare said Juliet was the sun, then Tatum was the whole fucking sky.

"Caspian?"

The thought of Brady seeing her like this made my blood boil.

"Are you alone?" I asked her.

The rumble of an engine coming to life answered my question. Tatum heard it too, because she made the mistake of looking over her shoulder toward the front of the house where

Brady had just cranked his truck. Before she could look back at me, I was already making my way around the house to the front door.

I caught her bounding down the stairs as I opened the door and made my way inside. She stopped on the bottom step, one hand on the wooden rail, breathless and staring at me.

I closed the door behind me. "Why was he here?"

She straightened her shoulders and narrowed her eyes. "Why are *you* here?"

So that was how it was going to be? The thought of her challenging me again made my cock jump.

I took a step toward her. "Did you fuck him?"

Her chest moved faster as her breath quickened. A pink heat crept up her neck and onto her cheeks. "What I do with Brady is none of your business."

I took another step. "Maybe not. But what you do with *my* pussy is my business."

Her nipples peaked against the thin chiffon fabric of her dress. *Checkmate, baby.*

Another step and I'd made my way across the foyer and into the living room where the staircase was. I was only a few feet away from her now. "Did you fuck him?" I repeated.

"No." Her voice was barely higher than a whisper.

"Prove it." I took another step.

Her eyes grew wide. "What?"

"I said, prove it." Another step. Now we were inches apart. I was close enough to see the pulse throbbing in the hollow of her delicate throat, close enough to hear her stuttered breath. Her nipples taunted me, begged me to put my mouth on them. "Take off your pretty little panties. Spread your thighs. And prove you didn't just give another man what belongs to me."

She swallowed hard then clenched her teeth. "Fuck you. Nothing about me belongs to you." Her voice burned with conviction.

There was my little troublemaker. Always testing me.

I grabbed her by the chin, forcing her to look up at me. "Let me make one thing perfectly clear." I let my hand glide down her throat, inside the V of her dress, to palm her breast. She closed her eyes, tilting her head back when I rolled her nipple between my fingers. I slid my other hand around her hip, lifted her dress, and grabbed a handful of her ass, making her whimper when I gave it a hard squeeze.

With my mouth on the shell of her ear, I whispered, "You. Are. Mine."

She opened her mouth to argue, but I lifted her up, carrying her to the living room then flopping her on the couch. She tried clamping her thighs together and crossing her legs. *Not so fast, sweetheart.* I wrenched her knees apart, positioning myself between her legs, then reached beneath her ass and ripped her panties off. They landed on the floor beside the couch. She fought to scoot up and away from me as my hands slid along the sides of her body, inching up her dress and exposing her sweet, perfect, fucking pussy. I loved that fight. I lived for it. She loved it too, because she was soaking fucking wet.

My fingers dug into her flesh, keeping her in place.

Her hands flew to my head, tangling in my hair the moment I positioned my face between her thighs. "What are you doing?"

I glanced up right as she licked her lips. "Making sure you don't taste like him." I leaned in, dragging my tongue in a long, lazy trail right up her dripping wet center. Fuck me. She was ambrosia, nectar of the gods, and I wanted to feast on her forever.

She yanked on my hair in a weak attempt to pull me away, but her thighs clenched on either side of my head, and a moan escaped her lips. A paradox if I'd ever seen one.

"Caspian, stop."

No fucking way. No fucking how.

I gripped her inner thighs and spread her folds open with my thumbs. Her fingers tightened in my hair, trying to push me away, but her hips lifted off the white couch cushion beneath her, begging me for more. Her body was at war with her mind, and I was about to plant my fucking flag on the battlefield.

I ran the tip of my nose along her slit. "Making sure you don't smell like him."

She didn't. She smelled like pineapple and white wine with a hint of musk. Like salvation and sin.

"I said stop." Her hands left my hair to press against my shoulders.

I looked up. My gaze drifted over the bare pussy in front of me, to her stomach, then to her breasts as they heaved with every breath she took. My eyes narrowed when they met hers.

"Say it like you mean it, and I'll think about it," I said with a smirk, then brought my lips together and blew on her clit while I held her stare. A soundless whistle against her slick flesh.

"I mean it." Her voice was too breathless to be confident, and her ass cheeks flexed as if she were trying to control her body's reaction.

"Nice try."

I speared my tongue and plunged inside her. Her body relaxed as she opened up for me. I threw one of her legs over the back of the couch to give myself room.

There's my girl.

I prodded and speared and fucked, trying to go deeper and deeper until my face was covered in her juices from my nose to my chin. It wasn't enough. It would never be enough. I needed this, needed her.

I ran my tongue up her center all the way to her clit, then shoved two fingers in her tight little hole. Her hips rolled up as her body writhed, and she rode my fucking face. Hungry. Desperate. Needy.

So. Fucking. Perfect.

Slick sounds, wet and hot, filled the room. I wanted it louder. I wanted it wetter. Four years of waiting for this had created a monster, and now he wanted to be fed.

My fingers plunged deeper. Harder. Faster.

My tongue worked her clit. Then my teeth. Flicking and nipping. Kissing and sucking. All I tasted was her. All I breathed was her.

She arched her back and moaned. It almost sounded like she was in pain, but I knew better.

"Oh, God," she cried. "Oh, fuck." Her body quivered around me, and her hands gripped my hair so tightly my scalp burned. Her thighs gripped my head in a vise.

That's it, baby. Come on my face.

I wanted her everywhere.

I wanted to breathe in and still smell her later. I wanted to lick my lips and still taste her on the long drive home. She was like a sickness in my blood that I never wanted to cure.

Tatum closed her eyes and threw her head back, letting the orgasm shake her body. God, she was beautiful like this—mouth open and panting, delicate throat exposed to me.

I pulled my black joggers down enough to release my dick.

She opened her eyes and lifted her head to see my fist wrapped around my cock, giving it hard, urgent strokes.

"You like that." It wasn't a question. I could tell she liked it by the look in her eye.

Stroke.

Her lips parted. I squeezed tighter.

Stroke.

"You're looking at my dick like you want it in your mouth." I grabbed the back of the couch for support and thrust myself into my hand. Fuck.

Stroke.

She opened her mouth, but no words came out.

"Soon, Little Troublemaker. Very soon." Then with a few final pumps, I came all over her stomach and sweet, sweet pussy. It was still swollen and red from me devouring it minutes ago. Now it was covered in ropes of milky white.

I slid my hand under her dress to her breast, leaving a trail of cum that had spilled onto my fist all over her skin. "He can't give you this."

She arched into my touch when I squeezed her tit, then pinched her nipple between my fingers.

"No one can." I moved my hand over her stomach and down to her pussy, smearing my seed into her skin. Then I took my cum-coated finger and eased it inside her, not giving a single fuck about birth control, not anymore, not with her.

She lifted her hips to welcome me as a whimper left her lips. The mask she tried so hard to hold in place slipped when she was with me. The predator lurking beneath the surface licked his lips as he eyed his prey, so vulnerable yet so strong.

I pulled my finger out and wiped it on the front of my pants. "There. Now you smell like me." *And I smelled like her.*

"You're insane." She pulled her dress down, covering up my masterpiece.

"Maybe." I pulled my joggers back over my hips, tucking my dick inside. "But you're just as fucked up as I am. You crave what I can give—what *only* I can give."

She was everything I needed, and I wasn't giving up until I'd ruined her. Until I'd possessed her, body and soul. It wasn't a question of whether or not Tatum was going to let me destroy her. She wanted the monster. She craved the beast. The question was, could she stop me.

SIXTEEN

Tatum

Caspian came in and made his point. He staked his claim. It was just like him throwing me over his shoulder and carrying me out of The Chamber all over again. Only this time, I knew what to expect. I knew what it felt like to be owned by him.

The last time I saw him was in my studio when I'd told him to leave. I should've known he wasn't that easy to get rid of. I should have known he'd be back.

I was waiting for him to come back.

He showed up here, out of nowhere, wearing all black, thinking he could hide in the darkness. I knew it was him as soon as I'd stepped out onto the balcony. I felt his presence.

I should have looked him in the eye and told him "No" and meant it.

I should have sent him back to wherever he came from.

But this was what Caspian did to me. He eased his way into my veins like morphine, making me numb to the rest of the world. He crept inside my soul and conjured up my darkest desires.

Now he stood here, his intense gaze searing a trail from my head to my toes. His facial hair had grown out enough to create a sexy shadow along his jaw. I loved the way that shadow felt between my thighs. His plump lips turned up in a smirk. I loved the way those lips felt on my skin. His hair was a mess, but I loved that too, because I knew it was my hands that had made it look that way.

He was still beautiful.

He was still dangerous.

"We can't do this." I scooted up the sofa and held my dress over my thighs. The fabric clung to my skin where he'd smeared his cum.

He moved an oversized seashell to one side of the glass coffee table, clearing a place for him to sit in front of me. "Why not?"

"You know why."

Because you'll end up leaving again.

Because my father hates you and would never allow it.

Because you get to keep your secrets but demand I tell you mine.

"Because of Brady?"

God, no.

I'd just finished telling Brady that he deserved someone better than me right before I found Caspian in my backyard.

"Brady is a good man." Too good of a man to be with a woman who pleasured herself to sleep at night with dark thoughts of an even darker man.

"Then let him be good to someone else. You're taken." He leaned forward, resting his elbows on his knees and hypnotizing me with his stare. "Did you forget that already? Do you need me to remind you again?" He ran his tongue across his lips.

Yes. Please.

I swallowed. "No."

He cocked a brow. "No?"

I shook my head, knowing *no* didn't always mean *no* with Caspian and wondering what he would do next.

He didn't do anything, though—just locked his fingers together and held my gaze. "Then tell me *why* we can't do this."

"My father and your father would both—"

He cut me off, his jaw clenching at the mention of our fathers. "Do you trust me?"

"Yes."

No.

Maybe.

With everything but my heart.

His eyes softened. "Have I ever done anything to hurt you or put you in danger?"

My mind flashed back over the years all the way to the very first time I'd met him.

"Never."

He leaned forward until we were face to face, then cupped his hand at the nape of my neck. "That throbbing ache between your thighs? My scent on your skin? Get used to it." He ran his tongue over my bottom lip the way that he always liked to do. "Because we *are* doing this." He smirked, then gave me a kiss. "I need to go now, but I'll see you soon," he said with a wink, then he got up and walked out the door.

My father was a United States senator. I'd spent my whole life around powerful men. None of them held a candle to Caspian Donahue.

The night I gave him all my firsts, he'd told me he would destroy me. I'd dared him to try.

At the time, I had no idea what I was asking for. Now I knew. I'd known for six years.

I was ruined.

He was right.

I craved the depravity he brought with every breath of mine he stole.

And I loved the simplicity of the life I'd built.

I reveled in challenging him.

And I found joy in keeping the peace with my family.

I needed his chaos.

And I cherished my structure.

It was as though two different women lived in the same body, bound together by the same desire—we both just wanted to be *free*.

I wasted more time over the next few days thinking about Caspian than I should have. I stood on the balcony outside of my bedroom every night, waiting for him to return.

He never came.

I sat on the sofa, staring at the front door, waiting for him to burst through it.

He never did.

Brady called twice, and both times it broke my heart to assure him I'd meant what I said. Both times, I wished it had been Caspian on the other end of the line. Both times, I questioned my sanity.

Not long after I graduated, Dad had bought an old theater on 42nd Street and had it remodeled to look exactly the way it did in the 1940s. He said it was to keep Lincoln out of trouble and to give my students and me a place to perform. Lincoln was big into MMA, so he hosted tournaments and amateur fights there. Three times a year, I scheduled a public performance for my students. It gave us all something to look forward to and helped Dad save face since neither one of us went to college. This way, we were still successful in the eyes of the world—his world.

Our next performance was in a few weeks, which meant that starting today, I would be spending a lot of time in this theater. Lincoln even had a set of keys made for me, so I wouldn't have to bother him every time I needed in.

On the outside, the theater looked like an ordinary building made of brick and glass. There was a neon sign over a marquee and a set of large wooden double doors. On the inside, it looked like someone snatched the building right out of the middle of Paris and plopped it down in New York City. The walls were painted a creamy ivory with brown accents and gold trim. Every few feet on the walls high above the seats, there were colorful murals of cities with golden temples and people dancing. The balcony formed a half-circle overlooking the downstairs seating area. From up there, the seats below looked like a garden of red poppies blooming in front of the stage. A remarkable gold and crystal chandelier hung from the middle of the painted ceiling. It matched the sconces that hung on the walls. The massive, red velvet curtains were pulled open, showcasing the stage where I had just finished taping off quarter markers for my dancers.

Every year, we did the same three ballets—one for each age group. I knew the choreography by heart. I'd gone over it hundreds of times with different classes in the last few years. I didn't need to retrace my steps, but as the music played overhead and echoed throughout the space, I couldn't help myself from moving.

My body was operating on pure muscle memory. Spinning, stretching, and arching with the energy of the music and my emotions. Nothing else mattered when I was dancing. Nothing else existed.

Then the music ended. The theater went silent, except for the sound of my harsh breath.

And a loud, slow clap coming from somewhere in the house area.

Caspian stood with one shoulder leaned against the wall near the entrance. He wore a white T-shirt and dark jeans. Even casual, he looked like royalty. His stare burned right through my long-sleeved leotard and leggings.

I held my breath as I watched him walk down the center aisle between the rows of seats. I thought I'd spent the last few days missing him, but the truth was that he'd never left. He was always there, under my skin, in my bloodstream.

"You know you could always send a text or call." I smirked at him. "Unless the whole creepy stalker vibe is your thing."

He stopped in front of the stage and looked up at me. "You think it's creepy?" The glint in his eye told me he already knew the answer.

No.

I didn't.

I probably should have. But the thought of him watching without me *knowing* he was watching excited me in ways that were nowhere near healthy.

I bent down, grabbing a white towel from the stage to wipe my face and neck. "It's definitely not normal."

Caspian pulled himself onstage with minimal effort. Like hoisting himself up onto a three-and-a-half-foot-high platform was an everyday thing for him. He made his way over to the blue X I stood upon. I breathed in the scent of him, a heady blend of bergamot and leather. All male. All sophistication. The sheer power of his presence made my stomach flutter.

He brought his hand to my face and ran the pad of his thumb over my bottom lip. "Nothing about us is normal."

You can say that again.

He pried my mouth open, then stuck his thumb inside.

I curled my tongue around it, drawing him farther into my mouth.

Caspian pulled his hand from my mouth and cupped my ass, yanking my body against his. "I like watching you." His erection dug into my stomach. The fabric between us didn't even matter. I still felt him as though he were buried inside me. The air between us was charged, a magnetic force that refused to be broken.

I smiled. "I can tell."

He stroked my cheek with the front of his index finger. "I want you to dance for me."

I almost melted into his touch. "I just did."

"I mean when we're older, sitting in the living room. I want to shove the coffee table out of the way and watch you dance."

"For someone who likes to disappear, you sure are planning ahead."

He brought his other hand to my ass. "You're fucking right I am."

I met his stare. "And what if, in this imaginary scenario, I want you to dance with me?"

"I don't dance."

I trailed a finger down his chest. "You know, dancing is like making love, but with clothes on."

"We both know I don't do that either." He squeezed my ass tight with both hands, pressing me harder into him.

"We'll see," I said as I pulled away from him. My body immediately hated feeling his absence.

His loud groan filled the auditorium.

I walked over to the sound system and scrolled to the next song on my playlist. The soothing voice of Sara Bareilles filled the air as *Gravity* started playing.

"I'll walk you through it the way you did the first time you kissed me," I said when I went back over and stopped in front of him.

"That kiss landed you flat on your back with my dick in your cunt."

I turned around, pressing my back against his chest and my ass against his crotch. "Who says that's not my plan?" Something like a growl rumbled in his chest, making me smile. "Wrap your arms around my waist." He did, and I breathed in at the electricity of his touch. I lifted my arms in the air above my head. "Now, glide one hand down the front of my body." He slid his hand down, letting his fingertips skim dangerously close to my center. "All the way down my thigh." I closed my eyes and swallowed. "Trail your other hand upward." He moved his other hand over my waist then along the side of my body. "Up my arm." His touch was so smooth, so gentle, so careful. It was nothing like the monster I knew lurked within him—a side I would bet not many people got to see. "See how you can feel what I'm feeling without me saying a word? The energy moves from my body to yours with a single touch." I bent at the waist, dipping my body forward, and both of his hands instinctively flew to my waist. My body twirled around so that we were facing each other. I opened my eyes. "It's an unspoken language." I placed one of his hands on my lower back and held his other hand in mine. "Just like sex." Then I interlocked our legs, pressing my core against his thigh. "Move with me." I urged his hips backward with my own, then forward again, repeating the pattern until there was no more distinction between where he ended and I began. My heart raced, and my breath stuttered. "Take a step backward." He moved, and I moved with him. "Another." He moved again, and so did I, but our connection never faltered. He moved his hand from my back to behind my thigh, lifting my leg to his hip. I hooked my arms around his neck, and his whiskey eyes darkened.

Caspian licked his lips, then brought his other hand to my ass. As he was about to lift me up, Lincoln's voice echoed across the room.

"Get the man some tights and a tutu. He's a natural." He stood at the last row of seats, chewing on a toothpick in one corner of his mouth. His black T-shirt and jeans hung loosely on his tall, lean frame.

Caspian's grip tightened on the back of my thigh.

My heart thrashed wildly in my chest at the sound of Lincoln's voice. *He's going to tell our dad.* I couldn't think, couldn't speak, but somehow I pushed air in and out of my lungs, forcing myself to stay strong. My brother's eyes met mine, mischief dancing like fire in their depths. I didn't move, though. I stayed right here in front of Caspian, ready for whatever happened next.

Lincoln continued as he took a few steps forward. "I heard you were back from exile but didn't realize you were back to fucking my sister."

Caspian let go of me and took a step back. Tension rolled off him in waves. The atmosphere vibrated with it. "That was one. Disrespect Tatum like that again, and I'll make sure you have a matching scar on the other cheek."

I let out a strangled breath.

Lincoln ran his finger along the marred skin from his temple to just below his cheekbone. "Do your best, pretty boy. I never got to thank you for the first one. The chicks really dig it."

My mind ran circles around his words. *Thank him?* What was Lincoln talking about? The race? He blamed Caspian for the wreck? Ethan was driving the night of Lincoln's accident, and Caspian's car was a mess, too. Why would Lincoln blame him? If anyone, he should have been angry with Ethan.

"Stop being a dick, Lincoln. It was an accident."

The air grew thick with silence once the music stopped.

Caspian narrowed his eyes and studied my face.

Then Lincoln threw his head back with a laugh. The malice in it made my hair stand on end. "Oh, shit." His eyes widened, and he pulled the toothpick from his mouth with his tattooed fingers. "That's right." He looked at Caspian as he made his way down the aisle and toward the stage. "We told her it was an *accident*." He made air quotes around the last word. "But you wouldn't have known that because you weren't here."

Caspian's jaw ticked as his gaze shot to Lincoln. "Fuck off. You know why I wasn't here."

What the hell was going on? Why would Lincoln know why Caspian left when I still didn't even know?

I took a step toward Caspian. My mind was screaming, but I forced myself to remain calm. "What is he talking about? Why is he blaming you for the wreck? And why does he get to know why you left and I don't?"

"You wanna tell her, or should I?" Lincoln asked.

"I said, fuck off." Caspian's voice was cold and harsh.

"Ohhhh, that's it, Romeo. Show her who you *really* are." Lincoln moved along the front row and took a seat in one of the chairs. He propped a booted foot on his knee. "I can't wait for the show. Too bad I don't have popcorn."

"I'm not playing your games, you psychotic fuck." Caspian turned his attention to me and cradled my face in his hands. "We'll finish this later. I promise." The chill in his tone disappeared when he spoke to me, like a switch had been flipped.

I huffed a laugh. "You promise." Right.

His eyes darkened. "If I don't leave *right now*, I'm going to fuck him up, and trust me, that's not something you need to see."

Lincoln was unpredictable and maybe even a little crazy. He was like a tornado hellbent on destruction. But Caspian was like the ocean. On the surface, he was beautiful and calm. Underneath it all, he possessed the power to steal the life from your lungs without warning.

Animosity became a palpable presence in the room. It was then that I finally realized just how deep the hatred between our families was rooted. I'd always known. I'd heard it in conversations and seen it in my father's expressions. But I'd never actually witnessed it firsthand until now.

I had truly and wholly fallen for the enemy.

Lincoln knew it, and soon, my father would too.

Caspian leaned forward and brought his mouth to mine. My lips parted when he ran his tongue across the bottom one. Then he kissed me.

And I kissed him back, not caring that Lincoln was watching, or that this kiss was most likely Caspian's personal *fuck you* to my brother, or about the fallout that was inevitable.

He tangled his fingers in my hair, pulling until my scalp burned. Still, I gave myself to him. The tension in my body slowly melted away as he glided his tongue against mine the way he'd moved it against my clit the other night. He kissed me like he hated me—the pulling of my hair and the brutal way his lips pressed against mine—and he kissed me like he loved me—the way his tongue danced with mine, slow and tender. He kissed me like he'd die without tasting me and kissing me was his lifeline.

When he finally pulled away, he pressed his lips to my forehead, loosening his grip in my hair. "Everything I've done, I've done for you."

"What does that even mean?"

He tipped my chin up with his finger. "Later. I promise." He grinned at me, and I felt weightless.

My heart thundered as I watched him hop off the stage and walk past Lincoln without giving him as much as a glance, then out the door.

Lincoln stood and looked up at me. "He's dangerous."

"Tell me something I don't know."

"No. I *mean*, he's dangerous. You have no idea what he's capable of."

"And you do?"

"As a matter of fact, I do." He stuck the toothpick back in his mouth and rolled it between his teeth. "And if you'd think real hard, dig deep enough, you would too."

SEVENTEEN

Tatum

After my shower, I changed into a pair of tie-dyed shorts and long-sleeve shirt that fell off one shoulder. I tried reading. That didn't work. I flipped through the channels on the TV. Nothing held my attention. I even listened to music. My thoughts still strayed.

Ever since I left the theater, Lincoln's words kept echoing in my head.

Think real hard. Dig deep enough. You don't know what he's capable of.

I let my thoughts drift back to the first time I'd met Caspian Donahue. I was a little girl pretending to be a bride, and he was a bossy tyrant who dragged me away from my happy place. Then there was the time at Crestview Lake when he'd pulled me from the water. And the time before that at that same lake when he'd dragged me out of my cabin in the middle of the night. I didn't know why he pulled me out of bed or made me sleep in his cabin afterward. He never told me. All I remembered was how dark and ominous the water looked later when I'd gone back to my own bed. Other than that, I had nothing, but I wasn't sure why. *Because it was just a dream.* A sudden chill washed over me, covering my skin in goosebumps. *Dreams didn't give people goosebumps.* I may have forgotten the memory. I may not remember if what I saw was real or not, but I would never forget the feeling that something was wrong that night.

I walked onto the balcony outside my bedroom and prayed the fresh air would clear my head. A cool breeze that only the night could bring swept my hair across my face. I pulled it back and tucked it behind my ear, then leaned against the white wood railing. Looking out over the waves didn't give me the familiar comfort it usually did, and the sky seemed darker than normal. Maybe it was because there were no stars out yet. Even the moon was shadowed by clouds. Maybe a storm was brewing in the distance. Or maybe my thoughts only made it feel darker than it actually was.

I stared out into the nothing, watching the waves lap at the shore. It felt as if I were somewhere else, as if I wasn't standing on the balcony of a beach house waiting for the fulfillment of a promise I was almost sure he wouldn't keep. Instead, it felt like I was out there, in the middle of the darkness, adrift at sea.

My breath caught in my chest the moment the door slid open.

He came.

"I wondered how long it would take you to show up."

Caspian's smooth voice wrapped around me. "I made a promise."

"So, you did." I continued staring out over the water but felt his gaze on my back, all over my skin. I felt him *everywhere*.

"You left the front door unlocked." It felt as though he were chastising me, but his voice was hypnotic and seductive rather than cold and callous. He was behind me now. His solid chest pressed against my back. Searing warmth radiated from his body to mine.

I leaned back into him, seeking out the comfort the waves failed to bring. "I knew you were coming."

I hoped he was coming.

He moved my hair to the side. His breath tickled my neck, heating my skin. "You need to be careful."

"I'm not the naïve sixteen-year-old girl standing in your room begging you to kiss her after you carried her away from a party. I know how the world works. I don't need protection."

"No. You're the twenty-one-year-old woman standing outside her room about to beg me to fuck her." He dug his fingers into my hips and spun me around, crashing me into the wall of muscle that was his chest. "You don't have a fucking clue how the world works, and you *do* need protection."

Visceral need bloomed inside me at the thought of begging him for anything, much less to fuck me.

I looked up into his eyes. "From you, maybe."

He grinned and circled his arms around my waist. "Considering I was five seconds away from fucking you on a public stage before your brother walked in, I would agree."

I loved his smile. It made him appear almost boyish. Human.

"That doesn't change the fact that you're the daughter of a United States senator aiming for presidency, which makes you a target for people far more dangerous than me. Promise me you'll be smarter than this," he added, as if he knew things I didn't.

Add that to the list of questions.

"Speaking of promises..." I let my hand glide down the front of his white T-shirt.

He reached up to grab my wrist. "Promise me."

"Fine. Yes. I promise I'll lock the door from now on," I yanked my arm away from him. "Happy?"

"Very." He took my hand and brought my wrist to his mouth.

"Now, it's your turn. You promised me answers."

Caspian laced our fingers together. "You sure you want them?"

What kind of question was that? Of course, I wanted answers. Questions had been brewing in my mind since the morning he left that tray on the bed right after he took my virginity and ran. If he thought I was letting this go, he had another thing coming.

Apparently, my expression said it all, because he steeled his jaw and his stare grew dark. "Okay, but for every answer I give you, you give me something in return."

"What kind of *something*?"

"That depends on how deep you want to go."

There was a hint of something in his tone. A challenge? A veiled threat? Lust? I wasn't sure. I just knew I wasn't backing down.

"Deal."

How bad could it be?

"You should know the deeper you dig, the darker it gets."

"And? I'm not afraid of the dark." It was only a half-lie. I wasn't afraid of the darkness in general. I wasn't even afraid of the darkness I would find in him. I was only afraid of the darkness I might find in *me*. What if deep down inside he was the monster my brother claimed he was, and I wanted him anyway? What did that say about me?

Caspian lifted a brow.

I gave him a look. "What?"

He smirked. "Nothing. Start digging."

"Why does my brother blame you for his accident?"

He let go of me and took a step back. "Because it wasn't an accident. Your family lied to you."

What? My family didn't lie. We were the epitome of a Norman Rockwell painting. The evidence was in every framed photo that hung on the wall and every memory of my parents smiling and clapping at my recitals. My father had been in politics my whole life, and people loved him because there wasn't a pile of skeletons following him wherever he went. The only time anything had ever felt "off" was after Lyric's death. What happened to Lincoln had nothing to do with me, so why would they lie?

But I knew Caspian was telling the truth, and the fact that I didn't even question it spoke volumes about where I'd placed my loyalty.

Caspian cut off my train of thought, answering a question I didn't even ask. "Probably to protect you, which I agree with, even though I hate it."

"What really happened?" *Why would they need to protect me?* I was so tired of people "protecting" me.

"That's number two, and you haven't paid up for the first one yet."

"Fair enough. Your turn."

"How many times have you fucked yourself with the dick I sent you? With *my* dick?"

With his dick. Hot flames licked at my core, lapping and twisting, until I was wrapped in a web of lust. I was certain my body language gave me away before I ever answered. Heat traveled from the back of my neck to my cheeks. My walls clenched from the mere memory of it, and my whole body vibrated with need. This time I wanted the real thing, not a rubber imitation.

He didn't show it, but the low tone in his voice told me he was just as affected by his question as I was.

"What kind of question is that?" My voice was hoarse with need.

The kind a man who sends you a mold of his cock asks.

He repeated his question slowly. "How many times?"

Lying to him was futile. Besides, I didn't care if he knew. I *wanted* him to know. "Almost every day."

His expression changed in an instant. His features sharpened, and his eyes darkened. Pride. Possession. Lust. It was all there in deep seas of whiskey gold. The more he looked at me, the sharper my breaths became, the hotter the fire burned within me. That look alone nearly sent me over the edge.

Then he reached down to palm his cock—his unmistakably hard cock.

A tremor racked my body, and I swallowed hard.

"What happened to my brother?" If I didn't ask now, I'd never get the chance again. This thing, this current, would still be here once all the asking was done.

"I put that scar on his face."

"What? Why? How?" And why would my family cover that up? Lincoln seemed ready to jump at the chance to throw Caspian to the wolves. Why lie to protect him?

"That's three more questions."

"You aren't playing fair. You aren't even answering me."

"Yes, I am."

I threw my head back and groaned. This was like talking to someone who spoke a different language. I needed a decoder ring to figure his cryptic answers out.

"Fine. I'll give you this one. Lincoln showed up at my house the morning after I brought you there. He fucked up my car and started talking shit, so I fucked up his face and shut him up." He moved closer to the door, as if he was worried his truth would be the end of it—the end of *us*. "I gave him that scar with a piece of glass and my bare hands."

"Oh."

"I never said I was a nice guy, Tatum."

You don't know what he's capable of.

I did now.

I knew.

And I didn't care.

Because even though Caspian hurt my brother—and God only knew who else—I knew he would never hurt me. I'd dug deep enough to find the darkness, and I wanted to lay in it with him. Whatever that made me, I would accept it.

"I know." I took a step toward him. "I know what you are."

"Do you?"

Another step. "I do. I also know who I saw on that stage earlier today, and it wasn't the monster you pretend to be."

He narrowed his gaze. "You think I'm pretending? You think a few rare touches and a love song are going to change me? I'm not some broken hero who needs to be redeemed. This is who I am. This is who I was born to be." He was close enough now that the breath of his heated words danced across my face. "The monster will *always* win, because the thirst for power runs through my veins. It's time you accepted it, sweetheart. You didn't choose the prince. Hell, you didn't even choose the villain. You picked the motherfucking dragon none of them can slay." His chest heaved, and there was fire in his eyes.

"That's not true."

"No?"

I shook my head.

"Then maybe Lincoln was right. Maybe I need to show you." He reached up and casually twirled a strand of my hair around his finger. My eyelids fluttered shut, then opened again. I let out a shaky breath. He let go of my hair. "Here's what's about to happen. I'm going to count back from three—no—I'll start at five to give you more time. Do you know what happens when I get to one?"

I said nothing.

I did nothing.

I was frozen. Something akin to panic welled up inside me like wildfire, pulling my lungs tight. I believed he would never hurt me, but I'd also believed my family would never lie to me. *What if I was wrong?*

Caspian leaned in and whispered against my ear. "Do you want to know what happens when I get to *one*?"

I shook my head.

He leaned back and stood up straight. His lips curved into a satisfied grin. "Then I suggest you start running. Five…"

My heart hammered. My brain screamed at me to run, but my feet were nailed to the ground.

He ran his tongue across his bottom lip, the way a predator would after spotting his prey. "Four…"

A shiver razored up my spine.

Caspian tipped his head and studied me. His lips parted to say *three*, and I finally flew past him.

I tore through my room, flying around my bed and down the hallway. I swung around the corner, darting past a whitewood console table and toward the wooden stairs. One hand slid along the shiplap wall while the other gripped the rail as I bounded down the steps.

Footsteps sounded above me, heavy and determined, and I realized that it wasn't panic that had welled up inside me.

It was anticipation.

Even though every step I ran took me farther away from him, I knew I'd only made it this far because he'd allowed me to.

He was going to catch me.

I wanted him to catch me.

I glanced to my right, past the living room to the stark white kitchen cabinets and grey speckled granite. Then back across the foyer to the front door.

The footsteps grew louder. He was on the stairs. His footfalls mirrored my heartbeat.

Thud.

Thud.

Thud.

My adrenaline kicked into high gear. I sprinted to the door and threw it open. My bare feet slapped against the wide, wooden planks on the front porch. I flew down the steps and into the plush grass of the front lawn. The crisp night air burned my lungs when I stopped to breathe. The Hampton house sat on a six-acre lot surrounded by trees. No one would hear me if I screamed. They probably wouldn't care if they did.

Caspian's silhouette appeared in the doorway. The darkness of the night casted shadows across his face. He paused, only a moment, for just a beat, long enough for our eyes to meet. Like he was waiting to see if I'd given up.

I pushed off the balls of my feet and ran as hard as I could around the corner to the side of the house.

His arms wrapped around me, stealing all the air from my lungs and sending us both crashing to the ground. My senses were immediately assaulted with the bitter scent of dirt and grass. I was lying on my stomach, and Caspian was on top of me, his body rock solid against my back.

My fingers clawed the earth as I tried to crawl away, but he leaned further down, pinning me in place.

He growled against my ear. "Would a good guy chase a princess out of her tower and tackle her to the ground?"

I tried getting up on my knees, but he straddled me, locking my legs between his.

"Would a good guy be thinking of all the ways he wants to fuck you right now? Of all the ways he wants to ruin you?" He brought his mouth to my bared shoulder and bit down so hard I was surprised he didn't draw blood. His words were unapologetic and full of promise.

I needed to be fucked.

I wanted to be ruined.

But only by him. Always him.

My body went limp beneath him. My bones turned to liquid and my blood to lava, burning with the awareness of what was to come. We were hidden by the shadow of the house. Out here, in the darkness, everything was heightened—his touch, his scent, the sound of my pulse thrumming in my ears.

Caspian took the opportunity to ease his thigh between my legs. He trailed the tip of his tongue over the spot he'd just bitten, all the way to the back of my neck. I felt the relief of his weight on top of me, followed by the tug of fabric as my shorts and panties were yanked down in one fluid motion. I gasped at the sudden feel of cool air against my bare skin.

He palmed one side of my ass, kneading his fingers in my flesh. I was beginning to think he was obsessed with doing that.

"Is it sinking in yet?" he asked.

I moved to scramble away from him, not because I wanted to, but because I wanted to feed the monster. I wanted him primal and raw. I wanted to see his worst. I needed to know I could survive Caspian Donahue. More than that, I needed *him* to know I could survive him.

"Is that the best you can do?" I gritted through clenched teeth.

He grabbed my hair and jerked my head back, forcing a shriek from my lungs. "I'm just getting started." He leaned forward and brushed his lips against my cheek. "Don't fucking move." His voice was calm, dark.

The fabric of his jeans rustled followed by the sound of a zipper being pulled down.

Oh, God.

I swallowed hard. This was it.

He held his palm in front of my face. "Lick it."

He loosened his grip in my hair, allowing me to move my head forward and do as I was told. I flattened my tongue and lapped his skin from wrist to fingertip.

"Fuck," he rasped. His hand disappeared for a moment, then reappeared in front of my face. "Again."

I licked his palm, and his fingertips began massaging my scalp. I leaned my head back, giving into this rare act of tenderness.

He pulled his other hand away from my mouth, then brought it back a few seconds later. "Spit in it."

What the hell?

His grip tightened in my hair, and on instinct I hurried and spat in his palm.

His hand disappeared, followed quickly by a low growl echoing in the air. He let go of my hair, and I started to turn my head to see what he was doing, but his hands on my ass, spreading my cheeks apart held me in place.

No.

"Caspian…"

The hard length of his cock was heavy between my cheeks, slick with what was no doubt my saliva, gliding back and forth, rocking slowly along the crack. It felt so dirty, but Jesus did it feel good. Everything inside me tightened with need.

He placed his hand at the small of my back. "You're mine, Little Troublemaker. All of you. Even this." In one small movement, the thick crown of his cock was at my pleated hole.

I vehemently shook my head.

I was wrong. I wouldn't survive this. He was too big, and I'd never done anything… *there.*

He would tear me apart.

I braced my hands on the ground and scrambled away from him.

He grabbed my ankles and dragged me back. The earth and grass burned my skin as my shirt pulled up over my breasts.

"No," I cried. "Please." My breath was ragged, and my heart lunged to my throat. "I'm not ready."

He flipped me over and plunged his middle finger inside my pussy. His mouth curled in a grin. "No?" He added a second finger, sinking in all the way to his knuckle. "You feel ready to me."

I arched my back and pushed against his hand as he worked his fingers in and out. The sounds my body was making. God. *The sounds.* I was so wet, and the sound of it only seemed to urge him on. His thumb pressed against my clit, and I began to unravel. My body felt like the ocean waves behind us, building and surging, ready to crash.

"Oh, you mean *here*." He slid his fingers out and trailed them over my hole, over *that* hole, the forbidden one, circling and circling until I was soaked, then finally easing a fingertip inside.

My body quivered as my walls clenched around him. The pressure was so foreign and at the same time so welcome.

He smiled again. "You like that." He wasn't asking.

Did I like it?

The way that tightness in my belly exploded into fiery sparks told me I did, even though my mind was in denial.

He pressed in all the way to the next knuckle.

Oh, God. This was wrong, indecent, animalistic.

But so good, so *very* good.

My skin felt like it was being pricked by a thousand electrifying needles then licked by flames. I tightened and clenched around him, both terrified and exhilarated. *"Stop,"* I wanted to scream, but the words got caught in my throat. I wanted to push him back out yet push against his hand and draw him in.

"I'm going to fill all your holes. Every single one," he said with a drawn-out growl, seeming drunk off the power he exuded over me. He moved his finger deep inside that forbidden place, and the familiar twinge of pleasure began building in my stomach. Tight. Hot. Fierce.

I was right there, right on the edge. Just a little more…

He eased his finger out of me and wiped it on his pants. "Soon."

I stared up at him, unable to speak.

Or think.

All I wanted to do was *feel*.

There was a feral, untamed wildness in his eyes as he yanked my shorts and panties the rest of the way off then positioned himself between my legs. He held his dick in his hand, rubbing the tip over my clit, pressing hard enough to steal a moan from my lips. This need, my need for him, was like nothing I'd ever felt. It bubbled and burned inside me until I was sure I wouldn't survive another second without him fucking me.

He rubbed his crown over my sweet spot again, then along my slit, over and over, tying me in knots. He stopped teasing to slide inside me just enough to send a shudder across my skin before slipping back out.

I pushed against his chest and tried scooting away from him. "Wait. Stop. You don't have a condom," I said, holding onto the last thread of my sanity before it completely snapped and sent me over the edge. I wasn't worried about pregnancy. I was on birth control, but I had no idea where he'd been or what he'd been doing the past four years.

He gripped my hip with his free hand and held me in place. "No stopping. No more waiting. I craved this sweet little pussy —*my* pussy—for four fucking years. I'm here now, and I'm taking what's mine." Then he thrust himself inside me.

Raw.

Primitive.

Violent.

I gave up the fight and offered him everything.

My body.

My soul.

The ground was hard and unforgiving as Caspian slammed into me. I tried to push myself up, and his hand was immediately at my throat, shoving me back down. His fingers gripped my neck, stealing my breath, but I'd never felt so alive. I welcomed it—all of it.

He leaned in and nipped his teeth on the shell of my ear. "I'm going to come in you, on you, all over you." He scraped his teeth along the column of my throat. "And you're not going to stop me. You know why?"

My entire body quivered with a pleasure more intense than anything I'd ever felt. I could live forever off this high. I never wanted to come down.

I closed my eyes and shook my head, then felt his lips on my skin, soft and tender.

"Because I own you, Little Troublemaker."

He did.

He owned every piece of me.

Caspian reached down and hooked his arms under my thighs, lifting my ass off the ground and spreading me open even wider. His pelvic bone ground against my clit with every thrust, sending tiny little shockwaves from my core to my toes. His groans turned into grunts as his thrusts turned more violent each time he reared back and slammed into me again. Like he couldn't go deep enough, couldn't fuck me hard enough. The waves inside me grew higher and higher until they roared and crashed. My body trembled as the orgasm tore through me, but he didn't stop. He didn't let up.

He drove into me, over and over, until he finally came with a loud "Fuck" and a slow hiss.

We both stilled, and he stayed inside me for what seemed like hours while we caught our breath. His heartbeat pounded against my chest, as wild as my own. He leaned up on his elbows and swiped my hair from my forehead then pressed his lips there. My eyes flitted closed.

"You're fucking perfect," he whispered against my forehead. He brought his mouth to my neck. "So fucking perfect."

Then he slid out of me, making my body mourn the loss of his fullness. He pulled his pants up to fasten them, then lifted me up and carried me back inside the house—all the way up the stairs. And then he placed me on my bed while he ran a bath.

I watched him check the water temperature and pour bubbles into the tub, and my heart swelled as I realized that, whether he admitted it or not, underneath the monster was a man, tender and kind.

And I craved them both.

EIGHTEEN

Tatum

My entire body throbbed from head to toe. I wanted to stay here, sunken into the plush softness forever, but the dirt on my chest and in my hair didn't pair well with my white and gray comforter.

I groaned when I stood up and lifted my top over my head, then dropped it on the floor next to my shorts and panties.

Caspian hitched in a breath as he watched me walk from my room into the bathroom.

His gaze heated every inch of my skin as his eyes raked over my body. "Jesus, Tatum." He ran his hand over the back of my hair, a mess no doubt.

My stomach flipped at his scrutiny. *Did I really look that bad?*

He grabbed the hem of his shirt and pulled it off with ease. Bold, black lines swooped and swirled across his chest in a breathtaking tribal tattoo. I had seen it once before but didn't remember it being so bold, so intimidating and virile—so *him*. It continued across his shoulder, stopping at his bicep. There was a phrase in Latin script, *Post Tenebras Lux*. After darkness, comes light. I'd seen it on a coin once in my father's office and asked what it meant.

I wanted to trail my tongue across every one of those words, over every single line. I wanted to mark him the way the ink had marked him. I wanted to mark him the way he'd marked me.

I moved to look at myself in the mirror, but Caspian scooped me up and carried me into the Roman shower, stopping me before I could. I hadn't even realized he'd turned the showerhead on. He stepped inside, still wearing his jeans, and set me down under the warm spray.

"I'm not fragile," I said. With a man like Caspian I couldn't afford to be.

He grabbed a bottle of shampoo from the niche in the wall behind me. "Neither are diamonds, but people still treat them with care."

Touché.

He squirted two shots of coconut-scented keratin onto his palm, then massaged it into my scalp.

I closed my eyes and let myself get lost in the way his fingers rubbed my scalp and the hot water rained over my skin. I'd come down from my high, and now I just wanted to stay here, right here, under the warmth of the water and tenderness of his touch.

He detached the sprayer and rinsed the shampoo out of my hair. Trails of foamy bubbles carved a path over my breasts and down my stomach, taking the remnants of dirt with them.

Caspian reached around and shut off the water. The cool air on my naked skin made me shiver. He lifted me again and carried me to the bathtub. The minute my body sank into the water, I was warm again. Water droplets drew wavy paths over his chest and down his stomach. Goosebumps covered his flesh, but he didn't move, not even a shiver.

He sat on the edge of the tub. "All clean. Now, you can relax without soaking in a pile of dirt."

How thoughtful.

"Get in with me." I waved my hands under the bubbles. "The water's warm." I knew he had to be freezing.

"I'd rather spectate."

"Have it your way." I sank deeper into the water, letting it surround me in its warmth and draw the tension from my aching body. "There's only been Brady."

He visibly tensed.

"Other than you, I mean." I lifted my hand, watching the bubbles drip from my fingertips back into the water while I waited for him to give me something, anything.

He leaned in and lifted my chin, holding it between his fingertips. "There will only *ever* be me." He brushed his thumb over my lips, then dropped his hand and sat back up.

If he only knew.

"What about you? Did you…" I shrugged one shoulder. "…you know, date, while you were away?"

He smirked. "You mean did I fuck anyone?"

I answered with a hopeful stare. *Please, say no.* Not that I had any claim on him or any right to hope he'd spent four years alone. I didn't. That didn't mean it wouldn't crush me if he had.

"There was this one pussy I couldn't get enough of."

I squeezed my eyes shut, thinking if I didn't look at him I wouldn't be able to hear his words. *Nevermind. Don't tell me. I don't want to know.* I shouldn't have asked.

He let out a low groan. Like he was remembering something carnal. "Fuck."

Stop. Please. I don't want to know anymore.

I squeezed my eyes tighter. I wanted to sink into the water and drown in my humiliation.

"Look at me," he said, his voice gruff, demanding.

I opened my eyes.

"Every time I came, it was because I was thinking of you. Every time I wrapped my fist around my dick or slid my cock inside the opening of some bullshit rubber toy, I imagined it was you. I pictured your tight little cunt or that perfect, hot mouth sucking me, swallowing me, squeezing around me."

"So, there was no pussy?"

"Oh, there was pussy."

My heart dropped.

"But it was about as real as that dildo I sent you, just a weak substitute for the real thing. It was always you, Little Troublemaker. Only you."

Holy. Shit.

I let out a slow, thankful breath.

What was I supposed to say to that?

If he'd spent the last four years thinking of me and only me, then why did he leave without as much as a goodbye? Unless…

"I know you made a deal with my father." I glanced up at him, and his jaw flexed. "I'm right, aren't I?"

He didn't answer.

I kept going with my theory. "That's why you left. Because of what happened with Lincoln. Because of what you did to him. It didn't make sense to me that my dad wouldn't go after you with guns blazing, considering…" I winced. "…You know." *He hates you.* "So, you must have made a deal. You agree to leave, and he makes up some story about an accident. No harm, no foul."

He shifted, still silent, but there was a glint of torment in his eyes.

"It's okay." I grabbed another handful of bubbles. "You don't have to admit it. I know I'm right." I had to be. Nothing else made sense.

But it was over now. He was back, and I knew the truth. No need for regret.

Caspian stood up and began unfastening his jeans. Something dark flickered in his eyes, and once again, I found myself wanting to break free from the carefully crafted upbringing of obedience and sophistication.

My body tensed and tingled, but I kept talking. I was so close to getting my answer, so close to hearing it from his lips. "And you didn't want to tell me because Lincoln is my brother."

He pulled his jeans over his hips. His movements were graceful, though I knew the denim was heavy and soaked with water. He slid them down around his ankles, then kicked them off. "No more talking."

I shamelessly stared at his body, at his thick thighs and heavy cock, at the V that looked like it had been chiseled from stone. "Because I'm right?"

He grinned—at my blatant appreciation of him or at my statement, I wasn't sure. Didn't care. I wanted his smile any way I could get it. "You know more than you should."

"I knew it!" I lurched up quickly, sending a surge of water splashing over the edge of the tub and onto the floor.

Caspian swallowed hard as his gaze dropped to my now exposed breasts, covered in a few wayward suds. He licked his lips, and a shudder bolted through me as I imagined him licking my nipple. I sat up straighter, resting my back against the tub and giving him a better view.

He held out a hand. "I think bath time is over."

My eyes stayed trained on his cock as he helped me step out of the tub onto the plush bathmat. The thick head and veins that were just begging to be licked. His thighs were powerful and strong, and I remembered the way they kept me pinned to the ground outside.

I caught a glimpse of myself in the mirror when he turned to the linen cabinet to grab a towel. There were teeth marks on my shoulder, right by my collarbone, and bruises the size of handprints on my thighs. There were scratches on my chest and stomach, small, but enough to leave a mark. I couldn't see my back. I wasn't sure I wanted to.

Caspian squeezed his eyes shut.

I brought a hand to his face. "This doesn't scare me. *You* don't scare me."

"I should." He wrapped the towel around my body.

"Have you seen my feet?" I chuckled and glanced at my battered toes. "Apparently, ballerinas are masochists."

After I'd dried my skin and patted the towel over my damp hair, I climbed in bed next to Caspian, who had been lying with one hand behind his head and the covers pulled up to his waist like he belonged there.

This was my haven—this house, this room. Aside from dancing, this was my escape. Sometimes I opened the balcony doors and let the sound of the night air and the ocean drift into my room and lull me to sleep.

This was the only room in the house without agreeable gray painted on the walls—the ones that weren't covered in white shiplap, anyway. As soon as I'd moved in, I chose a soft blue-green to offset the white furniture in the room. Sheer, white curtains billowed in the breeze while my gray and white pin-tucked comforter kept me warm.

This was my sanctuary.

And I was sharing it with Caspian.

He stretched out his other arm, offering me a place to rest my head.

I laid on his shoulder. "You mean you're actually staying this time?" His body tensed at my words, so I wrapped my arm around his waist and looked over at him with a smile. "Relax. I'm kidding."

I'd long since gotten over the fact that he'd left me to sleep alone that night.

The tension left his body as he pulled me closer. "I told you everything I did, I did for you, and I meant it. You weren't ready for me." He moved his hand and trailed a finger over the bite mark and scratches that tainted my skin. "For *this*." He shook his head. "Not then, at least."

Could I have handled him at sixteen?

Part of me felt like I was made for this, made for him, and that I could have handled him at any age. Another part wondered if he might have been right.

"As long as I don't wake up to a tray of fruit and a morning after pill, we're good."

His eyebrows shot up.

I smiled. "Yeah. I figured that out too." It took me a while. Over two years, to be exact. When I'd first gotten on the pill, my doctor explained all the different courses of action to me, and I knew then what Caspian had done to prevent me from getting pregnant at sixteen.

When I'd first learned what he'd done, anger pulled at every part of me. I hated him for taking away my right to choose. I grieved the possibility of a new life being ripped from my grasp without me ever knowing. If I had gotten pregnant, would I have kept it? The thought weighed on my mind for months until reality sank in, and I knew the answer.

No.

My father would never have allowed it.

A pregnant teenage daughter would have been a disgrace to our family. Having his daughter carry the child of his enemy's son would have been even worse.

Caspian did me a courtesy. He knew it then. I knew it now.

"You're on birth control now," he said.

"How did you—" Of course, he knew. Somehow, he knew everything.

He smirked. "I saw it on your bathroom counter when I was running your bath."

Oh.

It felt as if the weight of the world had been lifted from my chest, and I could finally breathe. Peace settled within me. We'd made so much progress. So many of my questions had been answered. Now we could finally walk away from the past and toward our future.

His fingertip brushed over my nipple. "If you're finished with your trip down memory lane..." He ran his hand down my side, over my stomach, finally placing it over my pussy. "...I'd love it if this hot little cunt would come over here and keep my dick warm."

The morning sun flooded the room with light, and the warmth of a naked body pressed against mine from behind. I eased from under his arm draped over my waist and rolled out of bed. If I thought my body was sore before last night, it was nothing compared to how it felt now.

I watched Caspian sleep. Peaceful features smoothed his usual guarded expression, and his chest rose and fell with a calming ease. I grabbed my phone from the nightstand and captured the moment with my camera, then slipped on a T-shirt—no panties—and headed downstairs to make us breakfast.

NINETEEN

CASPIAN

One of the benefits of being subjected to the world of the Obsidian Brotherhood at such a young age was that I'd spent the last twelve years of my life watching, learning, and storing away every tidbit of information in the darkest parts of my mind.

Work in silence. Let your success speak for itself.

I'd also learned to keep a secret.

Dad had maintained the empire given to him through blood, sweat, and sacrificing a piece of his soul—or maybe the whole damn thing. I was building mine on secrets.

I looked out the floor-to-ceiling windows of the penthouse loft at the Manhattan skyline. The space was vast and open now, but I pictured it the way I wanted it. A white grand piano there, in the corner where the windows met the wall. There, on the other side of the room, a sectional big enough for both fucking and sleeping when we're too spent to walk up the stairs. And a twelve-seat table over there, right under the chandelier, where I would pull Tatum to the end and let her legs hang off the edge while I sat in my chair and feasted on her pussy like it was the Last Supper.

It had been three weeks since the first night I'd stayed at Tatum's Hampton house. I stayed there as often as I could, but I kept waiting for her father or Lincoln to show up and catch me chasing her naked ass down the beach. The shit would surely hit the fan at that point, and Chandler and I still had some things to work out before I could let that happen. I also couldn't risk bringing her to my father's house again, not right now, not while I was busting my ass making him believe I'd fallen for his lies.

I needed a place of my own.

We needed a place of our own.

I stuffed my hands into the pockets of my dark blue suit pants and turned to face the realtor. "I'll take it."

The tall, thin blonde flashed her perfectly practiced smile. "I knew you wouldn't be able to resist." She walked over and stood beside me, looking out the windows at the city. "Exceptional men have exceptional taste." She turned her head to face me and licked her lips.

Nice try, but my dick is spoken for.

I pulled my phone from my pocket and Facetimed Tatum, taking in her surroundings when she finally answered. She was at the theater, where she'd been every day for the past three weeks working with artists and lighting consultants to make sure the upcoming ballet would be perfect.

"I want to show you something," I said, then flipped the camera to show her the view of the city.

"Wow, Caspian, that's gorgeous."

The realtor watched as I zoomed in on one particular section of window.

"See this?" I tapped a finger on the glass, then ran my palm over it as if I were caressing her body. "I'm going to shove your naked body against that spot and fuck you in front of the whole city, so that everyone knows you're mine." I flipped the camera back to show my face.

Tatum hitched a breath, and the pink heat I loved so much flushed her cheeks. She licked her lips. "And if I say no?"

My little troublemaker.

I smirked. "Then I'll take it." My cock swelled at the simple thought of it. "Try to run from me. I dare you. We both know what happens when you do." I watched the pulse in her throat quicken. "See you soon, sweetheart," I said as I ended the call.

The realtor stood staring at me, her eyes wide and mouth open.

"You're right." I shoved my phone back in my pocket. "I do have exceptional taste." I showed myself to the front door. "Tell your boss my attorney will be in touch to handle the paperwork," I said as I walked out.

The house was quiet when I walked in. No surprise.

I made my way across the foyer, down the hall, and toward Dad's study. The door was open, so I took a deep breath and steeled myself for what needed to be done.

He was standing in front of his bar cabinet, pouring a glass of scotch from a crystal decanter. I caught his side profile. His light gray tie rested perfectly straight against his white button-up shirt. Every hair was in place, and his jaw was smoothly shaved. He looked every bit the part of the powerful presence he emanated—on the outside.

"Should I pour you one too? Are we celebrating?" It was almost as if he'd been expecting me.

I walked into the room. "I'm twenty-five years old. I can't live with my parents forever." I didn't even ask if or how he knew about the penthouse. It didn't matter.

"Twenty-five," he repeated. The words sounded like a curse spewing from his lips. "Twenty-five." He accentuated each syllable. "That's the magic number, isn't it?" He was baiting me. He wanted me to show my hand.

Fuck him.

"I thought the magic number was three, but what do I know?"

Three. The number of completion. Past, present, future. Beginning, middle, end. Birth, life, death. It all came in threes.

Dad turned to face me. The smooth lines of his face grew hard, and his eyes darkened to soulless orbs. He lifted his glass as if to agree, then drained the contents in one drink. "He's going to take her from you, you know."

Okay, Dad. I'll bite.

I crossed the room and rested one hip against his desk. "Who?"

His lips curved into a malevolent grin. "Huntington." He angled his body to pour himself another drink. "He's running for president."

I remembered the hunt and Malcolm's promise that when Jacob's term was up, he was taking the reins. I guess I hadn't realized so much time had passed already.

I squared my shoulders, now curious where the rest of the conversation was going.

"Your great-grandfather started all this." He held his hand up in a swirling motion, indicating our surroundings. "He was a self-made billionaire." Dad took a sip, hissing when the liquid coated his throat. "Until the government—one of Huntington's ancestors—decided it wasn't fair for one man to have it all. One man shouldn't be so powerful." Another drink. "So, they made him split it up, sell it off piece by piece." He chuckled. "They made him share." He spoke the last word as if it poisoned his tongue.

I knew this already. Grandpa Donahue started Donahue Oil, which was later split into other companies like Chevron and Exxon. What any of this had to do with Tatum or me, I wasn't sure, but I had a pretty good idea where he was going with it. If I was right, I was going to march right out of here and snatch the life out of Malcolm Huntington's body.

"Always fucking with us, those Huntingtons. Always taking what's rightfully ours. Since the very beginning." Dad gulped down the rest of his drink, then set the glass on the cabinet top with a heavy thud. "He's going to give his daughter to Khalid.

Then he's going to shut down our pipelines and shove import/export regulations down our throats again."

I didn't give two shits about the pipelines. All I heard was *he's going to give his daughter to Khalid*. Fury bubbled within me. Rage roiled in my chest, and hatred coiled around my heart like barbed wire.

"He's going to cut us off, give the industry to Khalid, along with a nice little care package to make sure he still gets his piece of the pie."

That motherfucker.

Shut us down. Force the U.S. to get our oil from Khalid, fattening his pockets. Hand Tatum over as a consolation prize to make sure Huntington gets his share of the profits without breaking any rules. They would technically be Tatum's shares, but at that point, no one would give a shit. No one would care that she'd be degraded and cheated on by a man who murdered anyone who dared to fight for women's rights. No one cared that the fire in her eyes would be stripped away with every set of rules he gave her or if he sliced off her clit to keep her from pleasuring herself.

Whoever decided money should have been green was wrong. It should have been black because that was exactly what it did to people's souls. It sent them into the darkest pits of hell until they came out as nothing more than a pile of ash.

I was going to kill Huntington. Slice his throat, then piss on his corpse before I carved him into pieces and fed him to the family dog.

I would have said my father was bluffing if it weren't for his unsettling demeanor and the drinking… and the fact that he rarely ever bluffed. If Kipton Donahue told you something, you could believe it as truth. He had no use for gossip.

Dad laughed, the sound maniacal in contrast to his distinguished appearance. "Well, I guess it's Khalid who will be getting a piece of the pie, isn't it?"

I clenched my teeth. "Shut up."

He took a step toward me and smiled, like he was proud of his next words. "How does it feel to know that pussy you're willing to give up everything for is going to be riding the cock of the man trying to steal our empire?"

I fisted his shirt in my hands and slammed him on the ground. "I said shut the fuck up!" I knelt over him and grabbed his tie, then wrapped it around his neck, ready to choke the fucking life out of him.

Someone cleared their throat in the doorway.

I glanced up, temporarily distracted by the sound. Dad took the opportunity to shove me off of him. I laid flat on my back and stared at the ceiling, forcing my demons back into their cage. I tried to remember a recent time when my father had been warm, when he'd seen me as a son rather than an enemy. All I came up with were memories of seething anger and resentment.

"Good afternoon, Judge Flannery," Dad said as he stood and straightened his tie.

I followed his gaze as he grinned at the heavyset man with gray hair and glasses.

"Just the man I wanted to see." He stood over me, peering down. "You see, son, Huntington is wrong. It *is* possible for one man to have all the power, and Judge Flannery is here to make sure that man is me. We just need to sort through some pesky paperwork first." Dad carefully placed his Italian leather shoe on my throat, pressing down hard enough to make it uncomfortable to breathe. "If you even think about touching me again, I will kill you and not even flinch. Understood?"

I narrowed my eyes and did my best to spit on his shoe. The trail of saliva just ended up falling on my chin.

Dad laughed, then removed his foot and held out his hand.

I slapped it away and stood up on my own.

The judge stood in the doorway, watching the whole thing transpire in silence.

Dad cleared his throat, then walked over to his desk. "Please, have a seat." He motioned to the chair on the opposite side. "Damn shame about Bradshaw." He shook his head as if he cared about our dead attorney. I knew better. "But hopefully you can clear a few things up for me. Some technicalities."

Like my three-billion-dollar trust.

He looked over at me. "That's all, son. Close the door on your way out, would you?"

Gladly.

I shut the door behind me, then pulled out my phone and found Chandler's name.

"It's me," I said when he answered. "He's coming unhinged. We're going to need to speed this shit up a bit. Meet me at the club. You know the one."

TWENTY

Tatum

Twenty-one days.

It seemed like a blink and a lifetime all at once.

It had been nearly twenty-one days since the first night Caspian spent the night in my bed. Twenty-one days since I'd started preparing for the ballet at the theater. It wasn't a professional production, not like the New York Ballet, but I took pride in making it unforgettable. The costumes, the set, the choreography, and the music all had to be the best they could. The weeks leading up to a performance were always my favorite. Instead of only spending three days a week at my studio, I was there every day.

During the last twenty-one days, I'd grown to look forward to the rehearsals. I lived for the moments when everything started falling into place. I waited for the nights when Caspian would show up and take whatever he wanted, then put the monster to bed as he slept next to me.

The last three weeks had blown by in a flash.

The end of the next three weeks seemed forever away.

Twenty-one days from now, Caspian would sign the paperwork on his penthouse. From what he'd shown me, it was perfect for him, all hard lines and fierce masculinity. I was excited for him. I knew he didn't mind staying with me, but I could tell he wasn't entirely comfortable with the knowledge it was still my parents' house. I also knew he was growing restless underneath his father's thumb.

It was also twenty-one days until my oldest class would perform the ballet, *Romeo and Juliet*.

Twenty-one days felt like an eternity, but I was already coming up with all kinds of ways for Caspian and me to celebrate, not including his comment about fucking me against the window.

I stood on the stage in the theater now, listening to the score for the balcony pas de deux. Every year, I was more amazed than the last. Nicholai Volkov, the set designer my father hired, had done a phenomenal job recreating sixteenth-century Verona, and Sergio's music gave me chills.

Lincoln walked in and placed a bouquet of red roses on the apron of the stage. He had transformed the floor above the theater into an apartment, so it didn't surprise me that he was always here.

I glanced at the flowers. "You're supposed to save those for the end of the performance."

"They aren't for you."

"Oh? Who's the lucky girl?"

He shrugged. "If my math is correct…" he mentally counted the flowers, "…there will be twelve lucky girls."

"You're disgusting." I walked over and pressed *Stop* on the playlist.

"If being a gentleman is disgusting, then okay." If Lincoln was a gentleman, I was the queen. "I give one to a random chick after every fight I win."

"And that gets you laid?"

"I don't need flowers to get laid, but yeah. They sure as fuck don't hurt."

"You need to find someone decent and settle down." I walked along the length of the stage, mentally mapping out where to put the landing lights.

He snorted. "You mean like you did? Did *Mr. Decent* ever get his panties out of a bunch?"

I cut him a glare. "Stop talking about him that way. He's not what you think."

"No, Tatum. He's not what *you* think."

"Why? Because he fucked up your face?"

He hopped up on the stage and stood in front of me. His stare was harsh and his jaw tight.

I tilted my chin up and met his glare. "Yeah. He told me what happened. And I also know that's why he left."

He stared at me for a moment. "He told you that's why he left?"

"No. But he might as well have."

Something flickered in his eyes. "During your little confession session, did he also tell you Lyric was at his house the night before she died?"

The breath left my lungs in a whoosh, and a sharp pain fisted my chest. His words were a punch to the gut. Why would Lincoln say that?

He canted his head to one side. "Didn't think so."

No.

It wasn't true.

My brother was lying.

He was lying the same way he'd lied about the scar on his face.

Caspian wouldn't have kept something like that from me. *Lyric* wouldn't have kept something like that from me.

Right?

The rush of memories of Lyric's death and the sting of betrayal—of constantly being trapped in a web of lies—were like ice water flowing through my veins, freezing me in place.

The deeper you dig, the darker it gets.

Had I not dug deep enough?

I looked at Lincoln as he studied my reaction. I wanted to hit him, to hit *something*. I wanted to claw my way out of the suffocating wall of anger and hurt that was closing in on me. I wanted to scream so loudly it blocked out all the thoughts that swarmed in my head. My heart was racing, and I had the urge to run. Like I needed to escape before all the emotions that were bubbling up inside rose to the surface and exploded, destroying me in the process.

Lincoln closed his eyes and inhaled a deep breath. When he let it out and opened his eyes, they were kind. He was the Lincoln I'd built blanket forts with in the living room again, not the tattooed lunatic who fed his dog raw meat and set things on fire for the fun of it. "Look, Tatum. I'm not trying to be a dick. I'm just looking out for you. I know you can handle your own shit. All I'm saying is be careful." He bent down, grabbed the flowers, and walked backstage toward the stairs that led to his apartment.

Anger continued to swirl within me.

Lincoln was looking out for me.

Caspian was protecting me.

My family had lied to me.

Was I that oblivious to the world around me?

You don't have a fucking clue how the world works.

Maybe Caspian was right when he'd said that. Maybe I didn't know how the world worked. But I knew I wasn't weak. I knew someone was lying. Who it was, and how tangled up those lies were, I wasn't sure.

Yet.

But I was quickly learning that the world was full of monsters walking around with beautiful faces.

When I left the theater, the last place I wanted to go was home. I had no doubt Caspian would show up, and I wasn't ready to see him yet.

My car seemed to drive itself down the interstate and into New Jersey. I heard myself singing the words along with the songs on my playlist. I watched the other cars on the highway as I passed them by. I saw the white, painted lines disappear with every mile I drove. But it felt as if someone else were doing all those things, and I was just a bystander.

The gravel crunched beneath the tires as I followed the road from the front gate down to Clearview Lake. Summer had come and gone, and the lake was quiet. There were no families having barbecues or rowers racing across the water. The leaves had just begun to take on their orange and scarlet tone, but most of them were still green. The freshly mowed grass covered the ground like a plush emerald blanket.

I parked my car at the top of the embankment near the boat launch. Down a pathway to my right, there was a row of cabins where we stayed every year—grown-ups on one end and kids on the other. I shared with another girl until Lyric started coming with us, then it was the three of us. Behind the cabins was a grove of trees that always made me uneasy. The trees towered over everything like watchful guards, capturing our secrets while hiding their own beneath a shield of lush branches. Dad told me to stay in the clearing. He'd said there were bears in those woods and other things that would hurt me. It was likely just another ploy to "protect" me because I never saw a bear, but I did see a man there once. He'd looked hungry, so I brought him some food. I remembered the pang of sadness I'd felt for him when Lincoln had told me the man was homeless.

I followed the walkway down to the big square platform where I'd first met Lyric. After the emotions that Lincoln dredged up, I suppose in some way, I wanted to feel close to her again.

I climbed into one of the boats and sat down.

"What happened to you?" I asked for the millionth time since she'd died.

Her warm smile and bright eyes were as fresh in my mind as if I'd seen them yesterday, as if it hadn't been over four years. The memory of her voice floated through the air.

"Don't you ever get tired of rich people stuff?"

I laughed.

She pointed to the white tent lit up by strings of clear lights and the people laughing and drinking expensive alcohol while a band played.

I broke off a piece of chocolate and stacked it on top of a graham cracker. "Your dad just won a Grammy, and he sells out stadiums all over the world. Pretty sure you guys do plenty of rich people stuff."

She pulled a marshmallow from the fire and pointed the poker at me. I slid it off the end and piled it on my cracker. Almost burnt on the outside, nice and gooey on the inside. Just the way I liked them.

She licked her fingers, then stuck another marshmallow on the metal poker. "I mean, don't you ever want to just escape?"

Was that what she'd done?

Was she trying to escape?

Was I as oblivious to her unhappiness as I'd been to the lies that surrounded me?

My vision blurred as tears filled my eyes. I didn't even blink them away. I let them fall.

I missed her.

I missed her so much I felt the ache all the way to my bones.

And I refused to believe she'd lied to me. The lies hurt worse than the grief.

I looked out over the calm, dark water, and a sense of dread circled around me like a vulture. There were secrets in that lake. I knew it. I'd always known it.

There were secrets everywhere.

―――

I managed to avoid Caspian for an entire week, only because I stayed in Lincoln's guest bedroom. I caught him standing at the double doors, watching our rehearsal almost every night, but he never followed me all the way upstairs afterward—not with Lincoln's one-hundred-twenty-pound rottweiler guarding the door. Caspian was a lot of things, but dumb wasn't one of them. That dog had a bloodthirst for anyone who wasn't considered family. Lincoln had made sure of it.

"I hate the guy as much as anyone, but you're gonna have to talk to him sooner or later," Lincoln had said to me one night while we sat on his couch eating Rolos and watching *Lucifer*—after whom he'd aptly named his dog.

He was right. I couldn't hide from reality forever. If Caspian was fucking my best friend before she died, I had a right to know.

At the end of Tuesday night rehearsal, the dancers all walked out, and Lincoln was upstairs, leaving me alone. Caspian leaned one shoulder against the door frame. His hands were tucked neatly into the pockets of his dark blue suit pants. His gray shirt was partially unbuttoned, with his tie unknotted and left hanging. He must have come here straight from work.

I sat on the edge of the stage, letting my legs dangle. The haunting sound of the final score floated through the air. Deep cellos and sensual violins told the end of a tragic story. I hoped it wasn't ours.

Caspian pushed off the frame and started walking down the aisle, stopping a few feet in front of me. God, he was beautiful.

My heart leapt to my throat, and my hands itched to touch him.

"You're not going to run and hide this time?" he asked. There were dark circles under his eyes, evidence he'd been sleeping as horribly as I had.

"I'm surprised you haven't tried forcing me to stay."

He huffed a laugh. "Forcing you is only fun when I know you want it. Otherwise, it's just me being a dick."

Heat bloomed inside of me at the thought of all the things he'd forced me to do.

"Aren't you going to ask me why I've been avoiding you?"

I was ready to get this over with, ready to get back to *us*.

"Sure." He sounded bored. "Why have you been avoiding me?"

"Did you have something to do with what happened to Lyric?" The question tore at my heart as I said it out loud.

His eyes bored into me, and his jaw tightened. "Christ, he's really got you drinking the Kool-Aid."

"Answer the question, Caspian."

"No."

The song hit its crescendo, and my stomach dropped.

"No, you won't answer the question, or no, you had nothing to do with it?" A heady cocktail of panic and fear brewed inside me while I awaited his answer. *Say no.*

"No. I had nothing to do with it. Next." He stepped closer to the stage where I sat.

"Why was she at your house the night before she died? Did you give her drugs?"

He scrubbed a hand over his face. "First, I'm a murderer, now I'm a drug dealer. Jesus, Tatum. Do you even hear yourself right now?"

The music stopped. The sounds that had always been a comfort to me fell silent, leaving nothing but my heartbeat thrumming in my ears.

"Why was she at your house, Caspian?" I hated the way our voices were raised.

"Who told you she was at my house? Lincoln? Because he doesn't know what the fuck he's talking about."

"So, she wasn't at your house that night?"

He ran a hand through his hair. "I'm trying to—"

I hopped off the stage and held a finger up to stop him. "Don't. Don't you dare say you're trying to protect me. I'm sick and tired of people lying to me, then using that bullshit excuse to cover it up. Stop treating me like a child. I'm a grown ass woman, and I can protect myself." I shoved at his chest. "*I* decide what I can handle and what I can't. Not my father. Not Lincoln. And not you." I strengthened my resolve and looked him in the eye. "Was. She. At. Your. House? Yes or no? It's that simple."

"Yes."

No.

No. No. No.

It was just a word. But it might as well have been a meteor crashing down on my world, because it left a gaping hole in my chest and the impact knocked the breath out of me. It felt as though the ground was giving out beneath my feet. My entire body went cold, and I wanted to vomit.

She was there. My best friend was with the man I gave my soul to the night before I let him have it, the night before she died. Now, he was saying he didn't know anything about it.

Well, I called bullshit.

"Why?" My question was barely audible.

"It doesn't matter."

"It doesn't matter?"

"No, Tatum. It doesn't fucking matter. She wasn't there for me. It doesn't concern us. And that's all you need to know."

So, he *did* know why she was there. He just *chose* not to tell me.

I squeezed my eyes shut, hoping when I opened them again, I would wake up in my bed, and this would all be a figment of my imagination, a result of working too hard. I took a deep breath, then opened them again.

It was real. I was in the theater, and Caspian was still here, still refusing to trust me with the truth. I was fed up with the lies.

"You should leave." I didn't know what to think. This was all too much. I wasn't sure how to process any of it.

He shook his head. "I'm not leaving." His eyes were dark but gentle when they met mine. "This isn't our fight. I swear if you'll just trust me, just give me some time, I'll find the answers we're both looking for."

Why would he *need answers?*

Time? He wanted more time? It had been four years, and her death still seemed to haunt us all.

I swallowed the lump in my throat. "How do you find answers when the only one who can give them to you is dead?"

TWENTY-ONE

Tatum

Someone famous once said, "The worst thing about heartache is that it never comes from your enemies."

Well, the worst part about mine was that it could never be mended. There would be no talking it out over ice cream or sending an *I'm sorry* text when one of us couldn't sleep. The ache would always be there. I was going to live the rest of my life with this permanent crack—this scar—because the person who hurt my heart was dead.

Lyric and I shared everything, at least I assumed we had.

What else did she keep from me?

Why would she be at Caspian's house if she wasn't there to see Caspian? And how did Lincoln know about it? What did any of this have to do with him? Is that why he was at Caspian's that morning? Is that why they fought?

I couldn't just stand here and go 'round and 'round with Caspian at the theater. I couldn't pretend everything was okay, either. Everything he said was cryptic at best, and at the end of the day it all boiled down to one thing: more secrets in the name of protection.

I needed room to breathe, and Caspian gave it to me. He promised to give me time to think, saying he had some things of his own to work out. I didn't ask what they were. They didn't matter, not right now, not to me.

I'd given up on the Sherlock Holmes expedition years ago. I'd accepted Lyric's death. I buried my questions next to my grief. I moved on.

Now, here they all were—ghosts swarming around and haunting me all over again.

Thankfully, this week was tech week, and on top of rehearsals, I kept myself busy getting all the last-minute details in order for the ballet. When I was moving, I wasn't thinking, so I made sure to keep moving.

Caspian showed up toward the end of the week. His handsome features were shadowed in something darker, something deeper, as if he were dealing with demons of his own. Our gazes caught, and my entire body thrummed with need. Even though I was upset with him, I missed him. He'd said Lyric's visit had nothing to do with him, and I believed him. I couldn't explain why. I just did. Maybe it was because every other time I'd made him promise me answers, he gave them to me. Why would this time be any different?

He leaned against the door frame, never pushing to come inside. And he was gone before rehearsal ended, leaving me with an empty feeling in the pit of my stomach.

When I wasn't at the theater or my studio, I was at home, walking along the edge of the ocean, begging it to bring me peace. The beach was pristine. The water was clear. The only trees were the ones hiding my house from the one next to it. There was no dark forest or murky water. There were no secrets here.

By the end of the week, after another long day of rehearsals, my body had become a vessel for pain. My limbs were sore, and my bones ached. My mind was exhausted from sleepless nights that flowed into busy days. But my heart—my heart was still beating. That had to count for something, right?

For the first time in a week, I just wanted to be still. I wanted to drown out the static in my head and be one with the heartbeat.

No more questions. No anxiety over the performance. No grief. Just silence.

I went home and sat in the sand, letting the waves roll over my feet. The crests came closer together as the ocean prepared for what was to come. The scent of rain was in the air, a whisper of an oncoming storm.

I grabbed my sandals and headed inside. After a long bath, I climbed into bed and buried myself in the comfort of my pillow and blankets. Then I fell asleep to the tapping of raindrops on my sliding glass doors.

The next week went by in a flash, and tonight was Opening Night. The theater pulsed with energy. The house curtains were closed to conceal the layers of scenery. I turned on a few heaters backstage for the dancers because it surprisingly didn't take much for the cold to settle into your bones. The dancers completed last minute touches on their makeup and costumes.

Even though this wasn't a professional performance, it was largely anticipated and respected among high society because of my family's name. On the other side of the curtain, men in tuxedos escorted women in cocktail dresses to their seats. I was pretty sure I even saw Brady at some point, with a beautiful blonde on his arm and a smile on his face. That made me happy. Servers handed out complimentary champagne in the foyer. Conversation floated through the air along with the low hum of classical music playing over the sound system.

I didn't have to wonder if Caspian was out there. I knew he was. His presence radiated across the distance between us and wrapped around me the way it always had, warming me from the inside out. I didn't see him, but I felt him—all the way to my bones. And on the stage, before the chaos of the evening began, there was a colorful bouquet of bright pink and white plumeria—

the kind you'd find circled around a tourist's neck in Hawaii—along with a note: *Nothing smells as sweet as you, but these are a close second.* I'd plucked one of the flowers and tucked it behind my ear.

I zipped back and forth between wings, ensuring everyone and everything was in place and ready to go. I was on my way to the control box when Lincoln stopped me.

"These are for you," he said as he pulled a bouquet of red roses from behind his back and held them out. He glanced up at my ear and smirked. "I wanted to be first, but it looks like someone beat me to it."

I fought a smile. "Do you not listen to anything I say?"

That was a dumb question. Lincoln never listened to anything anyone said.

"I know. Not until the end of the performance, blah, blah, blah. But with Dad having his party and all the excitement, I didn't want to forget."

Our father thought tonight would be a great night to announce to close friends and family that he'd decided to run for president. We all knew it was coming. He'd been talking about it for years. Tonight was about making it official. Mom had organized a post-ballet party to celebrate Opening Night and give Dad a platform to make his announcement. I didn't mind sharing the spotlight with him. If it was up to me, he could have it all. I liked it right here, in the wings.

I accepted the flowers with a slight bow. "Thank you."

Lincoln had actually dressed up for the occasion. He'd forgone his usual jeans and T-shirt and was wearing black pants with a black button-up. He even tucked it in and wore a belt. His curly hair was fixed, and he looked almost… normal—except for the tattoos snaking out of his collar onto his neck and spilling from his sleeves onto his hands and fingers. But his smile and the twinkle in his eyes softened his edges. A little.

"I overheard what went down between you and Donahue."

"I'd rather not re-live that conversation. Not tonight, anyway." I felt my excitement retreating and my walls going back up. I laid the flowers next to the control box.

His gaze followed my movement, then lifted to meet mine. "I know. And I promise I won't push. I just wanted to let you know —"

I cut him off. "Linc—"

He held up a hand. "Let me finish." He pressed two fingers to the bridge of his nose and closed his eyes for a long blink before he continued. "After hearing what he said and *how* he said it, I started doing a little digging of my own."

I clutched my hands over my racing heart, physically willing it to calm down. "I really don't want to do this right now."

All this time, I'd been running from my ghosts, and here he was, digging up bones. Something churned in my gut. I didn't know why, but I felt like Lincoln needed answers just as much as I did. It was right there in his voice and in his eyes.

"I know." He sighed. "I know." His usually detached voice was full of feeling. "I just thought you should know he's telling you the truth. He didn't know she was there. He wasn't even home that night."

A torrent of emotion rippled through me, equally happy that Lincoln just solidified my trust in Caspian—not that I'd needed him to—and agitated that we may never know the truth.

"Miss Huntington," the guy at the control box interrupted my thoughts. "It's almost time."

Right.

The ballet.

I shook away the secrets of the past and focused on the present. "You should go sit," I said to Lincoln.

He leaned in and kissed my forehead. "Knock 'em dead."

"It's *break a*..." I shook my head. "Nevermind. Go." I waved him off, then turned to the guy at the control box. "Let's do this."

The house lights dimmed, giving way to the spotlights overhead. The music quieted, and the atmosphere changed. The chatter grew silent as the house curtain slowly opened. The delicate piano notes of the first score trickled through the air as the first dancers tip-toed from the wings.

I took a deep breath.

Here we go.

A few hours later, we'd moved from the theater to the ballroom of a hotel across the street. As usual, my mother outdid herself with the party. My cheeks hurt from smiling and thanking all the guests who told me what an amazing performance the ballet had been.

I'd changed into a simple black dress and heels but taken my hair down from the bun to let it fall in dark waves over my shoulders—minus the flower. I didn't expect Caspian to follow us here. Mom sent out the invitations, and the Donahues, although allies in business, weren't exactly what my father would consider *close friends and family*. It didn't keep me from looking around for him, though.

Servers walked around with trays of hors d'oeuvres and champagne while the same band from my graduation party played a new set of modern tunes in classical form. The atmosphere was reminiscent of a wedding reception, with round tables scattered throughout and one rectangular table at the head of the room.

Dad made his way through the crowd and over to me. His face was beaming with pride, and there was a man I'd never seen before at his side. He was young with handsome features. His light eyes were bright against his olive skin, and dark hair smattered his sharp jaw.

"Beautiful performance, as always," Dad said as he kissed my cheek. His grin widened, and his gaze shifted to the other man. "I'd like you to meet Prince Khalid Falih, from Saudi Arabia."

A sense of unease gripped me in a chokehold and made my skin prickle, but I smiled because it was what I'd been taught to do. "Nice to meet you, Your Highness. Thank you for coming."

Khalid took my hand and brought it to his mouth. His eyes held mine. "I assure you, the pleasure is mine."

Loud voices sounded from somewhere just outside the ballroom my mother had reserved for the evening, and my father's gaze moved over my shoulder to the source of the commotion.

His eyes darkened and narrowed. "Excuse me for a moment."

I moved to follow, but he let out a deep breath and clapped my shoulder. "Nothing for you to worry about, dear. Why don't you and Khalid go ahead and have a seat at our table?"

Our table?

This guy was sitting with our family?

Since when?

The man placed his hand at the small of my back. I hated it. I hated the possessive nature behind it and the way his eyes blazed when he looked at me as we made our way across the room. I didn't belong to him. I was capable of finding our table on my own.

Servers urged the guests to their tables. Mom took a seat in the center of the rectangle table, leaving the seat beside her open for my dad. Khalid pulled out a chair next to my father's and took his seat. I eyed Lincoln, who sat on the other side of Mom and shrugged, then placed his napkin in his lap. Claire sat next to Lincoln, leaving the only available seat beside Khalid.

Great.

My father walked back into the room, running his palms down the front of his tuxedo, smoothing the fabric and smiling as if everything was as it should be.

The music from the band slowly tempered down until the room was nearly silent.

Dad took his seat next to my mother after leaning down to kiss her on the cheek.

I unfolded my napkin and placed it in my lap. Khalid glanced at me from the corner of his eye, then rested his hand on my thigh. The room was warm, but I was chilled to the core. Anticipation and fear swirled around in a relentless chase until my stomach coiled and twisted, and my appetite was gone.

I wanted to slap his hand away, but I knew better than to make a scene, so I swallowed the bile rising in my throat and found something else—anything else—to focus on. This day was seven years in the making. My father had been waiting for this, working for this, for as long as I could remember.

The servers rolled out carts with covered dishes on each tier and waited at the back of the room.

Dad cleared his throat and stood. The room grew quiet.

My heart pounded against my ribs, and I forced myself to breathe.

Just make the announcement, so I can run to the bathroom and hide. Please.

I swallowed.

Khalid flexed his fingers against my thigh.

Hurry.

Dad addressed the guests. "Ladies and gentlemen, I would like to express my sincere gratitude for your coming out tonight."

Applause.

Dad reached for his champagne and held it close to his chest. "It seems we have a lot to celebrate this evening. First of all, my daughter, Tatum, and her remarkable ballet." He looked over at me, and I returned his smile.

More applause.

"I've been blessed to have such a beautiful and talented family. Now, I know as much as you are all here to celebrate my family, you're also gathered for a long-awaited announcement." He paused and swallowed hard. Something foreign flashed across his face, but I couldn't name it. "But I have something else I'd like to announce first..."

Khalid lifted his chin, and my chest tightened.

The double doors burst open, and Caspian barged into the room. Two security guards followed closely behind him.

What the hell?

My heart raced and thrummed like it was trying to claw its way out of my chest.

Khalid dug his fingers into my flesh, making me flinch.

My father white-knuckled his champagne glass so hard I worried it might bust in his hand.

Caspian blew out a breath and grinned. His eyes locked with mine. "Sorry, I'm late sweetheart." He cut a glance to the men in black. "Traffic."

My father, never one to make a scene, quickly recovered. "Mr. Donahue, so glad you could make it."

Caspian wove through the sea of tables, stealing the attention of everyone as he made his way across the room. Power incarnate. "I wouldn't miss it." He walked around the back of the table, stopping behind my chair. He looked over at my father and gave him a wicked grin. "I hate to interrupt your announcement, but all things considered, I'd really like to be the one to tell them if you don't mind."

Tell them what? I thought at the same time my father spoke.

"Tell them what?"

Caspian settled his hands on top of my shoulders. "That I'm going to marry your daughter."

TWENTY-TWO

CASPIAN

In my world, appearances were everything. Who you were and who you appeared to be weren't always one and the same. Everything on the surface was a well-choreographed illusion crafted to show the world what we wanted it to see—and *only* what we wanted it to see.

To this room, Malcolm Huntington was the doting father, accepting his future son-in-law with a smile on his face. To the unsuspecting masses, two powerhouse families would finally unite. Tatum and I were two people brought up in the same world who ended up falling in love. Not a single expression on anyone's face disputed it. Not even Khalid's.

It didn't take much to piece everything together when I saw Khalid at the theater and heard Malcolm was having a party in which he'd planned on making a special announcement.

I gave Malcolm the benefit of the doubt. I waited in the wings —despite his security detail's attempts to make me leave. I held my tongue. I assumed the man would at least have the decency to warn his daughter first.

Instead, he was standing here, ready to throw her to the wolves, in a crowded room—with a smile on his face. I wanted to rip him apart with my bare hands.

At least with me, it wasn't a total shock to her system. We did have a history. As far as I knew, she'd never even met Khalid before tonight.

As soon as he sat at their table, and Malcolm brought up *family* and adding to it, the thread that bound my self-control snapped.

Tatum tensed under my touch as soon as the words left my lips.

Khalid ground his teeth together so hard it could be heard from where I stood.

Lincoln smirked, then lifted his glass of champagne. The rest of the room followed.

Malcolm lost all color in his face, and I noticed sweat beading across his forehead.

Still, they all smiled and toasted the occasion.

While Malcolm pretended to congratulate his daughter and me, I leaned down close to Khalid's ear.

"Thank you for keeping my seat warm." My lips curved up in a slow grin. "You may leave now." My gaze fell to where he pulled his hand from Tatum's thigh. "And if you ever touch her again, I will cut your fingers off one by one with a dull blade."

Tatum gasped, and I gave her shoulders a reassuring squeeze.

Khalid scooted his chair back and stood. He feigned a handshake and a smile. "You didn't put out the fire. You've just doused it in gasoline."

Little did he know, I wasn't afraid of a few flames. I would burn this whole motherfucker down before I'd let him take her.

I shook Malcolm's hand, then took Khalid's now empty seat.

Malcolm looked me in the eye and smiled.

In hunting, there was a warning. When an animal felt threatened—like a snake or a lion—it would bare its teeth. It was a display of aggression or dominance, a reminder of their ability to fill your bloodstream with venom or rip out your throat.

I remembered that warning as I bared my teeth and smiled back.

Malcolm turned his smile to the room full of guests. "Thank you." He rested a hand on his wife's shoulder, and she placed hers on top of it. "We're thrilled to finally bring our two families together." He lifted his champagne again. "And for the final announcement of the evening, I wanted you, my closest friends and family, to hear it first. This spring, I'll be officially announcing my campaign for United States president."

Khalid stood against the back wall with his arms folded across his chest, unphased. Applause erupted throughout the room, followed by a few whistles and shouts of congratulations.

I didn't care about any of that. My only concern was the woman next to me.

Tatum refused to look at me. Her posture was perfect, and her expression gave no hint to her emotions. She raised her champagne glass to her lips and took a long drink. She faced the room with a smile as she set the glass back down and clapped along with everyone else. Then, with practiced grace, she slid her chair from the table and walked quietly out the door.

I moved to follow her, but Huntington grabbed my elbow and halted me.

He leaned in and whispered in my ear. "You have no idea what you've done."

I turned to face him, clapping a hand on his shoulder. Anyone looking on would have assumed we were simply two people having a friendly conversation. A man congratulating his soon-to-be father-in-law.

"My way was the easy way," Malcolm said, and I laughed.

Sure, if selling her to the highest bidder was what you called easy.

"You don't get to threaten me with exile this time. Now, if you'll excuse me, my fiancée seems to have run off." I dropped my hand and stepped away from him.

He lowered himself to his seat and mumbled under his breath. "Let's hope she can run fast."

I smiled to myself as I walked out the door.

Go ahead and run, Little Troublemaker. We both know I'll always catch you.

Outside, in the hallway, Tatum leaned her back against the wall. Her little black dress exposed her toned legs, her chest heaved with every breath she drew in, and the column of her throat was exposed to me as she tilted her head and rested it against the wall. The monster living inside me roared to life at the sight of her delicate, flawless skin. I imagined how it would look broken from my teeth marks or bruised by my fingertips. Her eyes were closed, and I wanted to know what was going on behind them. What thoughts were flitting through her mind? They were unlikely to be the same ones going through mine.

It had been almost three weeks since I'd tasted her, and the fire within me was raging out of control. But the separation was necessary. She'd needed time to deal with a truth that nagged at the back of her mind. Whether Tatum wanted to accept it or not, her best friend had been living a lie. And I needed to give her time to miss me. I needed the burning inside her to match my own. I needed her strong for what I had planned.

Tatum opened her eyes and lifted her head. She turned and froze when her gaze locked with mine.

Gotcha.

I hated the way she looked at me—the pain and anger swirling in the depths of her big, brown eyes—but I didn't feel the least bit guilty for the cause. She thought she hated me.

I knew better.

I was no saint, but I was nowhere near the sinner her father was, and I was done hiding the truth.

The last time I was with Tatum, she told me she wanted people to stop handling her with little kid gloves. She wanted to decide for herself how much she could take.

I was about to give her everything I had.

Her shoulders set in determination as she glared at me.

There was a pulse in the air between us, a steady thrum. The vibrations of it grew stronger with every breath. Time seemed to pause for long seconds.

Tick.

Tick.

Tick.

Then it happened.

She ran.

In a rush of sharp breaths and footsteps, I chased her.

She darted around the corner and down the next hallway. She stopped running the moment she reached the lobby, but her pace was still swift.

I followed her all the way to the revolving doors that led out onto the sidewalk.

She politely smiled at the doorman as she exited the building and rushed outside, quickly blending in with the crowd.

The night air was crisp and cool. The heavy crowd of daytime traffic had thinned out but still flowed in a busy current. Bright lights lit up the city street and Manhattan skyline.

Tatum wrapped her arms around herself as she hurried toward the closest crosswalk.

The signal turned just as she approached, and she rushed across the street.

I wasn't so lucky.

I kept my gaze trained on her as I waited on the crosswalk signal to change back. My phone buzzed in my pocket, and I had two guesses who it might be.

I pulled it out and glanced at the screen.

"That didn't take long," I said when I answered.

"You need to apologize to Huntington for that outburst," Dad said on the other end.

Bright numbers popped up on the crosswalk signal, counting down from ten. I didn't have time for his bullshit.

"Does the lion apologize to the antelope?"

Eight.

Seven.

Something like ice clanking against the side of a glass sounded in the background.

Five.

"And which one is your precious Tatum?" he asked. "A lion? Or an antelope?" A sound close to a chuckle followed by the swirl of liquid echoed over the phone. He must have taken a drink. "I guess we'll find out soon enough." He ended the call right as the counter hit zero.

I didn't have a chance to answer. I didn't need to. His question was rhetorical. It was meant to taunt me—probably some kind of veiled threat.

She disappeared inside a building.

I pushed through the crowd.

A church.

She'd run into a church—a massive, Gothic structure made of bronze and stone. I felt judged for what I was about to do before I ever pushed through the heavy bronze door.

Didn't matter. I was going to hell anyway.

The cathedral was empty apart from Tatum and two other people. Apparently, most people chose to pray in the light of day. Or maybe the church was closing soon. I couldn't be sure. I didn't spend much time here. Maybe that needed to change. Maybe a lot of things needed to change.

The altar at the end of the center aisle stood majestic and proud amongst the white marble arches, and reflections from the stained-glass windows glittered on the wooden pews. Near the end of the aisle, off to one side of the altar, was an ornate, wooden structure with a door in the center of two arched openings. The openings were shrouded in heavy purple curtains.

Tatum stood next to this structure, staring at the carvings in the wood trim. I watched as she traced her finger along one of them. She looked like she belonged here, with the angels, even though we both knew she wasn't one of them.

As I got closer, I noticed a tear trailing down her cheek. She looked so vulnerable when she cried.

And maybe I was fucked up because it made me wonder what she would look like on her knees, with my dick down her throat, fucking her mouth until her eyes watered. It made me want to desecrate her, right here, right now, in this sacred place.

How many Hail Marys were required for having an erection in church?

I closed the final inches between us, stopping to stand beside her, and whispered in her ear. "Are you looking for sanctuary?" I brushed the front of my finger over her tear-stained cheek. "Or perhaps for someone to save you?" I brought my finger to my mouth and tasted her tears. I wanted to take all of them until there was no more sadness left in her.

"I don't need saving." Her voice was quiet but firm.

Maybe not now, but you did. I kept my thoughts to myself.

"Good. Because there is no salvation when your soul belongs to the devil."

She turned her head. "I don't belong to anyone." Her mouth was so close to mine that I could almost taste the champagne on her breath.

I arched a brow and ran my tongue over my bottom lip. "No?"

Her eyes fell to my mouth. "No."

"Wrong." I pushed the velvet curtain aside and backed her into the confessional. "You belong to me." I swept the pad of my thumb over her mouth, smearing her red lipstick. "This belongs to me." I moved the small wooden stool aside with my foot, then pushed her back against the wall.

"Get off me." She shoved at my chest.

I tried to remind myself that we were in a place of reverence, where morals and virtue were as important as the holy sacraments.

I tried to remind myself that I came here to talk, to explain what had just happened.

I tried to tame the beast.

The beast won.

My hand moved across her collarbone, then inside her dress and to her breast. I pinched her nipple through her bra. "This belongs to me."

She tried grabbing my wrist, but I took both her hands and pinned them above her head.

I leaned forward, hovering my mouth over hers. "You wanna try that again?"

"I swear to God, I'll scream."

I grinned. "Good."

I wanted her to scream.

I wanted her to cry.

I wanted her to forget to breathe.

Her words told one story, but her eyes told another. Her breaths came in shallow pants, and her gaze darkened. She parted her lips, and I took what was mine, letting my mouth punish her for challenging me. She gave as good as she got.

I let go of her hands and lifted her dress up over her hips, leaving nothing between us but the thin fabric of her panties and my clothes. I unfastened my belt and pants, then pulled them down, freeing my cock.

Fuck.

My mouth moved from her lips to her jaw, where I nipped her with my teeth.

She grabbed my hair and tried moving my head away.

Not a fucking chance, Little Troublemaker.

I stroked my dick with one hand and yanked her panties down with the other.

She kicked them the rest of the way off. Her hips rolled toward mine, drawn to me by an imaginary thread, an unbreakable bond.

I grabbed her thigh and hooked one of her legs around my waist. "It's kind of remarkable isn't it? That I'm about to fuck you in the place where darkness comes to light. Where the deepest desires of the heart are set free." My other hand slinked up her body, over her breasts, stopping at her throat.

"I hate you."

I positioned myself at her entrance. Fuck. Just as I thought, she was wet as fuck against my tip. Her body quivered against me. "You want to hate me." I flexed my fingers and held her stare. "But you can't." Without warning, I shoved inside her.

She arched her back and sucked in a gasp. Her pussy was so hot. It felt so fucking good. Every thrust led me further and further into my damnation, but I gladly let her be my undoing. Her eyes flitted closed.

"Look at me." I gripped her throat harder, feeling the pulse throb at my fingertips.

She opened her eyes, and I refused to let up.

Not when she clawed at my chest and moaned, "Harder."

Not when her head fell forward, and she bit my shoulder.

And not when she threw her head back again and cried out, "Oh, God."

"That's it, sweetheart. Pray for me."

I drove into her, primal and unrelenting, almost positive I'd leave bruises between her thighs.

"Caspian." She breathed my name, and fuck if I didn't need to hear it again.

My grip loosened on her neck, and she took in a deep breath. "Fuck yeah, baby. Let it go."

She leaned her forehead against mine, and her hands gripped my biceps. Her cunt tightened around my cock, and I pounded into her as deep as I could go until she shattered right here in my arms.

"I told you, Little Troublemaker. You belong to me," I said through gritted teeth as I came deep inside her.

TWENTY-THREE

Tatum

I didn't know what I wanted, or what I expected, when I ran from Caspian earlier, but standing here now, looking in his whiskey eyes with my thighs coated in his cum, feeling his ownership wrap around me like a warm blanket, I knew this was it—I wanted to be his.

That didn't mean I wasn't still angry with him, though.

"I'm pretty sure you're going to hell for this," I said as I bent down to grab my panties.

He smirked, not the slightest hint of remorse in his expression. "I'm going to hell for a lot of things. Add this to the list." He tugged his pants up.

I pulled my panties up over my ass. "Yeah, well, I didn't even have a list until you, so…"

He tucked his cock into his underwear, then zipped his pants. His top button was still unfastened, and his belt hung loose. The need to unzip his pants and taste him burned at me until my mouth went dry. God, I'd missed this man.

And I hated him.

But for reasons unknown, I couldn't stay away from him. Caspian Donahue was a brute force. He was power, protection, insanity, and chaos wrapped in a flawless package. I was paralyzed in his fierce, golden-brown eyes. The hunger for his touch was cemented in my bones.

He cradled my face in one hand and leaned in. "Oh, you've always had a list." He traced my bottom lip with the tip of his tongue. "You just didn't start checking it off until me."

I took a deep breath. This place—this holy place—smelled like sex and sin.

"Why did you do it?" I said the words as calmly as possible, though inside my heart was racing. From the orgasm high. From the closeness of his presence. From fear.

I wasn't sure I really wanted an answer for his unexpected outburst. It wasn't love. Caspian and I shared a lot of emotions, but I doubted love was one of them.

There was sex.

There was love.

Then, there was us.

We were somewhere in between.

Weren't we?

He watched me with the same dark intensity he had when he'd first backed me into this confessional. His hands worked to tuck in his shirt and fix his belt. He looked as if he'd just come from a business meeting, not like he'd just ravaged my body inside a church.

"Come home with me. We'll talk about it there." Confidence laced his tone the same way it had when he'd made his announcement to a room full of my father's family and friends.

"No. We're talking about it now. The damage you did can't be undone. My father has worked his whole life for that moment, and you stole it from him. He will never forgive you." I knew that without a doubt. Malcolm Huntington didn't forgive and forget. "And for what reason? To prove a point? To win some kind of pissing contest between our families?"

His jaw flexed and clenched. "You think that's what that was about? You think I did what I did to ruin your father's campaign announcement?"

"Didn't you?"

I knew Caspian wasn't petty. That wasn't his game. But what other reason was there?

"This isn't the time or place."

"It's the perfect time and place." I gestured at the tiny space we were in. "Bring the darkness to light, right? Isn't that what you said?"

He placed a palm on the wall behind my head, then leaned in and spoke against my ear. His tone was low and deep, almost menacing. "Tatum, this will be the one and only time you will ever hear me beg for anything. But I am asking you—*please*, just let me take you home. And I promise I will tell you everything." His scent floated around me, over me, seeping inside me.

Home.

He said it as if it were a collective place for all of our troubles, for all of our fears, and all of our happiness.

I stared up at him. "Okay."

He raised a brow as though he expected me to argue. When I didn't, he moved his hand to the small of my back and guided me out of the confessional.

On the other side of the purple velvet curtain, a priest was rushing down the aisle with a stern expression on his ghost-white face.

My cheeks were flushed. I felt it. My hair was a mess. I knew it. And my panties were soaked with a combination of our cum, although most of it coated my inner thighs. Not to mention the fact that we didn't even try to be quiet.

Shit.

Caspian's face lit up in an unashamed, boyish grin as he grabbed my hand and nodded at the priest. "We just got engaged," he said, as though the words were grounds for absolution.

The priest's mouth thinned in a firm line. "Get. Out." His words were clipped as he pointed toward the door.

I wanted to die.

I couldn't move. I felt like I needed to fall to my knees and ask for forgiveness.

Caspian tugged on my hand, and I snapped out of it long enough to follow him out the door.

We left my car at the theater where I'd parked it earlier and took Caspian's. Guilt weighed heavily in the pit of my stomach as the elevator door opened into his new apartment. I'd almost forgotten the other reason we were supposed to celebrate today.

"You moved in," I said, noticing the fully furnished and decorated penthouse.

He let go of my hand and moved past me toward the open kitchen. "Three days ago."

He must have closed early.

I followed him. "Why didn't you say something?"

He grabbed a bottle of wine from a wine refrigerator and an opener from a nearby drawer. "You had other things to focus on." He twisted the cork off the wine, then winked. "I knew we had time."

I leaned my butt against the kitchen island in front of him. "I like it."

The countertops were a polished stainless steel. The bottom cabinets were a dark espresso, and the top cabinets had glass doors. The floors were a slate gray that looked like hardwood but felt like tile. The kitchen opened up into the living room, where there was a massive U-shaped sectional on top of a fluffy white rug and a row of floor-to-ceiling windows overlooking the city. At the far end of the living room, in front of the windows, there was a beautiful, white grand piano. His home was as pristine and sophisticated as the man who owned it.

Caspian set two glasses on the counter, poured them half full, and handed me one. He placed the open bottle on the counter. "I'll leave this out. You're going to need it."

I brought the wine to my lips. "That bad, huh?"

He took a drink, then went still. His eyes closed while he took in a deep breath. When he opened them again, his stare was almost apologetic.

Anxiety twisted and pulled inside me. "Since when does Caspian Donahue wait for permission?" I tried to laugh it off, but my voice was weak.

He set his glass down. "The man who sat next to you at the party—"

"Prince Khalid," I interjected.

He clenched his jaw. "Yes. Khalid."

I noticed he left off the title, probably intentionally.

"He wasn't just a guest. His presence wasn't random. Neither was the fact that he sat at your table—at your *family's* table."

I remembered his hand on my thigh, and the acidic taste of bile rose in my throat. I swallowed it back down.

I put my glass down and straightened my posture. "And I suppose you know why."

I had my suspicions, and none of them were good. It wasn't the first time one of Dad's political allies had made a move on me, and I doubted it would be the last. I'd always spurned them off. This guy wasn't any different. I'd met my fair share of creeps and could hold my own against them.

"Before I walked in, your father was about to announce your engagement." Anger flashed in his eyes. "To Khalid."

What?

No.

I'd just met Khalid. That wasn't possible. My dad would never agree to that.

But I have something else I'd like to announce first...

Those were my father's words just before Caspian interrupted him.

Khalid sitting at our table. The possessive hand on my thigh. The way he and Dad shared a curious smile.

No.

I shook my head. "You don't know that."

"I do," he said, calmly.

My voice raised an octave and cracked a little. "You don't. Just because—"

"Tatum. I do."

The bile was back, and this time I was barely able to keep from throwing up.

"Why? Why would he—How could he—In front of all those people. He knows what that means." Reputation was everything in my father's eyes. You didn't make public announcements just to take them back. That was why he would never forgive Caspian for what he did. The words had been spoken. It might as well have been a decree.

Caspian stepped forward and pulled me to his chest. He held my head and rubbed a hand down my back. His lips pressed against my hair, and I choked back a sob. A single tear escaped and rolled down my cheek. I didn't stop it.

I moved my head to look up at him. His eyes were full of something that resembled sadness. His cold features had warmed. He flinched when another tear fell, as if the words had hurt him too. As if my pain were his pain.

"Why?" My question came out in a hoarse whisper.

He took a deep breath.

"I can handle it, Caspian. Just tell me."

And I could.

I could handle whatever he said next. I'd had enough secrets and lies to last me a lifetime. Now, I just wanted the truth.

"Khalid owns ninety percent of the oil surplus in Saudi Arabia. When your father becomes president, he's going to shut down our pipelines and give that business to Khalid. Your engagement was insurance—for lack of a better word—that both parties would make good on their end of the deal. And with you married to Khalid, and Khalid getting all the oil import business for the U.S, by default, your dad gets rich and Khalid gets richer."

Emotions swelled up inside me like a storm on the ocean. Waves of anger, pain, and despair rolled and crested until I felt as though I might drown. I trembled in Caspian's arms, and he pulled me closer. I wanted to be numb. Other than the feeling I got when he held me tight to his chest, the feeling of walking outside on a warm summer day or seeing a familiar face in a crowd of strangers. That feeling, I wanted to feel forever. It was everything else I wished would go away.

"He sold me."

He sold me.

I pressed my cheek against his chest, letting the strength and scent of him comfort me. "How did you know? About Khalid, I mean."

"My father told me. So, when I saw Khalid at the ballet, then again at the party, I knew it wasn't just an empty threat. I knew it was true."

Caspian didn't apologize for my father's actions. He didn't make excuses or try to sugarcoat the fact that he'd saved me from becoming what was basically nothing more than a high-class slave.

Because he knew.

He knew what men like Khalid—and apparently my father—were capable of. His father hadn't shielded him from it the way mine had. He'd seen it.

His former words came back to me. *You don't have a fucking clue how the world works.*

But he did. Now, I did too.

I hated that for him. My heart broke for the boy who had to become a man far too soon because of how his world worked—how *our* world worked.

"You stopped him."

Wasn't that what he'd always done? Hadn't he always shown up just in time to save me?

"I meant it, you know," he said, and I turned my face to look at him. "I *am* going to marry you one day." His pulse thrummed at the vein in his throat, and his breath quickened. "Our story was written before we were ever born. Our souls were destined to find each other. And if you think there was any other way for this to end other than you being with me, you're crazier than I am." His words crept inside me and flowed to all my darkest places.

He lifted a hand and pushed my hair off my neck, then brought his mouth there. His lips ghosted over my skin, sending a shudder over every inch of my body. My stomach knotted into a bundle of heat and nerves. My breath came harder and harder. His lips were soft, and his breath was warm against my neck as he let out a low groan. Like it was killing him to be so tender, but tender was what he wanted to give. The thick length of his erection pressed hard against my belly. His hands drifted down my back to my ass, where he cupped me and squeezed. I didn't want to fight him, not this time. I needed to challenge him, but I needed this too. We both did.

I circled my arms around his neck, then leaned up on my tiptoes and whispered against the curve of his throat. "I believe you promised me something about a window…"

As quickly as a heartbeat, the air shifted.

Caspian grabbed the hem of my dress, yanking it over my head and tossing it to the floor. He pulled back and let his gaze rake over my body, blazing a trail over my naked breasts and down to my black panties. My hands worked eagerly to unbutton his shirt while he undid his belt and pants. Once freed, Caspian gave his cock a long, lazy stroke while he licked his bottom lip.

"Over there." He nodded toward the living room window, his amber eyes going molten. "Hands against the glass."

I started to step out of my heels.

"Leave those on," he said as he rolled his thumb over the tip of his dick, pre-cum glistening on the thick head.

I held my breath as I walked over and palmed the window.

Caspian stepped behind me, close enough that his skin kissed my skin. He slid one hand up the side of my body, then cupped my breast. His other hand eased inside my panties, the tips of his fingers brushing my pussy. I arched back into him, and he used his body to push me forward, pressing me against the cool glass.

His fingertips ghosted my clit, rubbing slow, small circles. My palms flexed against the window, but I held perfectly still, even though my body was burning to press against him, to push back against his thick heat. He parted his fingers into a V, running them over my folds, massaging me, teasing me, but never entering me, not yet. My breath came harder and heavier, and my body felt like a bubble about to pop. And then, he was there, two fingers deep in my cunt while his palm pressed against my clit. He rolled my nipple between the fingers of his other hand.

"I'm giving you this because you need it," he said against my ear, then pulled the lobe between his teeth. "But you need to know that gentle is not in my nature." As if to drive his point home, he pulled his two fingers out of me and yanked my panties until the fabric ripped, leaving its mark on my flesh.

The need to be fucked by him tore at me, clawed at me until I felt like I was on fire.

He gripped my hip and pulled me to him, placing his head at my entrance. "I'm going to fuck you now, Little Troublemaker." The tip of his tongue ran up the side of my neck. "I'm going to show the whole world how I make you come."

I felt his every heartbeat, every ragged breath he took. And then he drove into me. Again and again, he pounded me, harder and harder, urgent and possessive, over and over. And over. Stretching and filling me until it hurt, but it was the kind of hurt that I craved, the kind that reminded me I was alive. His kind of pain was a drug. Until the tightness in my belly gave way to a splintering orgasm that stole the breath from my lungs.

Caspian was right.

This was home.

I woke the next morning to soft golden-brown eyes staring over at me and a fingertip running along my bare shoulder then down my arm.

"Sleep well?" he asked, ignoring the vibrating phone on his nightstand.

"Like the dead."

"Considering I fucked you into a coma, that makes total sense."

I rolled my eyes and stretched, like a lazy cat on the back of a sofa. The blanket inched down and exposed my breasts.

He lowered his head and pulled one of my nipples between his teeth. "I love it when you wake up smelling like me." He moved the covers to the side, letting the cool air dance across my hot, naked skin.

I tangled my fingers in his hair. The phone vibrated again. I arched my back, bowing shamelessly against his mouth. "You should get that."

He swirled his tongue around my other nipple and blindly reached over to grab his phone. "Or maybe I should let it ring," he said as he held the buzzing device against my clit, making my body sing with pleasure.

Holy fuck.

He looked up at me with a smirk, then swiped his finger across the screen. "Yes?"

The buzzing stopped, and I wanted to press my pussy against the cool glass of the phone, to grind against the smooth surface. The pressure inside me was building again, and I needed relief.

"Good morning, Mr. Donahue. This is Mrs. Talbot with Premier Title. We seem to be missing some of your paperwork, and we need you to come down and sign again as soon as possible."

Caspian bit the inside of my thigh, and I whimpered. "What do you mean *missing paperwork*? The woman at your office assured me everything was done."

The woman cleared her throat. "It looks like the deed wasn't signed. I can't finalize it with the county clerk's office until this is taken care of."

"Then send a courier here, and I'll sign it."

"Unfortunately, it has to be done at our office. I apologize for the inconvenience."

"Fuck. Okay, I'll be right there." He tossed the phone to the other side of the bed and spread my thighs wide. "Right after I make you come on my face."

He scooped his hands underneath my ass, raising me to meet his mouth. My body pulsed with heat as his tongue slid over my clit, down my center, to my waiting entrance. Again and again. He traced every part of me, like he couldn't get enough of my taste. And then he dug his fingers into my flesh and pulled me closer, letting his tongue dip inside my hole. I parted my thighs wider, shamelessly begging for more of his mouth. I writhed beneath him, ground against him until there was nothing else but me and him and the slick sounds of my pleasure filling the air. My hands fisted the sheets, grabbed his hair. It was too much and not enough. He moved his mouth to my clit, and my body shivered and quaked, then within moments, I was there, shattering, flying, coming apart with a ferocity I never wanted to end.

And then he was on top of me, crushing my mouth in a brutal kiss that tasted like me. Hot strokes of his tongue that were potent and urging, steel and silk, with a possessiveness that had me on the precipice of coming undone all over again.

He pulled away from my mouth, biting my bottom lip with a groan. "Don't even think about leaving. I'm not done with you yet." He gave my ass a squeeze, then climbed out of bed and walked across the room, not one bit bothered by his nakedness. Then again, neither was I.

I propped up on one elbow and watched him as he got dressed, jealousy gnawing at me that he was going to see another woman, regardless of who that woman was.

He leaned down and kissed my forehead. "I'll be back in thirty minutes. An hour, tops."

I smiled and tapped an imaginary watch on my wrist. "Better hurry. You're on the clock."

As soon as he was gone and the room was quiet, all the emotions I'd bottled up last night came bubbling back to the surface. The more I thought about what my father had planned with Khalid, the more my anger pushed past the pain. It ticked and ticked like a bomb inside my chest, ready to explode.

A mountain was only formed when the earth around it had been shaken. I'd been shaken plenty. Now I was ready to rise.

I threw on one of Caspian's T-shirts, then went downstairs and looked for my phone. I needed to call my dad and let him know I'd be moving out of the Hampton house soon, and I couldn't wait for him to ask me why. I had no idea where I would go. Maybe I could stay with Lincoln until I figured it out. Maybe I would stay here. I just knew I didn't want to be *there*.

There was no sign of my phone anywhere. I mentally retraced my steps until it dawned on me that I'd left it in the ballroom. I was so intent on getting away from Caspian that I didn't think about grabbing it.

Shit.

The elevator doors slid open right as I was headed toward the stairs.

I twirled around and pulled my bottom lip between my teeth. "That was quick. You must have really missed me."

Fear pricked the back of my neck all the way down my spine when he walked into the room. His smile was wide and malicious, and his soulless eyes held me in place.

I swallowed. "Mr. Donahue. Caspian didn't tell me you were coming."

Caspian's father strode toward me, and my heart flailed around wildly in my chest. "Of course, he didn't. I'm not here for him."

TWENTY-FOUR

CASPIAN

I texted one of Chandler's guys to pick me up. My car wasn't to be trusted, not now, not after my father's phone call last night. Maybe it was a ploy to get me out of my house so that he could snoop around or plant a bug—or worse, making sure I ended up charcoaled like our dead attorney. I wouldn't have even left Tatum there alone if I hadn't paid the security guard downstairs five hundred dollars to make sure no one but me stepped foot near my apartment until I got back.

Missing paperwork.

Something in my gut told me that wasn't an accident. Dad was fucking with me. I just didn't know exactly how yet, but I was determined to catch him in his game.

A guy I'd only met once before—pretty sure his name was Alec—pulled into the parking garage in a car identical to mine. Out on the street, the sidewalks were already bustling with tourists taking selfies, men in suits on cell phones, and women in pencil skirts and stilettos. The sky was blue and clear, and traffic was light.

I stared out the window, thinking about last night and wondering about the future, if Tatum would want to be a part of what I had planned. After what she'd learned about her father, I hoped she would.

I knew Tatum wasn't breakable. I'd known it from the moment she'd called me a *stupidhead* as I dragged her down the hallway when she was six years old. There was always a spark in her. All she needed was a little friction to turn it into a full-blown flame.

It wasn't that I thought she couldn't handle the truth. I was afraid that *I* couldn't. I'd spent most of my life protecting her from the darkness. I didn't want to be the one to shatter her with it. I couldn't stand the thought of pushing her away.

She wasn't naïve. She was simply one of the rare jewels that chose to see the light in the world over the darkness. She let the good outweigh the bad. She chose peace over chaos. Optimism over cynicism. Her inherent belief that the world was a good place with good people in it didn't make her weak. It made her strong. After all, heroes—true heroes—weren't the people who won the first round. They were the ones who lost and kept on fighting.

My girl was a fighter.

She proved it last night.

When I told her the truth about Khalid and her father, the pain in her eyes nearly crushed me. I knew that pain—the sting of betrayal from the person who was supposed to love you the most. I'd felt it ever since I was thirteen years old.

But she didn't break. She opened up like a flower after the rain and handed me her pain. Right there against the tinted windows that no one could actually see through.

I'd been taking steps to earn her trust, wholly and completely, since I came back from Europe. I gave the truth to her in small doses, preparing for the ultimate climax. The one she needed to be strongest for. The truth to end all truths.

Soon.

I would tell her soon.

"Pull around to the back and wait for me. I won't be long," I told Alec once we made it to the title attorney's office.

The receptionist at the front desk smiled widely when I walked through the door.

I scanned the office, already bored and ready to get this over with. There was a naked goddess in my bed waiting to be fucked.

"Caspian Donahue. You should have some paperwork for me."

She thumbed through a stack of files, then held up a single finger. "One second, Mr. Donahue." Her smile never faltered as she rolled her chair backward and got up to find whatever it was that I'd been summoned here to do.

She was back less than a minute later. "Good news." Her eyes glittered. "Your paperwork was filed yesterday." She leaned over the counter and showed me her tits. "Is there anything else you need?"

The fuck?

"Mrs. Talbot." I glanced around the room, reading the gold nameplates in each door. "Which one is her office?"

Her drawn-in eyebrows bunched together. "Mrs. Talbot?"

My heart dropped to my shoes, and I slammed a fist on the wooden desk. "Fuck!" *I knew it.*

I bolted out the door and back to the car. "Get the fuck back to my apartment. Now!" I ran my fingers through my hair and leaned my head back on the headrest, squeezing my eyes shut while I prayed to fucking God that he hadn't gotten to my apartment and found her yet. If he touched a hair on her motherfucking head, he was dead. I would murder that motherfucker and not even flinch.

Alec dropped me off in the parking garage, then I sent him to go pick up Chandler and be on stand-by.

"Everything good?" I asked the security guard standing outside the elevator that went straight up to my apartment.

He nodded. "Yes, sir. No problems other than some bum trying to sneak into the fitness room to shower."

I stopped breathing. "The fuck did you just say?"

The guard shook his head. "Oh, he didn't try to get on the elevator. Just creeping around the fitness room."

All brawn. No brain.

"But you left the elevator to go throw him out?"

He swallowed as realization widened his eyes.

The elevator doors opened, and I rushed inside, giving him a burning glare before they closed again. I jabbed a finger his direction. "Don't you fucking move. Because if anything happened to her, I swear to God, I will kill you myself."

I quietly scanned the open space the second I stepped inside my apartment, looking for anything out of place. Dread sneaked in and coated my veins, freezing my bloodstream and chilling me to the bone with every step I took.

How could I have been so fucking stupid?

I should have taken the car and left Alec here. I should have made Tatum come with me, but I'd thought it was a trap.

And it was—just not for me.

I knew Dad was playing head games with me when I got the phone call. My mistake came in thinking his mind fucks were small ball. I assumed this was another paperwork trail he wanted me to chase, like the one he'd started with my trust. He wanted to keep my future dangling just far enough in front of me that I could see it but not reach it.

The thought even crossed my mind that maybe it was a lure. Maybe he'd stage a robbery-gone-wrong or some other fucked-up bullshit ploy to try to scare me.

I was ready for that.

I was wrong.

He had bigger plans, and they didn't involve just me anymore.

Downstairs was empty. No sign of a struggle. Nothing out of place.

Before I reached the top step, my phone rang. I pulled it out of my pocket and damn near cried when Tatum's name flashed on the screen.

"I thought I told you not to leave, Little Troublemaker."

"Yeah, well, we both know I'm shit at following directions."

Lincoln.

Not Tatum.

It was Lincoln's voice on the other line.

"Why the fuck do you have Tatum's phone?"

"Why the fuck did you call her a troublemaker?"

I pinched the bridge of my nose. I didn't have time for this bullshit.

My bedroom was empty. The covers were still a tangled mess from last night and this morning. Her scent still filled the air. But she was gone. My heart tried clawing its way out of my chest.

I walked into the bathroom. "I have to go." It was empty. The shower hadn't been used.

"Wait. Where's my sister?"

I gritted my teeth. "Good question. Why don't you ask your piece of shit father and his new friend Khalid?" I said, then ended the call.

My phone immediately rang again.

Both guest rooms were empty.

She wasn't here.

Downstairs, her dress laid in a pile on the floor where we'd left it last night. Her heels were by the stairs where she'd kicked them off as I'd carried her to bed.

Fury and the thirst for vengeance boiled and bubbled within me, awakening demons I didn't even know existed.

My phone kept ringing.

She was gone.

Red.

All I saw was red. The color of my rage and their blood surrounded my vision on all sides.

My fucking phone kept ringing.

"What the fuck did you not understand about *I have to go*?"

"Where is my goddamn sister?"

The demons seduced me. They circled around me, licking at my skin and running their hands all over my body until I reveled in their darkness, until I was consumed by their flames.

"They took her."

Lincoln convinced me to let him come over. He said he had something important to show me. The first thing I did when I got off the phone with him was call Chandler.

It wasn't my favorite plan, but here we were.

We all sat in the living room, waiting for a pin to drop. Chandler had his long legs stretched out and his feet propped up on the ottoman. I swirled the amber liquid around in my glass, contemplating just drinking straight from the bottle. Lincoln kept chewing on his toothpick and tapping his fingertips against his thumb as if he were counting or playing a melody only he could hear.

Finally, Lincoln pulled Tatum's phone from his pocket. "She left this at the party last night. I grabbed it off the table right before one of the cleaning crew picked it up. There's something I think you should see."

My gaze shot over to him, and Chandler sat up straight.

Lincoln tapped the screen, bringing her phone to life. After another few taps, he flipped the device around, showing us a generic picture of a woman's hand. On her fourth finger was a large pear-shaped diamond ring.

I took a drink. "What does that have to do with Tatum?"

Lincoln shoved the phone toward me. "Because that's her Instagram, you fuck."

My hand clenched the glass to keep from punching him in the throat. I squinted to read the caption.

T Hunt Official

Just like that, I belong to him. Can't wait to celebrate our engagement! #Huntington&Donahue

I read the caption over and over. It didn't make any sense.

"At first, I thought, dude, that's fucked up. She didn't even tell me she was going somewhere." Lincoln pulled the phone back and stared at the screen. "Then I saw when she'd posted it, and shit started getting weird."

"When did she post it?" Chandler asked.

"That's the freaky part." Lincoln's eyes went wild. "She posted it *after* you two left the party."

That wasn't possible.

"Someone else had her phone. Someone before you," I said.

"Congratulations, Caspian. Bob, tell the man what he's won," Lincoln said in a game-show-host-type voice.

Asshole.

The photo was generic, at best. It could have been anyone. The caption made no sense, and the hashtags were cheesy as fuck.

#HuntingtonandDonahue

Whoever posted it wanted the world to know what I'd said at that party—that we were together.

Can't wait to celebrate our engagement on the island.

What island? What the fuck did that mean?

They also wanted the world to know we'd be going somewhere. Remote. Quiet. Off the grid. An island.

Lincoln moved to shove the phone back into his pocket, but I held out my hand. He slapped the phone down on my palm. "You really are fucking obsessed." The toothpick rolled between his teeth. "But you've always protected her. Ever since that night at the lake."

Chandler shot me a glance, and I took another drink, draining the glass.

"We all did what we had to do that night," Chandler said. His voice was low, haunted by the demons that plunged us all from childhood into manhood.

"I think about it sometimes," Lincoln said, then plucked the toothpick from his mouth. "About how fucked up it all was."

I didn't think about it. I'd shoved the memory of that night away into the darkest parts of my mind. All it did was remind me who I really was, what I was really capable of.

I got up and walked to the kitchen to pour myself another drink.

Chandler propped his elbows on his knees and rested his head in his hands.

"It's this weekend, you know. The Brotherhood ceremony," Lincoln said.

Yes. I fucking knew. It was all I'd thought about since I realized they'd taken her. I thought I had everything mapped out perfectly, but I'd played right into their hand. I'd been so preoccupied with Tatum and getting her the fuck away from her father and Khalid that I'd forgotten it was that time of year.

Maybe that was part of their plan. Maybe they'd outsmarted me in that way. That would never happen again.

Every year at this time, all the members of the Obsidian Brotherhood congregated in the middle of a dense forest in upstate New York. They called it the Ceremony of Cares, and one year at Clearview Lake, when we were all barely teenagers, we got a small taste of exactly what it was they did. The sons were never invited to The Grove. It was an event strictly for the patriarchs of the families. But we'd all been initiated. We'd been prepped and groomed for the depravity of the Brotherhood our whole lives.

Lincoln cleared his throat. "You think that's where—"

I threw the glass across the room. It hit the piano and shattered into a million pieces. "Shut up!" My breath came in hot, heavy bursts. "Just shut the fuck up."

He bolted up from the couch. "Calm down, motherfucker. We're on the same team."

I cleared the space between us, stopping when we were chest to chest. "You fill her head with precisely the bullshit I try to protect her from. We are *not* on the same team."

Chandler lifted his head but stayed seated, always calm, always the voice of reason. "Both of you calm the fuck down. We're all on the same team. If we weren't, we wouldn't be here right now." When I took a deep breath and a step back, he continued. "Now, I need you to think. What does that post mean? And if they did take her to The Grove—"

I pinned him with a glare.

He held both hands in the air. "I said *if*, asshole." His hands fell to his lap. "What do you think they'll do with her?"

Can't wait to celebrate our engagement on the island.

The world is a jungle, Son. You're either the lion or the antelope. You either run or you take.

Which one is your precious Tatum? A lion? Or an antelope? I guess we'll find out soon enough.

All eyes were on me as I unbuttoned the cuff of my shirt sleeve and folded it over, rolling it up my forearm, then repeated the process with my other sleeve.

The pieces all came together, like one of those cube puzzles that didn't make any sense until that final part clicked.

I knew what we had to do.

"They're going to hunt her." My voice was ice-cold. I almost didn't recognize it. "Then they're going to kill me."

TWENTY-FIVE

CASPIAN

Twelve years prior…
age thirteen

The sky was dark. There were hardly any stars out, and the moon was hidden behind the clouds. The bonfire several feet away was our main source of light. It was quiet except for the croaking of some frogs and crackling of the fire.

We all stood on the bank with the lake behind us—me, Chandler, Lincoln, our fathers, and three strangers who were lined up on their knees with their hands tied behind their backs and a burlap sack over their heads.

My father stood behind the kneeling strangers. "Each of these people represents a burden that weighs on the world today. This man is poverty." He placed his hand on top of the first man's head, then pulled off the sack. I immediately recognized him as the same man I'd caught jacking off while he stared through the window of Tatum's cabin earlier. I'd pulled her out of there and made her sleep in my cabin when I saw her tiny little panties in his hand. Who knew what sick things he wanted to do to her. There was no way I was leaving her alone.

Dad moved to the next person, obviously a woman. He held his hand on top of her head and removed her sack. She was thin with sunken-in cheekbones. She looked like a skeleton with skin.

"She represents hunger." The woman visibly trembled, and he moved over to the next guy, yanking the sack off his head. This one was older with silver hair that shone in the night. He was well-dressed and looked nothing like the other two. *"This one represents greed."*

Chandler, Lincoln, and I shared a look that said we wanted nothing to do with whatever came next but knew we had no choice.

Dad moved to stand behind the three kneelers. The orange-red glow of the fire danced over his sharp features, making him look like a god among men.

Or a devil.

"It's our job to rid the world of these burdens," he continued, *and the woman—Hunger—started to cry. Dad smoothed a hand over her dark hair as if he were trying to console her. We all knew he wasn't.*

Malcolm Huntington spoke up. *"Every year, we each choose a problem we see in the world, a burden we want to focus on, a worry we want to banish. Our forefathers called these burdens our 'cares.' The rest of that year, we focus on that care. But on this night, Mischief Night, we begin with the desecration of a symbol, an effigy of that burden."*

A sacrifice.

They were going to kill these people.

Pierce Carmichael opened a small black chest. *"Normally, this would be more of a sport, but being that you're younger and this isn't an actual ceremony but more of an initiation, we're doing it a bit differently."*

A sport? What did he mean by "sport"?

The woman was sobbing. The silver-haired man had pissed his pants after he'd tried to crawl away, but my father kicked him hard in the gut. The pervert just kneeled there, his eyes black and his mouth in a snarl. Like he was mentally ripping us apart, piece by piece.

"Boys, tonight you will become men," Dad said.

I swallowed hard. My pulse pounded in my ears. Realization hit me like a freight train.

They weren't going to kill these people.

We were.

"Choose your weapons," Pierce said as he nodded toward the open chest.

Chandler took the gun.

Lincoln picked up an axe.

I chose the knife.

We held our weapons like a group of skilled warriors instead of teenage boys. There was no fear on Lincoln or Chandler's faces, just pure indignation. I recognized it because I felt it too. We would all change tonight. Our fathers had made sure of it.

I remembered when I was a toddler, barely learning to walk. My father took me out back to the pool and threw me in. I'd heard my mother scream, but Dad had simply stood there, waiting to see if I would swim or drown.

I swam.

I swam because even at a young age, I had to learn that in our world, you did what you had to do to survive. If you didn't you would drown.

As we stood here, holding our weapons and staring death in the eye, I wondered if Chandler and Lincoln's father had made them swim, too.

Dad smiled. "Now choose your care."

I didn't have to think about it. I knew which one I'd choose.

Fate had made this easy for me. My eyes narrowed, and I pointed my knife toward the man known as Poverty.

Lincoln pointed to the older man, leaving the woman for Chandler. Thank God, he picked the gun. He could make it quick.

Our dads each stood behind our respective 'cares' and grabbed a handful of their hair, holding them in place. They looked at us with a dark challenge in their eyes.

My dad was the one to speak next. "It's time. Rid us of these burdens."

Before I'd turned fourteen years old, I knew what it felt like to slice a man's throat.

TWENTY-SIX

Tatum

Beads of sweat coated my skin. My chest was tight. Heavy. I struggled to breathe. I moved to lift my arms, and a shockwave of pain exploded like fireworks, shooting from my temples to my toes. My mouth was dry. So dry.

Hands gripped my wrist, the touch forceful and harsh. Fingers pressed into my flesh. Another hand brushed my forehead, unsticking the strands of hair that had gotten lodged in the sweat.

"Go back to sleep. It's not time to wake up yet." The voice sounded far away, muffled.

I tried to open my eyes but quickly slammed them shut when a surge of fire pierced my vein and shot through my arm.

My eyes fluttered open for a split second. Then the world tilted, and I fell back into the black, inky abyss.

I woke to darkness.

Fire flickered in my peripheral vision. My body ached. I sat up, and that was when the cold air struck me. Everything was sore, and my head felt as though it weighed a ton. A Band-Aid taped over a cotton ball covered the inner crook of my elbow. My stomach curled.

I was moving.

No, not I.

We.

I looked up at the two hooded figures standing above me. They each wore a black robe, and they held a long pole.

A boat.

They were poling a small boat over water.

A tiny trill of fear laced my nerves as I sat up all the way. The hooded figures never strayed from their task. They didn't even look at me.

Caspian's T-shirt had been replaced with a thin, white robe—and nothing else. Following closely behind the boat I was on were four other boats. Each of them also had a fiery torch at the helm, two hooded figures and one white-robed person.

Something familiar tugged at the pit of my stomach, like I'd seen this before.

That night at Crestview Lake. All this time I'd convinced myself it was just a dream, but it was a memory. I'd seen Lincoln in his boat, poling just like this in the middle of the night. I remembered as my father held me in his arms, I looked over and saw Chandler and Caspian follow in their own boats. They each had something with them, something else in the boat, something covered in white that they all rolled over the side and into the water. *The secrets.*

Did they know about this? Had they seen it before?

I hugged my arms around my body to stop the sudden shiver.

In the distance, the shoreline was aglow with dozens of small bonfires and two massive fires in the background. Between the two larger fires was some sort of statue—or shrine—in the shape of a lion. It reminded me of an ancient sphinx. As we poled closer and closer to the bank, panic trickled in a cold line down my back. We were in the middle of nowhere. Nothing but woods surrounded this lake for as far as I could see.

No authorities to douse the fires.

No neighbors to hear the screams.

What in the hell was this place?

We pulled into a boat launch, and two men walked over to the ramp to help me out of the boat. They were shirtless, leaving their sculpted torsos on display. They wore black pants and heavy, silver masks—the Venetian kind you'd wear to an elegant masquerade ball—after it was dipped in malice and carved out of ruin.

I slapped their hands away and climbed out on my own. The hooded figure behind me snickered.

Once all the other boats had pulled in, the hooded figures moved back out onto the water, leaving us there with no way to escape but to run or swim.

On the side of me, there were four other girls about my age or younger. I recognized two of them from different events my family attended. They were like me, well-bred, probably oblivious to the darkness of our world. But they were terrified. I wasn't. In front of us, there was a crowd of nearly fifty men, all in suits, all wearing hooded cloaks.

This was something you only saw on documentaries. This didn't happen in real life.

But it was happening. It was happening to me.

Leading the crowd were five men—one I didn't know, one I recognized as the King of Ayelswick, Kipton Donahue, Pierce Carmichael, and my father.

My father was here. Why was my father here?

Caspian's father was here.

My head spun.

"Welcome to the Ceremony of Cares," Kipton said with a grin plastered on his face, as though he were welcoming ten-year-olds to a birthday party.

"Fuck off," was on the tip of my tongue, but I held it in until I knew exactly what this was and what they planned to do.

The girl closest to me blinked in confusion. "Where are we?" Her voice was hoarse. She must have just woken up from being drugged, too.

I cut my gaze over to her. "Sshh."

She closed her eyes for a long beat, then opened them again. "I'm going to pass out."

I grabbed her elbow. "You're going to be fine. Just breathe. That's it. Slow and deep." I talked to her the way I spoke to my newer ballet students.

"Oh, look. We already have some bonding," Kipton said, then his eyes narrowed at me. "Too bad it won't save her."

I looked at my father.

His eyes darted to the ground.

Coward.

"Do you really think you can get away with this?" I shouted. Whatever *this* was.

Kipton stepped over to me, pinching my chin between his fingers. "Darling, I could slit your throat in the middle of Times Square and get away with it. Remember who you're fucking with." He let go of my chin and walked back to his place. "Normally, we make an example out of our effigies. We release them back into the earth. We set ourselves free of their burden." He spoke low and deep. "But this year we're doing things a little differently. This year is special."

Effigies. As in something that represents something else, something bad, something some cultures burn to release negative spirits.

We were effigies.

I glanced at the fires around us, and my stomach dropped.

Five of the shirtless, masked men appeared from the shadows. They were carrying something—horns. They each carried a set of horns, ridged and long with a delicate curve then a sharp point at the end. Like an antelope's horns.

Khalid stepped forward from the background, and my heart lurched to my throat. His cloak was different from the rest. His bore a lion's head as its hood.

The men strapped the horns onto our heads. One of the girls started to sob and beg.

I didn't. I knew it wouldn't do any good. I knew the only way out of these woods… was to go into them.

Other men started moving forward from the crowd, at least twenty of them, all of them wearing the lion cloak. Twenty of them. Five of us.

Kipton's wicked grin grew wide. "This year we're going to let them keep you." He glared directly at me. "This year, they'll make you their bride." *That explained the white robes.* "What happens after that is fair game." His tone lightened, and he threw up a hand. "Now, in the spirit of the hunt, we've placed weapons throughout The Grove. All you have to do is find them—if you dare to stop running long enough to look." He laughed, and the crowd laughed with him.

Sadistic bastards. Was this what they did for fun? How many times had they done it before? I didn't even want to know.

My father stepped in front of me. His eyes were filled with something—not regret, not remorse. Resentment. His gaze burned with anger. "All you had to do was stay away from him." He was talking about Caspian.

"Why? So you could sell me to the highest bidder?" Did my mother know what kind of man she married?

"I'm only going to say this once." Kipton inhaled a deep breath, as if this either exhausted or bored him. His eyes found me. The reflection of the fire danced in the black, soulless depths.

The word tore from my throat before I could stop it. "Run!"

Everything that had happened over the past years, from Lyric's death and Caspian leaving to my father's betrayal had helped prepare me for this moment. I'd learned to embrace my pain, physical and emotional. I'd learned how to be independent and cope on my own. And I'd learned that not everything was as it seemed.

There was a certain kind of beauty in that—in knowing that pain made me stronger, that death made me want to live, that all the things that were meant to break my heart made me a warrior instead.

My feet pounded the forest floor. Leaves and twigs crunched beneath my bare skin, but the sharp stings didn't bother me. My feet had seen worse. It was dark and hard to sweep the branches away before a few of them whipped my face. The horns kept getting caught in the trees and yanking my head back, so I yanked them off and kept running, keeping the horns held tightly in my hand. Right now, they were my only defense against whoever might catch me. I ran hard, faster than I ever had. Cold air burned my lungs, and my chest felt heavy. Anger and rage fueled my steps. I pictured my father's face as he stood there, allowing this to happen. I worried for Claire. Would she be next? Or was this my punishment for choosing Caspian?

Hurried footfalls sounded behind me, rustling branches and leaves. In the distance, someone screamed. I said a silent prayer for the one of us who had been caught.

I remembered all the times I'd run from Caspian, wishing it were him chasing me now instead of a real monster. I worried about him and wondered if he was okay. I had no idea what day it was or how long I'd been gone. If they'd taken me, what had they done to him? I had to survive. I had to get out of here, so I would know, so I could be the one to save him this time.

My foot dropped into a hole, twisting my ankle and sending a sharp bolt of pain splintering up my leg.

Another scream. This one was quickly muffled by someone's hand.

Dear God.

My eyes watered from the weight on my ankle. I just needed to make it to whatever was on the other side of these trees.

Out of the darkness, strong arms wrapped around me and tackled me to the forest floor. The impact stole the breath from my lungs in a hard thud. My chin slammed against the dirt, knocking my teeth together and making me bite my tongue. A flash of white light burst behind my eyelids at the pain, and I immediately recognized the metallic taste of blood. The horns tumbled to the ground as I threw my head back, trying to headbutt whoever was on top of me.

He grunted and pressed his body hard against mine. "You and your boyfriend are about to learn I'm not a man to be fucked with." He yanked a fistful of my hair, making my scalp sting, and I let out a yelp.

Khalid.

He'd caught me.

I tried to elbow his ribs, but he grabbed my arm and pinned it to my side. "I'm going to take you home with me and treat you like the filthy slut you are." He pulled my head back and forced me to look at him, his dark brown eyes narrowed slits of evil. "The world will call you a princess, but we'll both know you're just my whore."

I threw my other elbow up, aiming for any part of him I could reach. "This is the last time you will *ever* put your hands on me."

Air filled my lungs in a satisfying whoosh as the weight of his body was lifted off me. I pushed up off the ground and flipped myself over, flinching when I tried to push up on my ankle. Relief quickly turned to panic when one of the hooded figures from the boat towered over me.

Khalid swung at him and missed. "Find another whore. This one's mine."

The hooded man grabbed the antelope horns from the ground, then pushed them into Khalid's stomach, angling them upward. Blood poured from the wound and soaked his hands.

My mind was telling me to run, but my body didn't move.

I wasn't afraid of this man.

He tilted his head, inspecting his handiwork. "And the antelope slays the lion…" His voice was calm, proud… and familiar.

Caspian.

Oh God.

Caspian was here.

A long breath heaved from my tired lungs and tears began streaming down my face.

He was here.

He was okay.

Khalid jerked and twitched, and Caspian grabbed him by the shirt to keep him from falling. He leaned forward and looked Khalid in the eye. "You don't get to take what's mine. Don't ever, *ever* think you're capable of that." He grabbed Khalid by the hair and forced his head back, making his chin jut out. And then he pulled a knife from inside his robe and jabbed it upward from the bottom of Khalid's chin to the roof of his mouth. "That's for calling her a whore."

My body convulsed as I lurched forward, needing to empty the contents of my stomach but dry heaving because there was nothing there.

Caspian held his hand out to help me up. "As much as I love chasing you, Little Troublemaker, this isn't exactly what I had in mind."

I stared down at the blood that now covered us both, and my hand trembled in his.

"It will wash off." He gave me a tug. "We have to go. Someone will figure this out soon, and we need to be long gone when that happens."

I nodded. The words got trapped in my throat. I kept staring at the blood.

It wouldn't wash off. We might get rid of the evidence with soap and water, but the blood would always be there.

We ran through brush and jumped over fallen branches. My ankle was on fire, but I wouldn't slow down. I couldn't. Caspian was here, and I wasn't risking us both getting caught.

By the time we made it to a clearing, my vision was blurred with tears, and my foot hurt so badly it was numb.

Two more hooded figures pulled up in a bigger boat, this one more like a fishing vessel with a motor.

"Fuck. You're hurt," Caspian said as he lifted me onto the boat.

I shook my head. My stomach was knotted into a ball of emotions. "We can't leave them." My breath was shallow as it fought to escape my lungs.

There were three more girls in there, three lives just as important as mine, three other people worth saving.

He pulled me onto his lap. "We can't go back."

I struggled to break free. "We *have* to go back." My focus turned to the guy at the wheel as the engine revved. "Stop! We can't leave them." Tears streamed down my face because I knew what waited for those girls, what would've been waiting for me.

Caspian nodded toward my foot. My ankle was bruised and swollen from the angry bone. He ran a finger over it, and I hissed.

"There's no way you can outrun them if they catch us, and I'm not leaving you on this fucking boat alone." He jabbed a finger toward the woods that were getting farther and farther away. "Going back in there is glorified suicide." He glanced at the other two hooded figures in the boat. "For all of us." His eyes found mine again. There was the same firm determination in them I'd seen the night he'd told the world I was going to be his bride. "I'd risk a hundred lives—including my own—to save yours. But this, going back there, would all be for nothing because they would find you, Tatum. They would take you. And they would make sure I wasn't around to save you next time."

No. I couldn't lose him.

But I couldn't bear the thought of those other girls being caught.

"They'll catch them." My voice trembled.

Caspian held my gaze as he took my face in his hands. "They will." His eyes softened. "And we'll do everything we can to find them and set them free."

Was that even a possibility? Did he have that much power?

How long would it take? What would those women have to go through until they were found?

I closed my eyes and nodded because I knew he was right. And I believed him when he said he would try to help them. "Okay." It wasn't like he'd given me a choice anyway, unless I wanted to jump into the water and swim back to shore.

Once we were a good distance away from the forest, the other two figures tugged their hoods down.

My head snapped up. "Lincoln?" I looked between him and Caspian. "You two were in this together?"

He tipped his head back and smiled. "Somebody had to make sure he didn't fuck it up."

Chandler took his focus off driving the boat long enough to glance back at me. "Yeah. That's what I'm here for." He smirked.

"How did you know where to find me? How did you—"

Caspian grinned and brushed a hair away from my forehead. "We'll talk about that later. Right now, I'm getting us the fuck out of here. I have it all set up. There's a plane waiting on the runway. We're going to be okay." He pulled his hood off and cradled me against his chest. "There was no other way."

He was talking about Khalid.

I looked up at him, at his chiseled jaw and plump lips that were perfect for kissing or whispering vulgar things in my ear. Brown eyes with just the right hint of amber, eyes that held dark promises and gave nothing away unless he wanted them to. And I saw him—*really* saw him. He was pleasure and pain. Cruelty and tenderness. Peace and chaos. Darkness and light.

He was a reflection of me.

"I know."

"Are you afraid of me now?" There was a pain in his voice that wrapped around and pierced my heart like thorns on a vine.

"No." The blood, the malice, the pain, none of it mattered. All I knew was wherever he was, I wanted to be there too. If he needed to be fire, I would be rain. If he needed a sword, I would be his shield. There was no force on earth stronger than what we had together. An entire ocean couldn't even keep us apart. From the moment he'd first kissed me, my soul was home. "I'm in love with you."

If I was honest, I'd been in love with him since I was six years old.

Exhaustion and emotions caught up with me, and I let myself melt in his arms. He pressed his lips against my forehead and whispered, "I'm in love with you too. I always have been."

That was the last thing I remembered before waking up to him carrying me onto a private plane.

KIPTON

Kipton Donahue

Despite Khalid's monumental fuck up—the bastard went and got himself killed—the ceremony at The Grove was a success. We forged deals and made alliances over good bourbon and even better blow jobs that would never have been made in conference rooms or office buildings. That was the way it had always been done. Since the dawn of enlightenment, mankind needed a group of leaders to guide them, steer them, keep them in line. The way a parent would a toddler. We kept them from eating too much, spending too much, having too much. The world required balance, and we gave it to them.

People, as a society, were lazy. If one person said the sky was blue and another said it was gray, humanity spent more time arguing over who was right than walking outside to find out the truth for themselves. Truth was what we told them. Truth was *our* job, not theirs.

That was what the Obsidian Brotherhood was about.

There was an order to things, and we did what we had to do to keep it that way, no matter the sacrifice.

I buttoned the top button of my coat, then tugged on my sleeve, adjusting my cuff links.

Grace, our housekeeper, met me in the kitchen and handed me a cup of coffee—strong and black, just the way I liked it. I gave her a friendly swat on her plump, round ass when she walked away—just the way *she* liked it.

I'd had a small TV installed underneath one of the cabinets so that I could always start my day with the morning news. I pressed the remote and the screen came to life.

I stood in front of the kitchen island and took a sip of my coffee without sitting down. Early morning meetings didn't allow time for breakfast, and this morning's meeting was top priority. The hot liquid warmed my throat.

Joanna, my favorite morning news anchor, faced the screen with a solemn expression on her gorgeous face. Pity. She was so pretty when she smiled.

"A search-and-rescue operation concluded this morning with tragic results after the crash of a Gulfstream G100 Saturday night. According to reports, the private plane was on its way to Barbados when it suffered engine failure and went down about sixty miles from the point of takeoff. Listed among the passengers was Caspian Donahue, heir to the famous Donahue oil dynasty, and Tatum Huntington, youngest daughter of Senator Malcolm Huntington. Also listed among the passengers was Prince Khalid Falih of Saudi Arabia. Falih was rumored to be a close family friend. Three crewmembers have also been reported as not surviving the crash. A private memorial will be held at Green-Wood Cemetery on Thursday."

I cleared my throat and clicked off the TV, leaving the rest of my coffee on the counter, untouched.

This was who we were. This was who I had to be.

I tried to teach that to Caspian, but he was too damn stubborn. He should have never gone after her. I knew he would, though. He let his feelings get in the way, and he played right into my trap. He was reckless. Untrainable. He didn't deserve the privileges that had been bestowed upon him.

I did.

The petite blonde smiled at me when I walked into the office. Her appraising look ended with one of approval. I liked her smile. She had a fuckable mouth. If she knew I was about to walk out of here three billion dollars richer, she would fall to her knees without me even asking.

"Kipton Donahue for Judge Flannery."

Moments later, the judge walked out of his office to greet me. "Mr. Donahue. Please accept my sincere condolences. Such a tragedy."

I'd been playing the role of grieving father for three days. At this point, I could have won an Oscar.

I closed my eyes and gave a brief nod, as if in remembrance, then inhaled a deep, calming breath before opening them again. "Thank you." I kept my voice low.

He clapped a hand on my shoulder. "Let's go to my office." He glanced at the blonde. "Hold my calls."

She nodded, then focused her attention back on me as we walked away. I would definitely have her on her knees later.

"Please, have a seat," the judge said, gesturing to one of the brown leather chairs in front of his desk.

"I know this may seem out of place, but timing is sensitive, you understand." I unfastened my coat buttons and made myself comfortable.

Judge Flannery settled into his chair and straightened his tie. "Of course."

"The paperwork is in order, then? For the trust?"

With Caspian dead and no other heirs, the trust automatically transferred to me.

He swallowed hard, then cleared his throat. "I'm afraid the assets have already been distributed."

Until now, patience had been my best friend. I'd waited twelve years for this moment. I woke up every morning anticipating the power I would hold in my hands. I sacrificed my own blood for it. Patience disappeared in a cloud of smoke with his words.

Sweat broke out on my back and my palms. I slammed my fist against the wooden desk in front of me. "That's impossible." I'd made sure of it. I'd killed for it.

The office door opened, and an armed police officer flanked each side. An obvious hint that this discussion was not up for debate. They weren't stupid enough to arrest me. I'd be out within the hour and neither one of them would ever work again.

"Who? When?" I asked, already knowing at least one of the answers. It didn't matter, though. I had the resources to find where he'd hidden it from me.

The judge smirked, and pride smeared across his old, wrinkly face. *Lying, backstabbing, bastard.* He was supposed to be working with me. "Your son. The day after his twenty-fifth birthday."

TWENTY-EIGHT

CASPIAN

Two months earlier...

Chandler was already at Club Stiletto when I walked in. He sat at our usual table, a circular booth in the back corner. The bar was empty, but most of the tables around the main stage were occupied.

The hostess pulled the curtain around our booth closed, then licked her lips. "Violet will be your entertainment tonight."

Soft neon lights glowed against the walls around us. The heavy, black curtain separated us from the rest of the club. A Rhianna song played on the sound system. I wasn't interested in the tall brunette who wrapped her legs around the silver pole in the middle of our table. Neither was Chandler. We came here for the privacy.

I slid onto the leather seat and rolled my head from side to side, cracking my neck.

"The fuck happened to you?" he asked, eyeing the blood on my hand from where Tatum bit me.

"You don't even want to know." I grabbed the tabletop tablet and tapped the screen to order myself a drink. Privacy was priority here. Waitresses only came to the table when summoned by this nifty electronic device with a seven-inch screen and a menu. You could play games on it too, like trivia or some shit, but who wanted to play a computer game when someone was waving their pussy in your face? Not that I gave a shit about anyone's cunt but Tatum's.

"No wonder it only lasted four minutes." He laughed, then took a pull of his beer.

I'd just left Tatum's dance studio after seeing her for the first time since the night I stole all her firsts. I wanted to steal more. Her breath. Her fight. Her screams. I wanted it all to belong to me. I wanted to make sure every time she clenched her thighs together because her sweet little cunt ached, she thought of me. She would need me, whether she wanted to or not.

The brunette dropped her head, letting her long hair swing across the tabletop.

I focused on Chandler. "I need your resources."

He leaned back in the booth, splaying his arms out on both sides. His bright eyes danced with mischief against his olive skin. Chandler was adopted by the Carmichael family as an infant. His birth mother was a beautiful blonde cheerleader, and his dad was a dark-skinned quarterback. As a result, Chandler looked like someone had taken a day at the beach, blended it with smooth silk and poured it over chiseled stone. Also, as a result, he would never fully inherit the Carmichael fortune, even though Pierce had given Chandler his last name. Which was why he started making his own way in the world. Chandler did business with people who wouldn't even do business with my father.

"If you need pussy until Tatum gives it up, there's one right here." He pointed his beer bottle toward the girl on the table.

The server showed up with my drink, and I wished I had ordered two.

"Fuck you." I took a sip and let the whiskey coat my throat. "A month from now, I'm going to be worth a lot of money."

"And you need my help spending it?"

I shook my head and chuckled. "I need your help staying alive. I'm pretty sure my dad is willing to kill me for it."

"Jesus. How much money are we talking?"

"Three billion dollars."

He choked on his beer.

The girl on the table stumbled on her four-inch heels.

I took another drink of my whiskey.

The song changed to something faster, and thankfully, louder.

"So, what do you think he's going to do? Stage a car accident?"

I shrugged. "Possibly." That was how he'd handled Huntington's last lobbyist.

"All right. Then we'll get you a car. It'll need to look exactly like yours though. If you start driving something different, it will tip him off that you know. You'll leave your car parked and use the clone to go wherever you need to go. I'll keep it at my office, so he won't have access to it. Text me when you need it, and I'll send someone to pick you up." He finished his beer, then set the bottle on the table. "This is good. We can do this. What next?" He grabbed the tablet and ordered another beer.

"I can't sleep at home. I'll have to get my own place."

Fake drug overdoses were a very real thing in my father's world. Wanna kill someone? Fake an overdose. Maybe that was fucked up, but the fact that we were even sitting here having this conversation was fucked up. Money was power, and power was everything. There was no way I was falling asleep under the same roof with Kipton Donahue once I turned twenty-five.

"You can stay with me until then. What about fires or robberies?"

"He fucked up and gave me an office right across from his. I'll just make sure I'm only at work when he's there." I rubbed my thumb across Tatum's teeth marks on my hand. Fuck, I'd missed her. "I doubt he'll burn down his own house or put my mom in danger. He does halfway give a shit about her." Not enough to be faithful to her, but enough to keep her alive.

The dancer bent over in front of us and ran her hands up her calves then between her thighs. Chandler gave her ass a smack, then turned back to our conversation.

"What else would he do?" he asked. "What are we forgetting?"

"Plane crash."

"You planning on going anywhere soon?"

I had one place in mind, a small island off the coast of Barbados, but I needed to make sure I got the money first because chances were once I was there, I wasn't coming back. I also needed to earn Tatum's trust. I wasn't leaving without her. Once all that was in place, Chandler could help me with the rest—fake passports and whatever else we would need.

"Nah, but that doesn't mean he won't send me somewhere if he wants to make it happen. Especially if I dodge every other bullet." I smirked. "So to speak."

"So, we set you up with a lookalike. The lookalike gets on your plane while you get on a different one at a completely different airport."

"Then the lookalike dies."

"That's the nature of the game, bro." He took his beer from the server when she walked in. "Trust me. He won't be an innocent player. I know some pretty fucked up people."

It was good to know we were only killing fucked-up people now. Christ.

"So, what? We just have this dude on stand-by? *Hey, wanna fly to Paris for the weekend?*"

He took a drink. "Why not? These guys don't exactly work nine-to-fives or have families to take care of."

This motherfucker may have been more heartless than I was.

"So, it's set, then." I knocked back the rest of my drink.

Chandler smiled like a kid on Christmas. "It's set."

And just like that, it was done. We had a plan in place to keep me alive until I could get Tatum and me the fuck out of here. All I had to do now was meet with Jonathon Bradshaw and establish a successor trustee—some judge his father grew up with—to handle my trust in the case of any "accidents." Because while I had the means to make sure *I* stayed alive, I had a feeling there wasn't much I could do for Bradshaw.

TWENTY-NINE

CASPIAN

I had always said Tatum Huntington was worth saving… even if it killed us both.

I stared at her now as she slept, letting my gaze follow the curve of her body, the dip in her waist and the swell of her breasts, and I knew I would risk it all over again. For her.

It was easy to get inside The Grove. Chandler made one phone call to a high-ranking military guy he'd sold some illegal weapons to, and the plan was set in motion. The minute they'd carried Tatum to the boat I'd hijacked, my stomach sank. She'd looked so pale, so lifeless. All of the fire that burned inside of her every time she was with me had dulled to flickering embers. It took all my strength not to just fucking kill them all, then take her home right then and there. But we had a plan, and none of it would work if I didn't follow it to the very last detail. The fact that Khalid got in the way was a bonus—for me. I'd been wanting to gut him like a fish since I was eighteen years old.

I didn't ask Chandler about the people who took our place on the plane, and he didn't offer. That was a conversation better left unspoken.

I even thanked Lincoln for playing his part, which mostly included beating the shit out of the actual hooded boat guardians, so we could take their place. I think the sadistic fuck even enjoyed it.

Tatum and I were on a boat now, just off the coast near her Hampton house. I had one more thing to take care of before we left for the island, and I wanted to give her time to say goodbye to the life she'd built here. She'd crept into the house during the night and grabbed some of her things, although not enough to bring attention to the fact that she'd been there.

She looked so peaceful while she slept. Everything quieted inside me when I was with her like this—everything except *that* monster, the one that wanted to make her scream.

I held the dildo in my hand, the one she didn't know I watched her grab from her house, the one I'd had made from a mold of my own cock, the one I'd had a second dick made to match. She stirred when I trailed the head of one of them down the front of her body, between her breasts and over her stomach. I tugged the covers down and dragged it across her clit. She lifted her hips off the bed, urging me to press harder. Her body writhed as her eyes fluttered open. She let out a soft moan and licked her lips.

The monster roared. I wanted to be greedy. I wanted to taste her too.

Need—raw and primal—ripped its way out of me. I moved up and pulled her lip between my teeth, biting down until she cried out. Her hands grabbed my hair, trying to pull my head back. My tongue swept over her lip, tasting her blood where I'd just bitten her.

I slid the dildo up the center of her pussy, between the smooth lips. She was so fucking wet already.

Her body rolled and bucked against me.

She wanted to be fucked just as badly as I needed to fuck her.

I grabbed her wrists and brought her hand to the rubber cock. "You're going to fuck yourself with this while I fuck your sweet mouth." I pushed the head inside to make my point.

Her hand replaced mine, and I knew the moment she slid it in deeper because her lips parted in a gasp. She sat up, propping herself up against the headboard.

I grabbed the second dildo from beside the bed. "I'm going to fill all three of your tight little holes."

She hummed her approval, arching her back in a bow. Fuck, she was dirty. Filthy. And I was hypnotized, knowing I'd made her that way. I'd been prepping her for this moment for weeks—testing her limits with my fingers and butt plugs. And she fucking took it. She craved it.

My lips curved in a smile. "You like that, don't you? You want me everywhere."

She didn't answer.

I wasn't asking.

I dropped the rubber dick on the bed, then got up on my knees and twisted her hair around one hand while stroking my dick with the other. I leaned forward, tracing the seam of her lips, smearing her blood over the head of my cock.

She licked my tip, and my thighs clenched. Fuck.

Her mouth opened, letting me ease inside. She flattened her tongue, and I gripped her hair tighter.

"Take it all," I said as I held her head still and pushed all the way to the back of her throat, slow at first, easy strokes as her mouth stretched wide and her cheeks hollowed.

Her hips rocked below me, restless and needy. Her tongue curled under my dick, and I tipped my head back. I couldn't think straight, couldn't see straight. My body was a livewire of tension and adrenaline.

My.

God.

I moved faster, thrust harder, holding nothing back. Tears sprang from her eyes and trailed down her cheeks. Saliva dripped down her chin. I hit the back of her throat with a forceful thrust, making her gag. *Relax or choke, sweetheart. I'm not stopping.*

God, she was fucking beautiful like this.

I tilted her head back, and she opened up for me, taking everything I had to give. Her hand worked her pussy while I fucked her face. She moaned on my cock, and I had to force myself not to come.

Her free hand clawed at my thigh, marking me the way I'd marked her so many times.

I didn't care about vengeance or trusts or faraway islands. I just wanted this. Her moans. Her tears. Her blood on my dick from where I'd broken the skin on her lip. Power didn't matter, because I had mine. Right here. Right now. I was a king, and her body was my kingdom.

And I claimed it. I marked it. I owned it. My stomach tightened, and my muscles clenched. Fuck. I was about to come.

"Open your eyes, Little Troublemaker," I said as I pulled out of her mouth.

Her eyes flitted open as she licked her lips, her gaze hot and dark on mine.

"Turn over."

She did as I said, climbing on all fours while I positioned myself behind her. Her pussy was swollen from the dildo and glistening with her juices. She was so open like this, so exposed. I leaned in and lapped my tongue over her slit, drawing a tremor from her perfect fucking body.

Then I brought my face between her thighs, stopping to admire the view as I pushed the fake dick—*my* dick—back inside her, of how her pussy stretched around it, of the way it glistened with her slickness every time I eased it out then slid it back in. *This is what it looks like when I fuck her.*

My hand stilled as I stared in awe.

"Don't you dare fucking stop," she growled. *That's my fucking girl.* She rocked her hips back, a whimper escaping her lips as I licked and sucked on her clit while I fucked her with the dick until her body quivered, and she finally came apart.

"Take this." I handed her the dildo that was just inside her. "Now, suck. Lick the taste of your sweet pussy off while I fuck you from behind."

Her full lips wrapped around the rubber cock, licking the head the way she'd licked mine minutes ago. *That's right, baby. See how sweet you taste.* Fuck. I wanted that mouth on me. I wanted it to be *my* mouth tasting her. Jesus Christ, I was jealous of a goddamn dildo. The fuck was wrong with me?

I slid inside her tight cunt, and my dick swelled as though being inside her was the very essence of life. As amazing as her mouth was, nothing, *nothing*, compared to this. Always so wet. Fuck. I leaned forward, grabbing a handful of her hair and shoving her mouth down the rubber dick while my teeth sank into the delicate skin on her shoulder.

I brought my lips to her ear. "You have one more hole that needs to be filled, Little Troublemaker. One more place that belongs to me."

Her head stilled beneath my hand, bringing a slow grin to my lips.

"Relax. I'll go slow." I drove my point home by easing my thrusts. "Now, suck." I pushed her head back down on the cock and started grinding into her at full force again. And again. And again. Until the line between sanity and madness was blurred. The monster was out, ready to fuck, ready to destroy, ready to own. Sweat trickled down my back and dripped off the ends of my hair. Her sweet fucking moans filled the air as her head bobbed on the dildo. I grabbed the second cock off the bed because I was about to come un-fucking-done. Her hands clenched in the sheets beside her head. Her perfect tits bounced and swayed as I pounded into her tiny body.

Fuck.

My lungs burned. My chest ached. Sheer fucking pleasure shot through me in fiery jolts, tightening my nuts and stealing my breath. I pulled my dick out just in time to release my load all over her back, over her ass, down her crack, watching with clenched teeth as thick milky white coated her virgin ass. Fuck yeah. Right where I want it.

My breath was ragged, and my legs were weak, but I took the other dildo, spreading my cum over her pleated entrance with the tip. Her ass clenched, so I smacked it, grabbing a handful of flesh.

"I'm not going to hurt you." I leaned in, pressing my lips to her temple. "I need you to trust me." I ran the dick over her back then up and down her ass crack, coating it in cum, feeling the exact moment her body relaxed. "See?" I nipped her earlobe as I brought one hand around to rub slow circles on her clit. "Let me make you feel good." I eased the tip of the rubber cock inside, just the tip, just barely, using my cum as lube. Tatum tensed for a second but quickly relaxed as I pushed it in a little deeper. Then deeper. I got almost halfway before stopping. She stayed like that for a moment, drinking it in, adjusting to the pressure. And then she rocked her hips backward. Fuck yeah. My greedy little troublemaker liked that.

"Fuck. Turn over." I grabbed her hips and flipped her onto her back. "I need to be inside you." Yeah, I was jealous of my own fucking dick. Sue me.

"Both of you?" Her voice was scratchy, raw from me shoving the cock down her throat.

"Both of me." I hooked her leg in the crook of my arm, spreading her wide, then slid back inside her. Jesus. The fullness of the dildo in her ass put pressure on my cock. Holy. Fucking. Shit. Her walls tightened around me, and the monster broke free. I slammed into her, the fake dick forgotten but still inside her, inching deeper and deeper with every thrust of my hips. It was feral. Brutal. But I couldn't stop it if I tried.

A single tear spilled from her eyes, leaving a trail of pain mixed with pleasure down her temple and onto the pillow. I thought I was going to break her. For a moment, I thought the monster had won.

And then she reached over, grabbed the second dildo, and brought it to her mouth.

Motherfuck.

My free hand inched up her body, stopping at her throat. "Your body was made for me." I tightened my grip and pulled her head forward. "Look." I slowed my thrusts. "See how I fill you, how *only* I can fill you?" I leaned forward and licked the dildo she had in her mouth, letting my lips mold with hers, my tongue tangle with hers. That was *my* mouth. It belonged on *me*. I slid the cock out of her ass and pulled the one away from our mouths. Now it was just me and her. Real against real. "Come for me, Little Troublemaker. Scream my name. Tell the world who you belong to."

"What are we doing here?" Tatum asked when I pulled into the circular driveway of my father's house. "I thought we were going to the airport."

Soon. We would be out of here soon.

I rubbed a hand over her hair. "Lock the doors, and don't get out. No matter what." I kissed her forehead. "I'll be right back."

The house was empty when I walked inside. Everything looked exactly the same, yet so completely unrecognizable. This wasn't home, not anymore. Chandler's guy had hacked into the security system to disable the cameras. I worried I might need him to unlock the door, but Dad hadn't even changed the code on the front door keypad. Then again, why would he? I was supposed to be dead.

I walked across the foyer and down the hallway to his study. The door was open, and he stood in front of his window with a glass of scotch in his hand, the way he always did, the way I knew he would be. I'd made sure to wait until my mother and the staff were gone.

"Hello, Dad."

He spun around at the sound of my voice. His face paled, and the glass in his hand went crashing to the floor, leaving a puddle of amber and ice at his feet. He held a hand on the bar cabinet beside him to keep from collapsing onto the pile of broken glass.

"I can see you're surprised." I took a few steps into the room.

"How did you—" He brought a hand to his chest. "You're okay. You survived. They said there weren't any survivors."

That wasn't relief. It was fear.

I walked over to his desk and pulled out his chair. "Here. You should have a seat. You don't look well." I opened the drawer and pulled out a pen and some paper with his letterhead.

When he didn't sit down, I walked over to him and dragged him to the chair.

I slid a pair of leather gloves into my hands. "You have two options." I pulled out my cell phone and set it on the desk next to the paper. "We can call the police and have a little chat." I looked up and to the side as though deep in thought. "What's the sentence for attempted murder?" I snapped my fingers and looked back at him. "Oh, and let's not forget about Khalid. I bet those prisons in the Middle East are a bitch." My dad set himself up for that one the minute he'd told the authorities Khalid was on that plane. I grabbed the gun from my waistband and sat on the edge of his desk. "Or we can end this whole fucking mess right now."

He huffed a laugh at the sight of the gun. "You won't use that."

I grinned. "You're right. I won't." I handed him the pen. "You will." I smirked. "Or at least everyone will think you did. It's all about the illusion, right."

Even if the cops suspected foul play, they couldn't pin a murder on a dead guy, and I was dead long before my father would be.

He tossed the pen onto the desk. It rolled across the wood, stopped by a paperweight.

"See, you were so distraught over losing your only son. The pain was unbearable." I picked up the pen and handed it back to him. "Write."

Dad jotted down the first three lines of his "suicide" note. "You took the money." His voice shook when he spoke. Whether it was anger or fear, I didn't know. Didn't care.

"It was my money to take."

"It will ruin you, you know."

"No, Dad." I poised my finger on the trigger. "It ruined you. *You* ruined me." And then I pressed the metal to his temple and fired.

After stopping by my room to change clothes, I tossed mine in a plastic bag and went to my parents' room. I looked at the framed family photo on the nightstand and asked my mother's image for forgiveness.

Then I placed a book on her bed—Greek Mythology, bookmarked on page 144, the story of Alethiea, daughter of Zeus, goddess of truth. Between the pages, I left her a note. It simply read: *Veritas Nunquam Perit: The truth never perishes.*

I grabbed my bag and went back to the landscaping truck we'd bought on eBay, flipping the bird to my father's corpse as I sped out of the driveway.

EPILOGUE

Tatum

Six months later…

People said that grief takes time, that one day, the hurt would heal and that dull ache you feel every time your heart beats would fade away.

Five years after her death, I still felt Lyric in my heart. But now there was something else there, too. *Love.*

The love I had for Caspian was extraordinary. It was unconventional and at times it felt forbidden, like we were breaking the rules because no one should be this happy. But it was eternal. I had given him my soul, and he had given me his. We truly were soulmates. And tomorrow, I would become his wife.

I held my sandals in one hand, feeling the sand between my toes as I walked along the beach. The breeze blew in off the sparkling blue water. The sun glinted off the diamond on my left hand as I brought it up to hold my floppy hat in place. My hair whipped across my face. I turned and smiled as I looked up at the beach house a few hundred feet away.

I couldn't see through the window tint, but I knew he was watching.

He was always watching.

Every day, I walked the shore while Caspian sat in his office upstairs, watching me through the windows. With the help of one of Chandler's friends, he'd started an untraceable, anonymous online group focused on spreading what he called *truth*. They called themselves "O", and their mission was taking down people like our fathers and Khalid, ripping the power from their hands, so they could no longer use it to hurt people. My brother even joined their cause.

The experience at The Grove had brought us all together. It gave them purpose. It gave me strength. It gave us all hope. Caspian reached out to Prince Liam of Ayelswick, and Chandler contacted some of his powerful friends, and together they formed their own alliances—a new Obsidian Brotherhood, one that would overpower the old one.

I left Caspian to his secrets and opened a dance studio in the village. He saw the world for what it was. I chose to see it for what it could be. I knew darkness lurked beneath the surface. I'd seen it. But I still chose beauty over cruelty, humanity over depravity. Maybe Caspian and his brotherhood could weed out all the evil. Maybe in the end, the good guys would win. Well, if they were to be called *good guys*. He was right when he told me he wasn't a prince. He wasn't a villain either. He was the dragon. Maybe the fairy tales got it wrong. Maybe the dragon never intended to hurt the princess. Maybe he was there to keep her safe.

I washed my feet off at the back door, then went inside. Our home was the perfect blend of both our personalities. We had lots of windows—because Caspian had a thing for fucking out in the open—and shiplap walls with white kitchen cabinets. His grand piano was in the living room, and my oversized tub was in our bathroom.

My wedding dress hung in the guest bedroom closet, away from Caspian's prying eyes. I had to threaten him with no sex if he'd dared to peek. I paused to look at it for the hundredth time.

The design was simple—a semi-sheer, beaded lace bodice with spaghetti straps and a chiffon bottom with a side-slit. It was perfect.

The bedroom door creaked open, a gentle push meant to be quiet.

"You really couldn't wait *one* more day?" I rolled my eyes and spun around.

The moment I turned to face him, my heart thrashed wildly against my chest. The air left my lungs, and the floor felt as though it might swallow me whole. I tried to breathe, but it just got caught in my throat. The sound of blood rushing through my veins pounded in my ears. An ice-cold tremor raced down my spine.

No.

This wasn't happening.

There was no way.

"You didn't think I was going to let my best friend get married without me?" Lyric's smile was brighter than the sunlight beaming through the window.

I sank to my knees because my legs could no longer hold me.

Tears streamed down my face.

With every breath I took, it felt as though I might pass out.

She hurried across the room and knelt beside me. Her slender arms wrapped around me, and she pulled my head to her chest.

A sob tore from my throat when I looked up at her. Her blonde hair was now a sleek, jet black, and her pale complexion was a golden bronze.

"How?" I asked her, my voice cracking on the word.

A thousand different questions roared in my mind, but I couldn't make sense of any of them with everything rushing to my head—my blood, my pulse, all of it. I would think she wasn't real if I hadn't heard her heartbeat when she'd pull me to her chest.

She sniffled and let out a short laugh. "Caspian."

My breath hitched. "Caspian?"

All the times I'd asked him about her, the pain he watched me go through, the grief... I fought to breathe. I fought so hard my body shook.

She held me close, rocking back and forth the way a mother would console a child.

This wasn't real. This couldn't be real.

He lied to me.

She was alive.

He knew.

She was alive.

She grabbed my face and cradled it in her hands. "I know what you're thinking, and he's not the bad guy here. We have all night to talk about that." She swiped her hand under my eyes. "Right now, I just want to see this dress on that gorgeous fucking body. Seriously, T." Her gaze fell to my boobs. "What the fuck?"

I laughed through my tears because she was back. My best friend was alive. It didn't matter how. All that mattered was having her here, holding her, knowing she was okay.

After Lyric told me everything that she'd been through, I confronted Caspian. I knew it was bad luck to see the bride, blah, blah, blah. But I needed to talk to him. I needed to know. I thought I'd seen it all, thought I'd seen the worst of the darkness, but what Lyric had experienced was much, much worse. She was dragged into the darkness. She told me that with Chandler's help, Caspian had saved her, that thanks to them it wasn't so bad anymore.

He was lying in bed with the covers draped over his lower half and one leg kicked out. The moonlight danced over his flawless face. It was hard to concentrate around him.

I sat down on the bed. "Why?"

"Why did I save her? Or why didn't I tell you about it?" He clasped his fingers behind his head and stared up at the ceiling.

"Why didn't you trust me?"

His gaze shot to mine. "It wasn't about trusting you, Little Troublemaker. It was about trusting *them*. That shit you saw at The Grove was only the beginning. Do you have any idea what they're capable of? What they do to women like you? To women like Lyric?" He moved his hand to my knee, and my body immediately reacted to his touch—a spark igniting in my core. "If I'd told you she was alive, you would have moved heaven and earth to see her, and I would've helped you because as powerful as I think I am, I am powerless when it comes to you." He inched his hand up my thigh, and a moan worked its way up my throat, threatening to break free. "The minute they found out that you knew what they'd done, they would've taken you too. And I might not have had time to save you back then. The only reason I knew to save Lyric was because your brother fucked up and came to my house accusing me of fucking her." His voice lowered to a deep rasp. "You think what I did to Khalid was ruthless? I would've burned the whole fucking world down, leaving a trail of blood and matches as I went, if they'd taken you." He slipped his hand through the leg of my pajama shorts, and his thumb found my clit through my panties. I parted my legs, unable to help myself, not even wanting to. I rolled my head back and bit my lip. Oh. My. God. "I had to wait until I had the means to keep you safe, until I knew there was no way they could get to you. If that meant hurting you to protect you, then that was a sacrifice I was willing to make."

I knew how important this all was to Caspian. He'd already told me the reason he'd gone to Europe was because if he'd stayed, he would have gone to jail and lost his trust money. Without his trust, there would have been no future. There would have been no *us*. I would be a princess slave to a cruel man, and Caspian would be a slave to his father. While I wished he'd just told me everything from the beginning, I understood why he didn't. I was a sixteen-year-old girl still learning the ways of a world he'd been thrust into when he was just a child.

"No more secrets," I said.

He ran his tongue over his bottom lip. "No more secrets." He moved the fabric to the side and shoved two fingers in my pussy, still circling my clit with his thumb. I grabbed his forearm and rode his hand, fucking his fingers, devouring every ounce of pleasure he gave until I went over the edge.

The air was crisp and cool, and the sun was bright, like the sky was giving us its blessing. Caspian stood beneath a wooden pergola on the beach. White sheer curtains hung from the corner rafters and flowed in the breeze. Tall metal lanterns framed the middle aisle. It was small and intimate. Only our closest friends and Lincoln were there. Chandler was the best man, and Lyric was my maid of honor. Until she showed up, that role belonged to Lincoln. I was pretty sure he was as happy as I was to see her.

"You ready for this?" Lyric asked as the music started. She handed me a bouquet of flowers just like the ones Caspian had left onstage the night of the ballet.

A calm washed over me, even though my heart was hammering in my chest. I took a deep breath. "I've been ready since I was six years old."

She blinked back tears. "You know I can't stay…"

I swallowed the lump in my throat. "I know."

It was dangerous for her to have been here for as long as she had. If she got caught…

I shook away the thought and forced a smile. I'd just gotten her back, and I was losing her again. But at least now I knew she was okay.

I took her hand in mine. "I'm just glad you're here now."

The music grew louder, and she squeezed my hand. "It's time."

I heaved a breath. "It's time."

Lyric and I walked down the aisle, hand in hand, stopping in front of the minister. It made perfect sense for the person I loved the longest to give me away to the person I loved the most. I handed her the bouquet and stepped in front of Caspian.

As soon as I placed my hand in his, he pulled me against him and crushed his mouth to mine. He kissed me with a fierce possessiveness that made me burn with feral need. Tightness fisted at my belly, and I clenched my thighs together as I tangled my hands in his hair.

He pulled away with a growl. "I don't need him," he nodded his head toward the minister, "to tell me you're mine." He licked my bottom lip. "You've always been mine."

I stroked his cheek with the front of my finger and smiled. "Can you behave? Just for five minutes?"

He grabbed a handful of my ass and squeezed, then he looked at the minister. "You have five minutes."

The tall, slender minister swallowed hard, then cleared his throat and began the ceremony. The words were nothing more than background noise. All I cared about was the man in front of me, his eyes, that smile, the way he was looking at me right now.

The minister stopped talking, and Caspian tilted his head toward me.

He swiped the pad of his thumb over his bottom lip. "Wanna know why I call you my little troublemaker?"

I swallowed. The heat was blazing now, coursing through my veins. My heart was pounding and full, so full of love for this man.

"From the first time I saw you, my heart knew it was in trouble. It was like Fate knew our souls were destined to wreck the world together. You're the only one who's ever challenged me and gotten away with it. You embrace the shit out of my insanity. You let me chase you into the darkness, then you sit with me there. You are the heart of my heart, the soul of my soul. And I will spend every second of forever—and then some—making sure you know exactly how fiercely I love you."

I didn't think I'd ever seen him so perfect, so beautiful.

I brought my hand to his face because the need to touch him was unbearable. "You keep me safe. I love you in ways that I never even knew were possible. You make me strong. You say I challenge you, but you're the one who challenges me. Those times when you think you're hardest to love, that's when I love you the most. There was never a moment I haven't loved you. It was always you. It will always only be you."

Caspian pressed his lips against my forehead, then lifted his head and turned to Chandler.

Chandler handed him a small, sharp blade.

Caspian took my hand in his and held my gaze. His eyes softened and glimmered with pride. "You ready?"

I opened my palm, steeling myself for the pain but ready for the rush. "Ready."

He slid the blade across my skin, and a sharp slicing pain shot through my hand, followed by a trail of blood. The edges of reality blurred for a split second before coming back into focus. He handed me the blade, and I did the same to him. We held our palms together, squeezing tightly, and Caspian licked his lips. I knew he was counting down by the fire that burned in his eyes.

Chandler handed him a white scarf, which he wrapped around our hands, binding them together, bonding *us* for eternity.

"Repeat these words: *Et sanguis sanguinem meum*," he said, and his eyes grew even darker.

"*Et sanguis sanguinem meum.*"

"Blood of my blood."

"Blood of my blood," I repeated.

Calmness and peace washed over me. Hunger and fire burned within me. But that was how it had always been with Caspian. I knew deep in my soul that right here was where I was meant to be my whole life.

His lips curved into a slow, wicked grin, and his eyes narrowed. He slowly unraveled the scarf from our hands, counting as he went.

"Five… Four…"

I took a deep breath. The minister, Lyric, Lincoln… everyone else was long forgotten. There was only him and me and the chase I knew was only seconds away. The chase that had been brewing since he'd touched me last night in our bed. The chase he'd been waiting for since I'd put my hand in his.

"Three… Two…"

My heart beat like a drum.

He dropped the scarf on the ground and raised his eyes to mine.

"Run."

BONUS EPILOGUE

Mischief Night…

Lyric

Malum Noctis, otherwise known as Mischief Night. It was the one night when rules were irrelevant, and consequences didn't exist.

The low timbre of the bass gave the underground room a heartbeat. It was this heartbeat that urged me on. Through the crowd, I watched Caspian Donahue carry Tatum out of this unholy place. She didn't belong here. I didn't either.

Blue lights created neon shadows on everyone's faces. Beneath the shadows were flashes of smiles and glints of eyes full of mischief. Strong, thick hands caressed my body, pulling me closer from all sides.

The bass called to me.

Da pacerne domine…

Thump thumpthump

In diebus nostris…

Thump thumpthump

There was an ominous vibration in the air, as if the walls of this tomb were issuing a warning. All around me, people renounced the spirit of morality and danced on the edge of depravity. White powder coated tan skin. Hands inched inside short skirts. Heads bobbed between parted thighs.

Harry Potter got it wrong.

This was the real Chamber of Secrets.

Someone grabbed me by the elbow and yanked me away from the warm body pressed against me. "Time to go."

I looked up into bright green eyes.

Chandler Carmichael.

"Fuck you. I was just getting started."

"Save your attitude for someone who gives a shit." He continued pulling me through the crowd. My flesh ached where his fingertips were undoubtedly leaving bruises.

Two hooded guys at the entrance—or *exit* in this case—opened the door for him as if he were fucking royalty.

He placed his hand on the dip in my back and pushed until I'd made it to the top of the stone stairway.

I contemplated running, but we were in the middle of a cemetery. Where would I go? "Where's Tatum?" I stopped and glared up at him. I knew where she was. I was just stalling.

Chandler was seriously hot. If you liked emotionless assholes with smart mouths.

I was also an emotionless asshole with a smart mouth, so the two of us were like oil and water.

"She's with Caspian." He smirked at me. "But you knew that already."

Okay, *intelligent*, emotionless assholes with a smart mouth.

"Where are you taking me?"

"Home."

He didn't say another word the rest of the way to my house, and I didn't bother arguing with him. He was Chandler fucking Carmichael. It wasn't like I could win, anyway.

I heard their voices.

I saw their faces.

I felt my dad's teardrops fall on my face.

I tried reaching out to him, but my hands wouldn't move—like my bones were made of concrete.

I tried screaming, but the sound was trapped in my throat.

My eyes were open.

My body was alive.

But I was frozen, lying on my bed while my father sat next to me.

My dad said goodbye. He asked me why. As if I weren't right here, staring at him, willing him to *see* me.

There was no pain, though it felt like there should be. Like I was standing in a room consumed with flames, yet none of them touched me.

What was happening to me?

My mind screamed. It screamed and screamed.

My body flailed. I thrashed and thrashed.

Nothing.

Not a single thing.

There was another man, a short, stout man, talking to my dad. I heard the words *drug overdose* and wanted to cry, but the tears never came.

No.

No, no, no.

The last thing I remembered was sending Lincoln home after he'd showed up with a line of cocaine on his dick, telling me to try it.

I let him fuck me, but there was no way I was putting that shit up my nose—or in my mouth. He ended up leaving trails of powder all over me, all inside of me. He fucked me, licked me, and kissed me until my body was covered in coke and cum, and he was too high to stay hard.

He knew better. As soon as I was able to speak again, I was going to curse him the fuck out.

But people didn't overdose from having a little coke in their vag.

Did they?

Dad leaned down and pressed his lips against my forehead. It looked like it pained him to even touch me, like the memories of the last time he watched someone he loved drift away from him were too much.

Why couldn't I move? I needed to let him know I was okay.

"I love you, angel. Daddy's so sorry he let you down."

No! Dad! You didn't let me down. This isn't right. Something is wrong.

Please, God—if you're awake and listening—tell him I'm okay.

He moved to brush a strand of hair behind my ear, but the stout man clapped a hand on his shoulder, stopping him before he could. Dad stared at me a second longer, and a single tear fell down his cheek.

I'd never seen my father cry. Ever.

He closed his eyes for a long blink, then stood up straight.

He and the man exchanged a few more words that were too quiet for me to hear. And then he was gone.

The door closed with a resounding click in the quiet room, and the man walked over to where I lied here paralyzed.

He leaned down close, as if someone else might hear, and whispered. "I'm sorry you had to see that. This will all be over soon."

He knew.

He knew I was awake.

Why didn't he tell my dad I was awake?

I felt a sudden, sharp sting of pain. And then there was nothing but blackness.

When I woke up, I was in a circular room, almost like a courtroom, but more sinister.

On a platform in the front of the room, there was a row of chairs behind a wooden table, or desk, or something. In shiny, gold letters across the front of the desk was the word *Tribunal*. Ten men sat on the platform, all young, most handsome.

The floor was a golden marble with a blood-red "O" formed out of a serpent in the center. The walls were the same golden color with tall white columns placed near arched openings that led to long hallways. Above us, there was a circular balcony, like the ones in theaters or opera houses.

I was lined up with nine other girls near one of the arched openings. Ten of us, all wearing solid white robes and nothing else. Down the hallway behind us, and on the walls of the circular room were stone bowls with the same flaming red glass I'd seen at the crypt in Green-Wood Cemetery.

An ice-cold chill shot up my spine, and a deep voice spoke against my neck.

"Welcome to Judgment Day, sweetheart. Do you have any idea why you're here?"

Kipton Donahue stood with his front pressed against my back.

I had a pretty good idea.

I'd tried touching the untouchable. I'd challenged the unchallengeable.

Two months ago, at a charity function designed to send aid for disaster relief overseas, I'd overheard a conversation. The medicine and food Kipton's "charity" was sending to this underprivileged nation was laced with a drug that caused infertility. He was knowingly prohibiting the growth of a nation just because they were "poor." It was genocide at its finest. The night before I "died" I'd shown up at his front door with my evidence. He'd asked me if I wanted money, and I told him he could shove his money up his ass. I wanted justice.

Now I stood here, shivering, a few steps away from a room full of predators, swearing I would still have my justice.

The girl in front of me walked out into the room, smiling and posing as if she were on a runway, like she was *happy* to be here. Like she'd *chosen* to be here.

"My dad will find me. My friends will find me," I told Kipton through gritted teeth.

He narrowed his eyes and grinned. He tightened a fist in my hair and yanked my head back. "No one is coming. They all think you're dead."

The walls started closing in on me, and a shudder chilled my bones. The floor felt like quicksand, threatening to swallow me whole. My heart raced, and tears stung my eyes. I wanted to fall to my knees, but I refused to let him win.

They all think you're dead.

It all made sense now.

Drug overdose.

My dad's tearful goodbye.

Being trapped inside my own body.

I'd been taken.

Kipton nodded his head toward the circular room. "I believe it's your turn."

A dark-haired man who looked to be about Lincoln's age looked up from his place at the table. "Name," he said simply. His voice was harsh as his gaze ran over me from head to toe.

I flipped him the bird.

Kipton walked to the center of the room, stopping right behind me. He brought his arm around to the front of my body, placing a blade just below my collarbone. "I would hate to make this messy. Give them your name."

"Grab a mop, asshole, because I'm not giving them shit."

He pressed down on the blade, splitting my skin open and slicing a trail down my chest, over my breast, stopping just above my nipple. A river of blood trickled down my flesh and stained the pure white robe. My eyes watered at the white-hot agony that sparked through my entire body.

"Should I keep going?"

"No! Stop. Jesus. It's Lyric. My name is Lyric Matthews."

The man on the end stood up. He looked like old Hollywood with his dark blond hair, piercing blue eyes, and perfectly symmetrical features. James Dean looks with Cary Grant style. His plush mouth twisted in a grin. "This one's mine."

Kipton wiped the bloody blade off on the leg of his pants and smiled. "Lyric Matthews, meet Grey Van Doren. He owns you now."

THE END

ACKNOWLEDGEMENTS

First of all—YOU! Omg. You. The one reading this right effing now. You are the fuel that keeps the fire burning inside me. You are the reason the words flow. You are my inspiration. All day. Every day. Thank you. Thank you for waiting so patiently for this release. Thank you for taking a chance on a new-to-you author. Those who have read me before, thank you for staying with me. If we ever meet in person, I may smack your a**. Be ready. It's coming.

To my alpha and beta bishes—thank you for letting me know when my train veered off the tracks. You guys are amazing.

To Serena Worker for shoving me in the faces of all your blogger friends so this book would be seen. You are a rock star. I owe you some TimTams—or whatever goodies you Aussies love a lot.

And Serena McDonald for blowing up my box with all the things. *cough* cunt tunnel *cough* Your messages give me life and I freaking love you. Thank you for being real. This is the beginning of a beautiful smutship. I can feel it.

Nancy and Nicole, thank you for smoothing out my rough edges and making this a seamless, shiny story for the world to see.

Elizabeth—thank you for making sure I crossed my I's and dotted my T's. Shit. You know what I mean.

Angie, you are my guardian angel and I can never thank you enough. You know what you did.

And to my girl tribe, Roux, Lee Ann, Amanda, and Coco Lynn—thank you for keeping me sane and making me laugh on days when I wanted to burn my laptop and never write another sentence as long as I live.

To my divas—You guys really bring it with the daily dick tok. Inspiration for daaaaays. Thank you for sticking with me. For making me laugh. And for trusting me to be not just another author, but also your friend. I freaking love you.

To all the bloggers who took a chance on this book— F*CK YES! Thank you! If I could sing like Mariah Carey, I'd write you a love song. And then I'd sing it. Sadly, I'm more like the people they kick out of the American Idol auditions, so I'll just tell you this: You are seriously the real MVPs. I can't thank you enough. I will never thank you enough.

To the makers of Verdi and Sunny D— You saved my sanity too many times to count.

To Shauna at Wildfire PR, thank you for all your hard work in helping me get this book baby into the right hands. You are amazing.

And lastly, to my family— You are the reason… The ending of this sentence is infinite. You are the reason for everything. *Every-freaking-thing.*

ABOUT THE AUTHOR

Delaney Foster is a native of the deep bayous of sweet Louisiana, not far from New Orleans, where eating, drinking, and dancing are much a requirement for citizenship. She loves all things romance, a good glass of wine, and Saturdays at the baseball park. She does believe leggings are pants and is a bit of a book whore. In her heart, Mr. Darcy will always be the ultimate book boyfriend. And in her books, you will find sexy alpha males and the strong women who love them.

Printed in Great Britain
by Amazon